Ne

Christopher Geoffrey McPherson

News on the Home Front
Copyright 2012 by Christopher Geoffrey McPherson

All Rights Reserved. This book may not be reproduced, transmitted, or stored in whole or in part by any means, including graphic, electronic, or mechanical without the express written consent of the author except in the case of brief quotations embodied in critical articles and reviews.

Cover design by Matt Hinrichs

News on the Home Front
is dedicated to the millions of women
who held together their homes and workplaces
during World War Two.

Prologue - Tuesday Evening

She sang a love song. The haunted woman opened and closed her mouth to form the words, her eyes looking as if they were capturing the eyes of the audience; they were, in reality, the window to a soul many miles away. She stood at the circular microphone only inches from her red-trimmed lips; her brilliant white teeth caught glimmers of light. The sequins trimming her deep red dress sparkled in the spotlight as it sliced through the heavy, smoke-filled air.

The final words of the song filled the Blue Panther nightclub. As the last faint sound echoed through the enormous dance hall, she felt a sting at the edge of each eye and the smooth warmth as a tear began the long fall down her cheek. The last strains of music played through the club. The couples, many of whom had only just met that night, clung to each other; the desperateness of the moment, the possibility that each serviceman might never hold another woman before he died, the possibility that they could all die tomorrow, made each movement, each moment vital, important. Many of these men, young boys really, were on leave -- due to return tomorrow; others were leaving for the first time. But for them all, now was the only thing that mattered. Right now, this place, this song, this woman.

The song ended, the couples stopped dancing, their applause filled the huge club with appreciation. The singer backed away from the microphone, turned and walked to her chair in front of the band, tears soaking her face. She sat there, the world revolving around her, unable to think of anything other than the telegram she received an hour earlier, delivered by an old man she had never met.

PART ONE
Christmas Eve, 1944

Her hand rested gently on the fine linen table cloth; her gaze took in the rich tones of the hand-worked wood of the ornately carved buffet, dining table and chairs. As she glanced around the room she saw, interrupted only by the French doors, the dense pine forest outside the window behind the buffet. Two fragile birds rested in the comparative safety of the ledge as the winter storm raged. She smiled. The sound of the strong wind reached her ears over the din of the assembled dinner guests. Merriment as guests enjoyed the food, their conversation rich and involved; pointedly devoid of any reference to the war -- even though friends and family were overseas, huddled in cramped trenches, fighting for the glory and honor of the country, eating their Christmas dinners from tin cans. Tonight was a night to celebrate. She was lucky, there was no denying that; but there was no reason to regret it. Each in his own way, her guests contributed invaluably to the war effort. She was surrounded by the sons and daughters of some of the wealthiest and most influential families along the eastern seaboard. They were the driving force behind the United State's success in Europe. But, for tonight, all thoughts of the war were banished.

Her hand moved gracefully to her glass, lifting it toward her lips. Her gaze dropped as the glass made contact with her full mouth; the richly decorated fingers on her hand flashed nails the same deep red of her lips. She drank in the rich wine, letting it trickle down her throat, her gaze lifting again, searching those assembled at her table.

Her eyes fixed on Philip. She inhaled deeply, her breath solid like stones in her lungs. She released it slowly, not wanting anything to disturb the moment. There he sat, dapper in his black tie and black dinner jacket. His pure blue eyes flashed as he talked animatedly with the woman next to him. The woman's father was the biggest munitions dealer in America, supplying guns and bullets for the boys overseas. The dim light from the candles on the table etched his strong facial features. She caught herself staring. Her glass lowered gently to the table, the sweet liquid still lingering on her lips. Her hand raised again and adjusted the yellow ribbon wrapped snuggly against the pure white skin of her neck. Her hand lowered to the gold chain attached to the ribbon and the two-carat diamond which glittered like a raging fire in the candle's light. Her fingers rested on the gem, rocking it back and forth against her neck.

She looked once again across the table, studying the strong profile of the man who loved her. Philip Craig: tall, urbane, erudite air corps pilot. She loved him with every fiber of her being; yet at the same time was able to resent him for being there, for being part of it. But for the fact she was not born a man, she would be there too, by his side, fighting back the encroaching enemy. He flew the planes, was part of the whole thing. She had hoped he would wear his uniform this evening; she was disappointed he did not. His black hair and the deep blue eyes were more than adequately framed in his black dinner jacket. So sleek, the line of the jacket, his arms as they moved within the fabric, his legs, as they strode purposefully into the room, clad softly in the wool slacks. It was a uniform, she concluded, a uniform of his civilian life.

She watched him speak to a woman. He turned his head and suddenly she found herself gazing into those blue eyes. She knew that her heart had stopped beating. He smiled at her a wide, strong yet graceful smile. It looked so right, that smile, that it should be there, exactly as it was. She wanted to look away but she was compelled to continue watching him as he reached out his arm, taking his wine glass in hand. With a small almost imperceptible salute to her, he raised the glass and drank from it; his lips, in the once-strong smile, now gently touched the glass's edge, the liquid glistening as it flowed through them. He rose from the table, excusing himself, and stood, regal, the uniform of black wool draping his lithe figure. He grabbed a knife from the table and lightly struck it twice against the crystal glass.

"Ladies and gentlemen," he began, his voice ringing clear and true through the noise of the crowd. "Please everyone, friends." With another tap of the knife the conversation ceased. "Thank you."

He looked at her and spoke. "Ladies and gentlemen. There is something of great importance I have to say to you all. My friends." He felt his face grow warm, his eyes felt soft; this was lost on no one present. His eyes met hers. "As you all know, your hostess and I have," he gestured vaguely toward her, "have been seeing each other for some time now. Her father seems to approve of me and," he laughed, "I guess for good reason." He laughed again, joined by the approving chuckles of the guests. He found himself in a suddenly uncomfortable position and smiled. "You see, I'm little good at these kinds of things. There is something I just must get out before the night escapes us." The table grew silent.

She looked at him as he spoke, her hand reached out and slowly lifted the glass of wine, her mouth suddenly parched. Philip lifted his glass, turned and raised it toward her. "Carole my dear. I know this is rather unexpected and sudden, but if you will have me, I would like for you to be my wife."

She felt the glass slip through her fingers, falling toward the table a mile below. Reflexively, her hand caught the glass as the base gently touched the table. There was a moment of stunned silence around the table, broken, suddenly, by the cheers and shouts of other guests as they stood, glasses in hand, toasting them both. Again Philip tapped his knife against the glass.

"Please friends." He turned toward Carole. "What do you say? If you want me to get on one knee, I will."

Stunned, she sat there, still. She felt her face burn white hot as her guests turned, en masse, expecting her answer. She surprised herself, and her guests, as she began to laugh, uncontrollably, and blurted out, "Yes!"

Light strains of music filled the ballroom. The two of them danced slowly. They danced many songs that night, all of them in the same room; Philip and Carole in the same position. She knew she was neglecting her guests and if it were any other situation it would greatly bother her; tonight, however, she knew her guests understood. This was a night to be alone with Philip.

Carole felt the side of her face grow suddenly cold as Philip pulled his face from hers. She turned, startled, and looked into deep, commanding blue eyes hidden partially by a few stray strands of jet black hair. She could not help but to return a smile to his.

His voice gently cooed into her ear, "Darling, walk with me onto the terrace. I want to see what snow the storm brought us this evening."

She shivered in anticipation of the bitter cold that would greet them outside. "Onto the terrace? It's still snowing."

"No, it isn't," he assured her and turned her so that she could see out the doors. "See? The snow's stopped as has the wind. It's almost nice outside."

She resigned herself to fate and nodded her head. He turned from her embrace and led her onto the terrace through the doors. Their feet made no sounds as they kicked up the freshly fallen snow. Philip stopped short and Carole continued to walk to the railing, a faraway look in her eyes.

"Philip," she began, her voice like snowflakes gently dusting the trees. "Is it right that I'm so happy at this moment? There's so much to be worried about, so much that should be making me unhappy, I -- "

He cut her short. "My darling Carole. The war is going to be over soon, I assure you. Since Normandy we are unstoppable. There's no way for the tide to turn against our favor now." He joined her leaning on the terrace railing. He wrapped one of his arms around her shoulders to provide warmth and comfort.

"Oh, l know that. Father's been so proud of our country,

how we have all put aside our petty differences and pulled together. He says we have done so much in such a little bit of time. But," she turned quickly from the railing, faced him, dared him. "But what if something does go wrong? What if we don't succeed?" She turned from him and back toward the railing, pounding it with her gloved hands. "It's never going to end, is it Philip? It's never going to end." She began to cry. "Damn it. Damn this war and you for being so smug about it!" Finally, it all came out: the great fear she held for the success of the war -- and the doubt, the constant doubt that plagued her mind more and more each day.

Philip gently turned her and looked into her hazel eyes. "We'll win, Carole. Never doubt that." He gazed longingly into her glowing face, flakes of snow dotting it as the storm picked up again, gently.

"I know Philip."

"Carole?"

"Yes?"

"Do you love me?"

She smiled as a tear welled into each eye. "Of course."

"And you trust me?"

The tears overflowed and coursed down her cheek. She tried to find control for her voice but it wavered. "Yes."

"I must tell you something."

She began to cry. "No." It was a simple quiet statement of realization.

"Carole?"

She pulled free from him, violently, forcefully, surprising Philip. The snow began to fall harder onto the open terrace, the wind blowing flurries across the tableaux before it. "I knew it!" she screamed at him, momentarily unaware of the guests inside.

"What?"

She paced away from him, her white pumps disappearing into the freshly fallen snow. "They're sending you away, aren't they?" She turned and began knotting her hands together in worry. "I knew it was too good to last. Ever since you enlisted three years ago." She laughed as she realized the irony. "It was three years ago. You enlisted on Christmas Eve, 1941. Damn you! And now they're sending you overseas!"

"Yes, Carole. It's true."

"But why?" It was more a command to answer than a request. She knew how the military worked. Her father, the latest in the line of one of America's greatest chemical manufacturing families, had been sent all over the world with at times no more than a few hours notice. Ever since rumors of war in Europe, he had been in the vanguard developing new chemicals and processes to help his country. His family was rich, wealthy beyond any need for him to work. But he was dedicated to helping the old world his family left and the new world he found. Carole knew the cost of freedom. She knew. "Why now? You've managed to stay in the states for this long. Why now?"

"Please listen to me Carole."

She stopped pacing, turned, looked at him, tears in her eyes.

"I got my orders not five minutes before I left for this dinner tonight. I can't tell you what it's all about -- security and all. But, it has something to do with Japan. Italy surrendered last year and they think Germany will surrender soon -- very soon. But the Japanese are set against it and something is being planned -- sort of like Normandy."

"But, you're a *pilot*! Why would they need you?"

He grabbed her forearms forcefully. "Carole. You know I can't question my orders. If they're planning a land assault against Japan, and they want me, need me there, I know there's good reason for it. I must go." He paused, released her arms. His arms fell to his side. "I'm sorry."

She moved closer to him. She could not stand the thought of his leaving. She knew, in her heart, that if he were to go, he would never return and she was powerless to stop the great machine in action. "I hate this war," she finally managed. "I hate what it has done to us all. I just hate it."

"I know you do Carole. I'll be back. You've already agreed to marry me," he added with a laugh. "I have a whole room filled with witnesses. You can't back out now."

He smiled, laughed.

"Yes, well, I was tricked into saying yes. You cheated."

"I guess so."

She looked at him, flakes of snow edging her lashes, her hazel eyes underneath glowing. She parted her lips to speak. Instead, she raised them to his and they kissed. "Yes, my love, I will marry you. Please hurry back. I don't know how long I can wait for you but I will." She knew, as she spoke those words, he would never return; her wait would be an eternity.

As their lips met again, a blast of wind threw snow against their bodies. Screaming like little children, they rushed through the tall doors into the ballroom where they were greeted by the amazed stares of the guests inside -- guests they had totally forgotten existed. As they rushed into the ballroom, wind and snow followed them. The doors were quickly slammed shut. The room grew silent as they entered; the silence broken by the heavy chiming of the mantle clock. Carole quickly turned her head toward the sound and saw both of the clock's hands pointing straight up. She smiled. "Merry Christmas everyone!" she shouted.

The room filled with cheers. She looked up toward her beloved and whispered those same words to be heard by Philip and no one else.

Christmas Day

The first rays of the morning sun pierced through the wooden shutters of her room, illuminating the disarray. As tired as she was after her long evening, Carole did not feel the strength to undress properly and put everything away for the maid to clean. So, she let her clothing drop where it might as she took each piece from her weary body. Her pumps right inside the door, her gloves draped over them. Her jewelry, the yellow ribbon with the diamond, all in a cluttered mess on the vanity. A slip here, a camisole there, the dress draped over the plush chair. Under the tousled sheets on the bed there lay a body. It was Carole.

A mumble emerged from under the mussed silk sheets. An arm appeared and pulled the sheets from her face. "Philip?" She lifted her head and looked around the room seeing the clock on the table and the time of 7:30. She fell back against the pillows, exhausted. To bed at 5:00 and awake less than three hours later. This was not a pleasant situation. She looked around, sure she would see Philip standing there, looking down to her. She sat up and remembered that Philip would have gone home. When did he leave? She couldn't even remember saying good night to him.

A heavy sigh escaped her lungs, her eyes squinted against the bright sunlight in her room. She carelessly reached for the telephone. Picking up the receiver, she dialed the number 9.

From the kitchen, the cook answered. "This is Mrs. Kennison," said the matronly cook.

"Mrs. Kennison." Carole ended the sentence there. She rummaged through the junk on her night stand, clearing off what did not belong. "Would you be so kind as to tell me how I got to bed this morning?"

"I beg your pardon, Miss?"

"Mrs. Kennison. It should be simple to answer the question. I'm here in my bed and don't recall how I got here."

"Miss Irene took you into your bedroom, Miss. Don't you remember that?"

She didn't, but she would not let on "Oh, yes, of course I remember. Did Irene get home all right?"

Mrs. Kennison was used to this pattern of conversation with her boss's daughter. She had been employed in the Trent household since before Carole was born and thought the young woman spoiled. She long held that the best thing that could ever happen to Carole was a marriage to Philip. "You asked Miss

Irene to stay the night. She's in the guest quarters. Shall I wake her?"

"No, please, Mrs. Kennison. Let the poor wretch sleep. Is breakfast ready?"

"Breakfast has been ready since Mr. Trent awoke at six this morning. He has eaten and already left." She paused. "Is there anything else I can do for you this morning?"

"No, Mrs. Kennison. That's fine. I'll be down shortly." She hung up the telephone. She threw her sleep-heavy legs over the edge of the bed and rubbed her tired eyes with the back of her hand. She reached again for the telephone.

After a few moments, a tired voice answered on the other side. "Hello?"

"Irene, dear? It's Carole. Are you still asleep?"

"What time is it? I know I just got into bed."

"Oh, Irene, dear. Are you going to sleep away the best years of your life? Get up! We're going riding this morning or did you forget that?"

"Oh, dear. Yes, I remember. Is Philip joining us?"

Carole pulled her tired body off the bed. The mention of his name turned the morning gloomy. He was going away shortly and there was nothing she could do to stop it. "No," she said. "I'm afraid he had to take the train to Washington this morning for some high-level meeting. He'll be here in time for dinner, though."

"That's too bad. I was looking forward to riding with him."

"Yeh," she sighed. "Me too."

She let the phone drop onto the cradle, thoughts of Philip filling her mind. She slipped out of her silk nightgown as she walked around the cluttered and brightly lit bedroom.

Shutting the door behind her she walked into the large bathroom and directly into the shower. Three nozzles threw steaming water onto her exhausted body. Carole let her mind wander away from Philip and the few days that they had left together. As she soaped her body, she felt hatred rage within her. "Damn it," she shouted aloud, punctuating the words with a thump as she threw the bar of soap across the shower. She rinsed herself and walked from the shower onto the cold tile floor, the plush cloth towel doing little to warm her.

She fixed her hair, put on a little makeup and trudged from her bedroom. The morning was fresh but brought little joy to her as she took the steps down the stairs one by one. She trekked through the living room and into the dining room, still unhappy.

She sat, alone, at the long dining table which had, just last night, been the site of so much happiness and joy. Now, she felt forlorn.

"Good morning," said Mrs. Kennison as she entered from the kitchen. "And what will you be havin' for breakfast this bright and beautiful mornin'?"

"Please, Mrs. Kennison. I've asked you not to be so bright and cheery before noon, have I not?"

The stout woman frowned. The product of a large family in Scotland, she knew a happy attitude was the first requirement for a productive life. "Miss Carole. You've got to learn to start the day with more of a positive outlook on things. Your father - -"

"-- is not me, Mrs. Kennison, as I have pointed out to you before. Now, would you please bring me some juice, orange preferably, a scrambled egg, no butter this time, some rolls, gravy, and some hot tea." With a scowl, Carole dismissed the woman who turned, in a mock huff, stomping out for Carole's benefit.

Carole sat, her shoulders slumped slightly forward. She looked around the now-brightly-lit room. So different from last night, she thought, when the atmosphere was so happy, alive. And here it is, Christmas morning and she was having breakfast all alone. She ran her hand over the finely polished wooden table top. The grain stood out in the sunlight's brilliant glare. It looked so beautiful to her. Why did she feel so down this morning?

Mrs. Kennison returned with breakfast. Carole spoke: "Mrs. Kennison," she said, her voice quiet.

"Yes, ma'am?"

Carole raised her head and looked at the woman who had been part of her life all of her life. "I must apologize," she finally said, "for being rude to you."

"Think nothing of it, ma'am."

"But, I haven't even wished you a Merry Christmas. I'm so dreadfully sorry. Can you ever forgive me?"

A tear formed in Mrs. Kennison's eye as she hurriedly wrapped her hands in the apron to give her something to concentrate on. "Oh, goodness, Miss. How could I ever not forgive you?" She sniffled and brought the hem of the apron to wipe the wet smear from her cheek.

"Now, now, Mrs. Kennison. Stop that immediately or I'll start too. Just please forgive my less-than-adequate table manners and get about your work." A smile played lightly across her mouth and she gave a sly wink to the older woman. Mrs. Kennison placed the tray onto the table and served breakfast. As she made to leave the dining room, Carole spoke again: "Mrs. Kennison?"

The woman turned. "Yes?"

"Will you be preparing your famous dinner for tonight?"

"Yes, ma'am," she said as she bowed forward slightly. "Duck with dressing."

Carole smiled.

"Fluffy potatoes."

Carole's eyes lit up.

"Yams, plum pudding, green salad with almonds."

Carole's stomach yearned in anticipation.

"And freshly made peach cobbler from peaches I put up myself."

Carole squealed, unable to restrain her eagerness. "Get out, before I charge into that kitchen and help myself." The two women collapsed laughing as the cook went about preparing for their traditional Christmas feast and Carole began to eat her breakfast.

Carole finished the last of her juice as Irene trundled down the stairs, through the living room and into the spacious dining room, her long, thick brunette hair streaming casually behind her. The light bounce in her step gave her a youthful, childlike quality.

She walked across the room to Carole, kissed her lightly on the cheek, and returned to the other end of the table where her breakfast awaited her. She plopped onto the heavy wooden chair, undid her serviette, raised her spoon and dug heartily into the fruit salad. She looked down the length of the table to her best friend. "Good morning, Carole. Merry Christmas to you. Where's your father?"

"Good morning, dearest Irene. Merry Christmas to you as well. Father had to go into Washington this morning on business, thank you for asking. Now will you please shut up?"

"Carole, dear. You are always gloomiest when the day is the brightest and the moment most happy. Aren't you excited?"

"Yes, Irene, I am." She was not. "Christmas is such a cheery time of year. They ought to have it more often -- say, once a month."

Irene laughed, finishing the fruit salad. She rang for Mrs. Kennison to bring the next course. "You are a charge, dear. Where did you say Philip was off to?"

Mrs. Kennison entered from the kitchen bearing a hefty tray filled with eggs, sausage, toast, rolls and fruit for Irene.

"He was called into Washington. Something big is going on and he won't tell me anything about it. It's dreadful, really." She attacked a piece of toast. "Mrs. Kennison," she called as the woman was about to leave the room.

"Yes, ma'am?"

"Why do you always insist on bringing me toast, when I ask for rolls and gravy?"

"Miss," the woman spoke sternly. "Did you eat the rolls and gravy I brought for you?"

"I can't remember," she replied, momentarily caught off

guard.

"And did you eat the toast I brought you?"

Guiltily, Carole surveyed the empty plates before her. No rolls, no toast, nothing left. "Apparently," she said, understanding Mrs. Kennison's tact.

"That's why. You don't eat enough, if I may say so. And one day, it's going to get you in trouble. One day." The point made, the stern cook turned on her heel and returned to the kitchen.

Laughing to herself, Irene said, "You'd better listen to her, Carole."

Carole snapped, lightly, "Oh, shut up, you. The two of you are in cahoots together." She rose, a glass of lemon water in hand, drank it. "Yes, Irene. That's it. Spot on. I'm going into the library for a while. Come when you've finished eating all that food, will you, and we can get down to the business at hand. She turned and began toward the living room.

Through a mouthful of scrambled eggs, Irene mumbled.

"What did you say?" Carole asked, turning.

Clearing her mouth, Irene repeated, "What business at hand, dear?"

Carole laughed, "It is Christmas, after all, isn't it? Let's see what Santa brought." She turned lightly on her heel and strode into the library, leaving Irene laughing and eating behind her.

Irene knocked twice lightly on the library door and entered. The room was dark, almost gloomy. Irene stood at the door a moment, allowing her eyes to adjust to the light, trying to see Carole. Sure that Carole was no longer there, Irene turned to leave.

"Please, Irene, come in."

Startled, Irene turned back into the room. "Where are you?"

The displaced voice came through the dark. "Here,

behind father's desk." A great, richly appointed leather chair swiveled around and Irene could see Carole in the dim light. She heard a click as Carole reached across the wide desk and snapped on a banker's light. The room of darkness was pierced by a small circle of light.

"Carole. Is something wrong?"

Irene approached the desk, seeing that Carole had been crying. The two women had known each other since early childhood. Irene didn't need so obvious a clue as tears to know something was dreadfully wrong. She gently perched her body on the side of the heavy mahogany desk, her arm lifted to stroke Carole's hair.

Sniffling back a tear, Carole tried to be brave. "Oh, Irene. I'm so afraid for Philip."

"Why? Has something happened?"

Carole smiled at her friend. "No, it's nothing like that. I mean, I'm so happy about him, me, us. But," she turned her glance away from Irene. "If he goes overseas, I don't think I will ever see him again."

Unable to do anything but provide some physical comfort, Irene said, "Carole, it's all right. I'm sure everything will be fine. This horrid war will be over soon. I know it. The two of you will settle down, here in this wonderful house, have children, be happy."

"It isn't that," Carole insisted. "I will be happy with Philip. But I just don't know if that opportunity will ever come."

"Now, now. How can you worry like that? What could possibly go wrong?"

Carole lifted her eyes to meet Irene's. She felt compelled to reply with a whole list of things that could go wrong. She wanted to remind Irene of what had gone wrong in her own life, the tragedy, the pain, the loss; but instead said only, "You're right. Nothing could go wrong. Nothing."

They sat there, surrounded by yards and yards of wrapping

paper. They were surrounded by the house staff whom they had invited to join them to open all their gifts to make the atmosphere more homey. Carole placed aside the gifts for her father and Philip. It left a number of presents for the two women to open to make a scene reminiscent of those many happy childhood Christmas mornings the two had shared.

Exhausted from the morning's work, Carole reclined against the couch as the house staff returned to their duties, chattering happily, comparing gifts, offering thank yous to Carole and Irene. She adjusted her new ermine stole over her legs, wrapping her hands in the lush, soft fur. "John?" she said to the houseman as he turned to leave. "Could you stoke the fire please? I'm sure it's dying, and the snow has started to fall again."

"Yes'm," he replied. The elderly man, one of her father's longest retained staff members, made his way to the logs by the fireplace, added several to the already roaring fire. The new logs settled, caught, and added a rush of warm air to the living room. As John made his way from the room, the snow began to fall in earnest. Irene rose from the floor and walked slowly, gracefully to the doors. She stood, framed by the light, looking at the beautiful, picture-perfect morning which surrounded them. The terrace was blanketed with the pure, white, powdery snow. She saw birds and a rabbit digging around for a few bits of food. She looked across the terrace into the woodlands that separated the house from the lake some distance away. She saw a family of deer: a buck, doe and a young-looking fawn which was apparently a late birth. She smiled as the family went about their daily foraging, nibbling at a branch, digging through the snow for a hidden sprig of grass. Turning from the doors, she walked back toward Carole. "To live here," she said. "You are so lucky, Carole. Your terrace is so long!" She laughed. The terrace ran the entire length of the south side of the house. One could walk into the living room, dining room, ballroom, or the hallways into the bedrooms from the terrace. It allowed each social room a piece of terrace. "And you should see the snow along it!"

Carole sighed, her body drinking in the warmth of the fire which crackled and spoke to her.

Irene joined Carole on the lush couch. "Still thinking of him?"

"Yes."

"Will he be here for dinner tonight?"

Carole looked at her watch. "Yes, I think so. He'll be here for dinner tonight. But there are still eleven hours until then." She brightened up. "Shall we go riding then? The snow's stopped."

Irene rose. "Great!"

Afternoon, Christmas Day

The two women walked the distance from the main house to the stables where the horses awaited them. The winter day was crisp and cold. No snow had fallen in the last hour, but the trail was lost to the white blanket which covered the forest floor as far as the eye could see. They crunched the snow underneath their feet. The silence of the morning was broken by the screech of an owl, the rustling of a deer, or the call of one bird for another. The light breeze pushed Carole's blonde hair into her eyes. Using a gloved hand, she repeatedly pushed the stray strands into place. Irene's thick, brunette hair, in an elaborate French braid, stayed in place. Carole's jodhpurs rustled as she stepped one foot in front of the other, the black riding boots trampling indentations in the new snow.

Carole's fashion style had been honed at the hands of an expert. When she was younger, she and Irene had been guests of Gabrielle Chanel. They had been in awe of this woman, the renowned fashion expert, from when she first met them dressed in a simple and elegant black and white wool jersey suit. In fact it was at this meeting that Carole received a gift of Chanel No. 5 from Madame Chanel herself. Carole never wore any other fragrance.

Irene, at Carole's side, stomped through the snow. Her grey slacks, white sweater and pastel blue blouse providing warmth against the brisk weather. As she walked along the path, her thoughts were elsewhere.

To Irene, Christmas as well as all the other holidays during the year held special meaning. Since the loss of both her father and older brother early during the war she had clung more and more to Carole and the Trent family to fill the void. Her mother, long dead, had been close to Irene, but her father had been closer and a much greater influence in her life. But, it was her older brother, Matt, who had been her life. Everything Irene did was done in his shadow. Matt had been the expert horseman, Irene merely a good one; Matt the brilliant student who received a scholarship to Princeton, Irene merely good but improving. In her eyes, Matt had been the perfect example of a father's son and Irene wanted to feel that pride herself. Yes, she was her father's daughter and one in which her father had held enormous pride; but she had to be better. Always better.

For Irene, each Christmas since their deaths was hard. With no other family, there was little to be cheerful about. She did the best she could, and Carole and her family helped.

For Carole, her thoughts were on Philip. She still held a deep feeling of foreboding about his impending trip. She had fought against his enlistment from the day Pearl Harbor had been attacked until the day he signed the papers. She had wanted him to finish his schooling; but his thoughts, as with every young man, were on fighting the Japanese and defending his country. Because of the influence his father had, Philip received a commission in the United States Army; but now, apparently, he had become much more important to the military than he had ever been before. She hated him for that; but she hated them more, the government and the military, for their dependence on him.

She clomped heavily through the snow. She broke off a branch from a tree and savagely whipped aside the brush along the path. Her hatred extended all the way to Roosevelt, the president, FDR. Were the rumors true that he knew the Japanese intentions to bomb Pearl? That he could have prevented it all, but was too set on America's entrance into the war? Could he have knowingly allowed so many to die just for the sake of helping our allies? She did not want to think that, but too much was being made of the quick change in public opinion. First, America would remain neutral; suddenly, after Pearl, America wanted war. It was too much a convenience to be mere coincidence.

After a long distance the two women reached the riding stables. Fully in charge, Carole marched to the stable boy who was combing the coat of her favorite horse, Monterey. The beautiful, chestnut colored horse had been her favorite since it was purchased by her father last year. The horse was lean, strong; a good jumper.

"Good morning, Clifton," Carole said to the boy who hastily removed his cap, turning to face the women. He had been caught off guard, unaware of their approach.

"Hello, Miss Trent, Miss Davis. I was not told you would be riding today. I'm sorry."

"Please Clifton," Irene offered, smiling. "Carole decided late last night that we would ride today if the weather permitted and neither of us thought to say anything. Is Bay Rum ready?" Bay Rum was her black horse which she put up in Carole's stable since her home across the lake had no riding grounds.

"Not quite, ma'am. But a few moments and I can have her dressed and ready for you, if you don't mind the wait."

"Not at all, Clifton," she said, offering him a smile.

The young man secured Monterey's lead to the stable door and made way to retrieve Bay Rum who was housed several stalls back. As the two women waited, Carole plopped her body against the stable wall.

After a moment, Irene asked: "Tired?"

"No, not really," Carole replied. I'm just a little winded from that walk, that's all."

Irene was surprised. "You? Winded? Not at all. You're

thinking about Philip again, aren't you?"

Carole's response was sharper than she had intended. "And if I am, so what?"

Irene backed away a step, surprised by Carole's outburst.

Carole pulled her body away from the wall. She walked to Irene, gently grasping her forearm. "I'm sorry Irene," she said, looking into Irene's eyes. "I am thinking about him. What can I do? I feel so helpless I feel like I'm going to burst." She released her friend and walked the length of the stable. She stood a moment then turned and walked back to Irene. "What can I do?" she asked, her voice barely audible.

"Carole, there's nothing you can do. It's out of your hands; all of our hands. The only thing to do is wait. Do as Philip says. I know it's hard; but, look, he may not go at all. You know how unpredictable the military is: orders today, counter orders tomorrow. There is little good that can come from worrying."

Carole cast her eyes down to the dirty snow floor. "Yes, there's nothing I can do." She looked up, quickly and sharply at her friend. "But, Irene, I love him! How can I not fear for him?" She began to sob, the tension reaching a fever pitch. Irene's gloved hand touched Carole's face, wiped a tear from her cheek. Carole's staccato breath created wisps of fog between the two women. "I just know he's going to die if he goes."

Irene, alarmed by this outburst, placed both hands on Carole's shoulders. "Of course he isn't, Carole. How can you think that?"

Irene calmed Carole as best she could, but her mind raced back to the day she received the first ominous telegram. She had been sitting at the window table, dutifully writing her weekly letter to her father, the letter to Matt already finished, when she heard the footfalls of someone walking up onto the front porch of her home. Irene started violently when the door buzzer signaled someone at the front door. She had heard so often tales of women who received telegrams about their loved ones and she did not want to ever experience that horror first hand.

She rested the fountain pen on the blotter, slowly walked through the dimly lit living room straightening her skirt as she walked. She opened the door and was surprised by the sight of the short, balding, older man who stood there, hat in hand. He reached out the telegram to her. "Telegram, ma'am," was all he said.

She remembered standing there, frozen in place. Even though it was only autumn, her body was suddenly bitter cold. "Who is it from?" she asked, wanting to hear any other answer than what she already knew in her heart.

The old man diverted his eyes; this was the part he always dreaded, knowing there was nothing he could say to offer comfort against the bitter shock that was to come. Again, he said only, "Telegram, ma'am."

She knew then all hope was lost as her trembling hand reached out to the proffered telegram. She thanked the man as his stooped figure retreated on the walkway.

Clumsily she tore at the telegram, her hands refusing to work in coordination with her brain. She opened it and read that a person she had never heard of before regretted to tell her that.... She did not remember anything after that, only that she began to scream. She heard the scream, the bitter horrible scream filling the neighborhood. She remembered one of her neighbors running across the lawn toward her, panic and fear the only message in her eyes. She had been upset by the telegram, but didn't even know who had died. Violently, she read the telegram again and saw that it was her father who had been killed. Inside of her, she felt the guilty happiness that it was not Matt.

The afternoon passed quietly, the neighbor seeing to Irene, making a small lunch, making her rest. Irene did not know what time of day it was when the doorbell rang again. Sure that it was only the neighbor coming to check on her, Irene rose fitfully, stumbling toward the door. She opened it and was greeted by another, different, old man who stood at the door, almost a silhouette in the sun's dying rays, a telegram thrust in her direction. He said only "Telegram, ma'am." She remembered the burst of pain as she hit her head against the porch railing as she fell in a faint. It had been, she would learn later, a telegram telling her that her brother Matt had been killed the same day as her father. As organized as the military was, organized enough to plan a successful raid on Normandy, they could not have foreseen enough to at least deliver both telegrams together. As desperate a blow as even that would have been, it would have been a shock suffered only once. This was inexcusable.

Now, barely two years later, Irene looked into the fearful, pleading eyes of her lifelong friend and felt a sorrow for her. Carole had every right to be afraid; Irene was no one to tell her differently.

Carole turned away as Clifton returned with Bay Rum.

"Miss Davis, your horse is all dressed and ready for you." Clifton smiled as he handed the reigns to Irene, confident he had done his job well. With a few added actions, Monterey was dressed and ready for Carole who took the reigns from the stable door and led her onto the riding path.

The two women led the horses onto the snow-covered path. The day had become bright, sunny, clear. Their emotions had swung from despair and fear to happiness and exhilaration. Without warning, Carole moved Monterey in front of Irene and Bay Rum. She signaled the horse to move from a jog to a cantor. After a moment she charged the horse into a rapid gallop, the wind blowing off her small black cap to float onto a small hedge. Her flaxen hair sprung to life behind her. Irene, still keeping Bay Rum at a slow jog, stared in surprise at the quickly departing image of her friend.

Carole's mind gave no thought to Irene as the distance between them grew second after second. She reveled in the freedom the ride gave her, the excitement of the moment; the rest of the world, her fears, her problems, were being left behind, as forgotten as her black cap.

The horse emerged from the sparse forest, Carole's face grew red in the chill wind. She gave no thought to her hair, other than to move it from her face when it whipped in front of her eyes. In front of her, almost as far as she could see, there lay nothing but clear, flat land: her family's land.

She charged rapidly, wildly, the world around her shooting past without clarity, two solid walls of blurred images. Her lips grew into a true, honest smile; she was happy to be free.

She slowed Monterey as she reached the other end of the clearing, dense forest in front of her. She turned the horse and kicked it into high speed again as she made her way back. Her lungs filled with the cold air, her breathing fast and short. The clouds of steam from Monterey's nostrils disappeared as quickly as they formed; Carole felt the expanding and contracting of the horse's massive sides as its breathing deepened to keep pace. Adrenaline filled her body making Carole want to ride faster and faster. She covered the ground faster this time. She did not slow down the horse. She turned Monterey to take a left, then a right bank around clumps of trees, naked without their spring clothing. She emerged from another right-hand bank and saw Irene, her startled face almost comic.

Then suddenly, everything turned black. Carole had seen Irene's face, but could not identify it as the face of her friend. Then the world disappeared. She remembered hearing Irene scream, but did not understand why. She slumped off the still moving horse and fell hard onto the snow-covered ground. Monterey, frightened from the scream, continued running, riderless.

Irene gave no thought to the wayward horse as she quickly swung her right leg over her horse, sliding to the ground. She ran the short distance to her fallen friend. A brief endless moment passed as Irene tried to make her hands react. They refused to move. She closed her eyes, took a deep breath, exhaled and opened her eyes again. Her hands cooperated. Irene knew better than to move her friend. With a swift motion Irene struggled to pull off her heavy wool sweater; her gloves a hindrance. She let escape a small sound of frustration as she put the fingertip of one glove in her mouth and tore it from her hand. She deftly removed the other glove and pulled the sweater over her heard. She wadded the sweater and gently rested Carole's head upon it.

Carole's face was pale, Irene knew shock was setting in. She rose, unsaddled her horse and took off the blanket which sits between horse and saddle. She placed the still-warm blanket over Carole's upper body and put the saddle under Carole's calves in an effort to improve the blood flow to her brain. Irene checked Carole's eyes. The pupils were uneven. Knowing she had done everything in her limited power, Irene mounted Bay Rum bareback, turned the powerful horse and headed for the stables. She pulled the horse back at the sight of Monterey galloping toward her carrying Clifton on its back.

Evening, Christmas Day

Dinner had been cheerless. It was forced, tense. The servants in the house moved about as if in a dream, their movements coming more from routine than choice. The light music from the Sonora radio placed to one side of the buffet didn't seem fresh, original. The atmosphere was one of despair, gloom. Philip arrived promptly, looking resplendent in his full air corps uniform; but he was now conspicuous in his absence from the dinner table. He had been at Carole's side since he learned of the accident.

Irene forced herself to remain at the dinner table, forced herself to maintain the pace of conversation. Around her sat Carole's father; William, a friend of Irene's; and several others all of whom had arrived not knowing of Carole's injuries. Some, upon learning of the accident, begged off the dinner, asked to leave; none of the guests wanted to impose themselves on the family. True to his nature, Carole's father had been insistent.

These were friends of his and his family's who had come to celebrate the season. He was intent to see that they did. After all, they did have something to celebrate: his daughter was engaged to be married; she had survived injuries which could have been far more severe. There was reason to be thankful.

The doctor had left Carole only minutes before the first guests arrived. He left behind two nurses to care for her until his next visit. The doctor had been full of praise for Irene. Her quick thinking actions, he insisted, probably saved Carole's life. Irene, welcomed as a hero, could not stop crying. Only being self-forced to remain at the dinner table allowed her the self control to remain calm. She knew the accident was her fault, although could not think how she could have prevented it. No amount of praise from the doctor or Carole's family could convince her she was not responsible for her friend's condition. If only she had stopped Carole from charging off. Now she sat, desolate, picking at the duck dinner, guilt the only thought filling her mind.

Philip was the last to speak with the doctor before he left; he was certain no permanent damage had been done. The bruising looked worse than the injuries really were, the doctor assured Philip. Again, he praised Irene's quick action. She'd be sore for a while, he insisted, but would recover fully.

The nurses had been brought in at the insistence of Carole's father who wanted to insure expert care should something go wrong.

Philip sat in the huge, overstuffed chair he had pulled next to Carole's bed, holding her hand.

The two nurses, opposite the room from him, sat reading in straight-backed, uncomfortable looking chairs. One of the nurses was reading "Mildred Pierce," the novel by James Cain. The nurse loved this book and had read it before; but she also read, in a recent issue of *Screenland*, that a film was to be made of the story starring her favorite actress Bette Davis. She couldn't wait; she devoured the book's pages with a thrilling intensity. The other nurse read a dog-eared copy of Daphne du

Maurier's "Rebecca." She had grown tired of checking out the book from the library and rushed out for her own copy when Pocket Books issued the less expensive paperbound copy. She gave Joan Fontaine's face to Max de Winter's wife, Laurence Olivier's to Max de Winter. She sat, enthralled, as Mrs. Danvers was about to be trapped in the flaming house. Although both women sat in rapture in their own literary worlds, they kept a watchful half eye on their charge; neither woman forgot her primary duty.

Philip rose from the chair to adjust a wall lamp so its bright light would not shine into Carole's eyes. From outside the room he heard a sound. He walked to the door which had been left ajar and saw Mrs. Kennison trundling up to the landing with a hefty, overflowing tray in her hands. With a smile, he opened the door for her, allowing her into the room.

"How is she, Mr. Philip?" she asked as she sat the tray on a table near the far window.

"Just the same as when you asked a few minutes ago, Mrs. Kennison." He smiled again.

"Yes."

"She'll be like this for a few days, the doctor says. He seems to think she'll come out of the sedative soon. A little sore, but fine."

"Has she awakened?"

"Yes. She woke and we talked. The doctor immediately gave her something to sleep. He thought the excitement would just make things worse." He took the old woman's hand in his, patting it reassuringly. "She's going to be fine. Don't worry about it."

"I know she will, Mr. Philip. I just don't know. Should she not be in a hospital or something? It don't seem right."

Philip hushed her. "The doctor said she's fine and we must have faith in his ability. She got a nasty blow to the head. That's all it amounts to. But, she's fine, now."

Mrs. Kennison smiled, weakly, and walked from the room, pulling the door behind her. At the door she turned back.

"Will you be needing anything else, Mr. Philip?"

"Thank you, no."

"Are they all right?" she asked, indicating the nurses.

"Yes, Mrs. Kennison. I'm sure you brought everything we'll be needing for a while. How's it going downstairs?"

"Well, it's very quiet down there. I think everyone wishes they could come up here and do something. Mr. Trent is very unhappy."

"Of course."

The woman turned and crossed the landing toward the stairs. Philip turned back to the room, walking to the dinner tray. He was right. Mrs. Kennison had brought enough food for a dozen people instead of the three that were in the room. He saw heaping plates of duck, dressing, salad, peach cobbler, bread and other foods.

"Nurse?" he said to them both. "Are either of you hungry?"

Dinner over, guests gone, Carole's father asleep, Irene sat alone in front of the large fireplace where just this morning she had been sharing the joy of Christmas with her friend. She had stoked the fire herself and now watched as the flames flickered and reflected off the fender. She sat, her legs covered by Carole's new stole. She found little warmth in the white wool slacks which covered her legs or the loose wool sweater over her body. A heavy sigh escaped her as she thought that she would have to go back to work tomorrow.

She was so tired of the war and although she truly loved her job in the factory, she was tired. She was tired of the bond rallies; tired of making due without silk stockings; tired of ration stamps for sugar, petrol, meat; tired of lipstick in plastic cases and then paper cases; tired of steaks that cost $3.50 in a small restaurant; tired of saving tin cans, aluminum foil, cooking fat; tired, tired, tired. The war had been such a drain on her as well as every other man, woman and child in the free world. The hatred she felt for the Germans and the Japanese made the sacrifices worthwhile. She felt a chill run through her heart as she thought of all the men who had died defending their country -- her father and brother among them. Yet, even though the majority of people in America were fighting the war here, on the home front, there was a great deal of discontent. Without fathers in a family, many of the children began to suffer discipline problems. Irene remembered walking down the streets of the city seeing children coming out of movie theaters after having been in them all day, their mothers working and unable to afford a sitter. She saw kids smoking, drinking, being arrested for delinquent behavior. She had, at first, been shocked. Now, it all happened too frequently to be a surprise.

More so, however, she was shocked the war was not over. There had been so much optimism that it would be over by Christmas; here it is, Christmas, and our boys are still overseas, fighting and dying.

For every success, there was a problem. There was a great deal of joy at home with the success at Normandy; but then there was the transit strike in Philadelphia in August. She thought it odd that our country would be over there fighting against the racism of Hitler and his Axis powers, yet not allow Negro people to drive buses. It made no sense to her. Restaurants for whites only, buses with sections for whites and for coloreds; smoking rooms for coloreds only. Hospitals would even turn away dying colored men or women: they would not service them unless they were white. She shivered at the injustice of it all. And now, even after all they had been through, her friend lay upstairs, injured. At this moment, life, to Irene, seemed so unfair.

Tuesday Morning

The sleek Rolls pulled away from the Trent estate just outside West Lake as the snow fell lightly around them. Secured and warm in the back of the light grey car, Irene huddled in one corner, her shaved-beaver jacket crumpled close to her bare neck. She turned her head and looked out the steamed windows as the scenery passed by. She sighed heavily as she thought of the holidays just past and her friend, still asleep from the heavy sedative, in the house. She turned away from the window, adjusted her left glove, tightening it around the base of her fingers, one finger at a time.

As the car wended its way through the snow-covered roadway, bypassing the city of Baltimore, she thought sadly about returning to her job. It was not the job which made her sad, it was the thought of another sad Christmas behind her which dampened her spirits. When she left the house this morning she could not bring herself to look at the gaily decorated Christmas tree secure in its own little corner of the huge living room. It hurt too much. At Philip's request, Irene had agreed to stay at the estate for a while until Carole fully recovered from the injuries. After her car dropped her at the plant, she would have the driver go home to assist the maid in packing several bags of her things. Philip suggested Irene take a few days off from work, but Irene refused. Thinking of the women at the plant where she worked, she would feel guilty and not very patriotic, if she took even one day off. There had not been one absence by any of the women in her plant for the past 150 days. Carole was in good hands; the plant needed Irene.

And it felt good to be needed. She turned her gaze back to the window and the scenery passing by, thinking of how long it had been since she had been needed by anyone. It had been too long. When word came women were needed to fill in for the men in the military at the factories and plants, she went right down to the first factory she came to and volunteered for work. They needed women for the swing shift and she agreed. Today, however, she had been asked to work day shift. It was a change which threw off her timing. She bristled, at first, at the thought of working in a plant. Her father and brother had been dead for several months; she looked at this opportunity (any opportunity, really) to get out of the house as a godsend. But, a factory?

When she had seen how much she could do for the war effort, however, all doubts she might have had quickly left her mind as she took off her silk jacket, threw it into the assigned locker and got to work. Now, after all these months, she was an important member of a team. A vital member of the working class. She was proud to earn a paycheck. The money left to her by her father and from her brother's insurance was all fine and good; but, to earn a paycheck was different. It qualified her to be a member of society now. And she was proud of it.

The car drove on. She saw streets congested with other cars going here or there. The driver knew the side streets. He turned off the main road and headed for the plant avoiding traffic. The car drew nearer the plant. Irene mentally prepared herself for the day's work ahead. Her car pulled up outside the Glenn L. Martin factory and slowed to a stop. Irene waited as her driver came around to open her door. She stepped from the car, gave a few quick instructions about which items to pack and walked from the car, her work boots crunching in the snow.

She could imagine how incongruous she looked standing next to the co-workers she waved to. They in their overalls, work boots, cotton coats and jackets; she in the same, but with a fur jacket. She walked up to the factory joining some of her friends as they entered the side door and walked to the locker room. She tossed her jacket and gloves into the locker, locked it securely. She punched in. She was met by her lead man.

"Davis," the older man called, gruffly.

"Yes?" Irene turned toward the familiar voice.

"What're you doing here so early?"

She stood as the grubbily dressed man in a blue overalls came toward her. "I could ask you the same question," she said, playfully. "What's up?"

"I've been moved to days effective today. They didn't tell me my crew was being shifted around too."

"I don't think it's the crew. From what I understand, it's just me -- and, apparently, you."

"What's your new job?"

"Have no clue," she replied, honestly. With the holidays and Carole's accident the thought never occurred to her that she didn't know what new job she would be doing. "I guess I'm going to have to find out, though."

She turned from her lead man and started walking toward the main office. She didn't know who to talk with, or what to say. She had to ask someone. She couldn't just stand around and wait.

She walked through the plant, closing her mind to the riotous noises from every corner of the huge, open factory. She saw planes in various stages of completion, from beginning to end. The great B-26 Marauder being built in this plant at Middle River, Maryland, would fly over so many countries in the world it sent chills down her arms. Her hands tensed as she remembered the feel of metal parts and tools in her hands. She felt proud as she walked past the partially completed planes. She walked by women she knew and more she didn't, busily executing their assigned tasks, making planes for the war effort. There had been some talk the government might be planning to use another aircraft and that production of the B-26 would be halted, but she didn't care. For now, these were her airplanes. She and her coworkers worked long and hard hours completing these machines.

She found and entered the office of plant supervisor. "Mr. Atherton?" she called, opening the door slightly.

A tired looking man looked up from his desk overcrowded with papers. "Yes?"

"Sir, I'm Irene Davis. I've been assigned to days, but no one told me where to report."

The old man, glad for this interruption from his work, rose from his chair. He motioned for Irene to take a chair at the side of his worn, metal desk. "Please, Mrs. Davis. Have a seat."

Irene took the chair, politely correcting him. "It's Miss, sir."

"Hmmm?"

"I'm not married. It's Miss." She sat, but tried not to seem too feminine or polite.

"Of course, Miss Davis. I apologize. It's just that so many of our workers have husbands in the military. I took it for granted, that's all. No offense meant."

"None taken," Irene said, smiling at this wonderful old man so obviously embarrassed by his slight error. It was a great change from the pointedly rude and arrogant men who worked by her side in the factory.

"So," Mr. Atherton said, returning to his seat behind the desk. "You don't know where you belong, is that it?"

"Essentially, yes. I had been a welder's assistant since I joined the Martin family. Is that what I'm to continue doing?"

Atherton ruffled through some papers on his desk, tempting fate as Irene watched one pile begin to lean to one side, seemingly overbalanced, ready to topple onto the floor. He found a yellowed file and straightened the leaning pile. He tipped his glasses to review a file Irene was sure the contents of which he could recite without difficulty. He finally spoke: "Well, well."

Irene looked at him, the ambiguity in his words perplexing.

"Hmm," he added. Irene's patience was beginning to fray.

More minutes passed with Atherton reading his file. Irene knew he was merely drawing out his little visit with her, but she was itching to get on the line. She decided it was time to say something. "Sir?"

"Yes?"

She said nothing, but moved her eyebrows a bit, tilting her head slightly. Atherton, old but quick, grasped the nuance of her movements and pushed his glasses back to his face. "Of course, forgive me. You're a rather good worker, I see."

"Thank you." She now wondered what he had been reading.

"These reports from your supervisor commend you and

your work highly. You seem to have volunteered to work extra shifts before others were asked, you learn quickly, adapt rapidly." He looked to her. "Well, Miss Davis, speaking as a representative for the Glenn L. Martin company, I thank you for having chosen to come work for us. You're a sight better than most of the men we have working for us."

Irene smiled, unsure how to respond.

"It appears that our crane man had a heart attack at his controls just before the holiday."

"Oh, dear."

"We've been working some men double shifts to fill in. That's why you were asked to come in on day shift today. It seems your lead man suggested you for the job. The other men in this plant all handle highly specialized jobs and cannot be spared. The job, then, like so many others, must go to a woman."

Irene sat in the rickety chair, surprised. She had only been doing her job, in her mind, and didn't think she was doing so much better than the women she worked with. But she quickly realized what this job would mean to her and the other women on the line, so she accepted. "Whatever you want me to do, I'll do. When do I start?"

The old man rose from his chair. "If you'll follow me, Miss Davis. We'll begin now."

Irene rose hesitantly from her chair and followed a few paces behind the man, warily. She knew what a crane was but had no idea how to operate one. Apparently, word had traveled quickly through the plant because she felt every head turn toward her as she followed the supervisor. She heard a few softly spoken yet obviously caustic remarks from the men that no woman ever ran a crane and none ever would; she heard other softly spoken words of support and encouragement from the women. Everyone in the plant knew the importance of this moment and no one wanted to miss the events about to unfold.

She ignored the insults and tossed a thumbs up to the compliments. With a wink, she cemented her comradeship with the other women in the plant. Since she had begun there she heard the insults directed to all the women, herself included. They didn't affect her then and would certainly not affect her now. She was good at her job -- that's what her file said -- and she could easily do this, or so she hoped.

She listened as her supervisor explained the operations of the big machine which carried oversized plane parts, wings and the like, from one area of the plant to where they would be assembled to the body of the plane. She took mental notes, trying to portray a confident, almost blasé image to her audience. Toward the end of the introduction period, her supervisor said something about sanding the tracks. She asked what this was.

The man looked at her, then pointed his grease-spotted arm up to the long rails over which the crane moved from one side of the plant to the other. "Those tracks up there, that the crane moves over, sometimes get too slick from all the lubricant used on the machinery. In order to prevent the crane from slipping along the tracks, sand is put on the rails."

Innocently, Irene asked, "And who does that?"

Amid laughter from the men, only slightly dampened by the icy stares aimed at them from the women, the supervisor said, "Why, Miss. You do."

This was a signal for the men to howl with laughter; insults hurled around Irene. "She'll never get up there," one said. "No dame is brave enough," added his friend. "No dame's got balls enough, you mean," was shouted in reply. Irene felt her face grow hot with anger. Controlling her impulse to hurl insults in reply, she assumed a calm air of efficiency and competence.

"Yes. How often must this be done?" she asked, hoping the twisted rope of nerves she felt in her throat did not affect her words.

"At the beginning of each shift."

Irene asked other questions, the amount of self control she needed to sustain a conversation allowing her to relax and surmount the initial shock. "Where is the sand kept?" "Where is access to the rails?" "What is the proper method for spreading the sand?"

The supervisor obliged, frankly surprised the conversation had come this far. He was sure Irene would have begged off the promotion. He had nothing against her or the women who worked in the plant; but a crane operator had always been a man: it was just too hard for a woman to do.

He explained everything in detail to her. He handed her the bucket of sand and walked her to the ladder which led to the rails. Without looking up she grabbed the ladder and started the climb upward. She stepped one foot over another. The nervousness in her legs made climbing difficult; she forced her mind to think of the job ahead, not allowing her fears to take over. The weight of the sand pulled on the muscles in her arm and she had to stop once to switch arms much to the amusement of the men below who had gathered to watch her ascent. After a long climb, she finally reached the safety of the platform.

She stood there, allowing a moment to catch her breath, and looked at the length of narrow railing which extended from her feet toward a point lost in infinity. She bent down and placed the bucket of sand ahead of her on the rails. She did not know whether she should walk along the rails or crawl. She looked at her supervisor below her. He looked up, anticipation that she might prove all the men wrong drying his mouth, making his heart race. He tucked his body into a half crouch and lowered toward the ground; Irene understood.

She got onto her hands and knees, pushing the bucket ahead of her, sanding the portion of rail behind the bucket and before her. She crawled, from one platform, across the plant's length, toward the safety of the platform on the other end of the plant. Going was slow, minutes passed, word spread through the plant. Wrenches were lowered, rivets were set onto the ground as men and women left their positions and headed slowly toward the center of the plant for a better view. Irene's progress took her beyond the half point; expectations rose. She refused to acknowledge the people standing below her; fear of falling prevented her from diverting her eyes beyond the width of the narrow rail.

She pushed the bucket, grabbed a handful of sand and spread it. Push, spread, inch forward. Push, grab sand, spread. Push, spread, inch forward. She pushed the bucket. It did not move ahead. Irene lifted her eyes and saw the platform's ledge blocking the advance of the bucket. She lifted the now-nearly-empty bucket onto the platform, pushed it to one side, and crawled the few final inches to safety. Her job done, successfully (as much to her surprise as that of those below) she stood, triumphant, on shaky legs, straightened her coveralls and flashed a thumbs up to her supervisor below.

The plant erupted with cheers and applause. Men, who only minutes before had goaded and chided her, now found themselves cheering and hooting in acceptance of her achievement. Nothing had been said of the not-a-few men who had attempted and failed or even refused to try what a woman had just managed.

Slowly, carefully, Irene climbed down the opposite ladder. Stained and dirty, her face smudged. She strode, confidently, through the crowd to her supervisor. Defiantly, she thrust out the empty sand bucket. It was a victory not only for Irene but for all the women who had suffered abuse and harassment at the plant.

Those who would remember this moment would clearly recall only two things: the huge smile which played across Irene's face as she accepted the acknowledgment of her co-workers and the change in morale and relations that affected everyone who worked in the plant from that day onward.

Irene would remember only one thing: how happy she was as she left the crowd and walked toward the crane that her coveralls were so loose fitting. No one could see, she knew, how badly her knees were shaking.

She sat at the window, in a small chair which had been her father's and her grandfather's. She gazed, absently, at the snow-covered forest which spread to the horizon of her world. She could not tell how long she had been there, in that chair, looking at those same trees. She had been watching the small animals go about their daily chores, digging through the snow, trying to find small morsels of food. A particular family of deer had held her attention for more than an hour. She had watched, through the years, this family grow and develop. She made a point to insure their food supply during the winter months, hiding clumps of grass and weeds just under the snow for them to find. She wasn't quite sure they knew she had planted it there; but the family was always around, keeping her company.

She felt a heavy sigh escape her lungs and watched the warm air collect on the window. She felt the warmth of the fire on her right cheek; her left cheek cold. Gathering her robe about her legs as she rose, Carole decided to try and eat some of the cold breakfast Mrs. Kennison had brought for her hours ago. Was it hours ago or only minutes? She could not be sure. Time merged, undivided, within her. Slowly, with caution signaled by the heavy thumping at the back of her head, Carole stood erect, her legs still watery from the sedative. She looked at the cold food and felt her stomach turn. Breakfast, she decided, was not such a grand idea after all.

She turned her head, gazed at the room around her, looked for Philip whom she knew to be gone from the house. She had felt his presence at her side all through the evening and night. She knew when he had left early this morning bound, by train, for Washington. She wanted him to stay but would not ask it of him. His devotion to his duty all encompassing; his desire for an end to the war a compulsion. For this, she loved him. She raised her left hand, slowly. It still ached from the fall. She felt the back of her neck. She felt pain even from this slight touch. Her head thumped with every heartbeat. And now, what?

She knew Irene was working, her father long since gone to his job in Baltimore. Philip, long gone to his appointed duties. She remembered, with some vagueness, the visits she had from each as they left for their days. She felt her cheek where Irene placed a gentle kiss; her forehead where her father gently touched his lips; her mouth, where Philip gently sealed their love. She knew she was very lucky. She walked toward the fire, grasping the top of her robe to her neck, feeling the piercing warmth through the fabric. She stood staring at the fire's leaping and darting flames. For a long moment, Carole stood there. Her world was all in that fire. For her, now, nothing else existed.

At the dim edges of consciousness, she heard a jangling. Again and again she heard it calling to her. She rose to full consciousness and turned toward the sound of the telephone. She walked to the table, lifted the receiver to her ear, and listened, saying nothing.

"Hello?" came the voice on the other end. Carole said nothing. She did not know what she would need to say, or why. Her mind still was on the fire. Again a voice asked, "Hello?"

"Yes?" came the feeble reply.

"Miss? Are you all right?"

"Mrs. Kennison? Yes, I'm fine. What is it you want?" Carole felt heavy, sedated, her mouth working slowly, the words coming from her mind in short streams.

"Did you touch a bit of breakfast?"

Carole's eyes roamed over the tray of uneaten food. She mumbled a negative response.

"Well," the hearty voice answered back. "I'm fixing to come up with some lunch for you. I'm equally fixing to stand over you as you eat every last bite. And that's a fact!"

Again, the thought of eating make Carole ill. "No, please. I don't think I could hold anything down. Please come and take this tray away. I'll let you know when I'm hungry."

"Now, Miss. I -- "

"Please." She set the receiver onto the cradle and slowly returned to her bed. She sat on the edge, unsure whether she wanted to lie down or just sit here, like this. She felt like going outside for a short walk to escape the confines of this room. She laid back onto the soft bed as she heard heavy footsteps. After several small knocks, the door opened hesitantly.

"Miss?"

"Yes, Mrs., Kennison."

"Is it all right?..."

"Yes, Mrs. Kennison. Please take it and go. Leave me alone."

The cook resigned herself that the carefully prepared breakfast was a total waste. She would give it to one of the stable boys who could always find place for more food. She understood Carole's difficult time and wanted so badly to help. There were times, she knew, when doing one's assigned job was all the help one could offer. She knew well that this was to be one of those times. She stepped carefully and lightly around the bed and retrieved the tray. She walked out of the room, checking the fire to make sure it was well stoked, the water pitcher filled, the windows closed, and walked from the room. She might do her duty day and night but she would never forget that, to her, Carole was the daughter she never had.

Philip looked through the generous window of the train's car at the wintry scene flashing by him, defeat ringing in his ears. He could still hear it in his mind: "The president has organized a strike force which will drop several bombs on key cities of Japan," the aide said.

"Bombs?" Philip asked, incredulous. "What good are bombs going to do?"

"The president has two plans. The first, a land assault like Normandy. The second, a raid by air."

"Look," Philip said, his patience wearing thin. "If bombs would have worked against Japan, we would have dropped them already. It isn't going to work!"

The aide eyed him cautiously. "These bombs," he began. "Are unlike anything you may know about."

Now, sitting on the train, those words rang in his ears. For months, Philip had heard talk of a special bomb. Key words would escape an overheard conversation, lodging themselves in his mind: heavy water, nuclear fusion, uranium-235, plutonium-239. There was always another word, mentioned in the same conversation: Alamogordo, a city he knew to be in New Mexico. It had all been and still was cryptic. But more perplexing: how could he, a pilot, be involved with it? What could he do? But, for the rest of this trip, he would turn his attention to Carole. His world was with her for now.

Tuesday Evening

She opened her eyes in the darkness of the room, not knowing how long she had been asleep. She raised her head only to lower it suddenly; the intense pain thumping a dull pang in her head. Slowly, she remembered where she was and sighed at her helplessness. She changed her gaze. Her field of vision now included the dying embers of the fire. It explained the chill in the room. She could remain in the bed, cold, and wait for someone to come and stoke the fire; or, she could lift her weary body from the bed to phone for someone to come up. Neither choice pleased her. She chose to stay in the bed and rest forever her tired body.

As she leaned back into the softness of the pillow, the bedroom door opened slowly. A sliver of light shot into the darkness of the room. She heard the sound of knuckles rapping lightly against the door.

"Carole?" A man's voice called to her.

She recognized the voice. Her body wanted to leap from the bed, run to him, hold him. But fear of the pain, and utter exhaustion of her body, forced her to combine all the emotion in one word.

"Philip!"

Philip walked slowly into the room, his eyes adjusting to

the darkness. He walked first to the fire, tossed a few logs onto it, then moved to the edge of her bed.

"How are you?"

"Fine. How was your trip?"

"It went well, but I didn't come here to discuss the vagaries of war. I came to bring good health to you. I saved some of last night's dinner for you, for us. When you feel up to it, we'll have our own little holiday celebration."

"If I had the strength. My brain is willing, but my body is against it."

"If only you had been a better rider, none of this would have happened," he joked.

"To hell with you, Philip!" Carole shouted, propping her body up to defend against this attack, indifferent to the pain.

Alarmed, he reached for her arm. "Calm down. I was only teasing. Don't carry on."

"Well don't," she said, lowering her body, and her throbbing head.

"I'm sorry."

"You had better be. It is still possible for me to withdraw my consent to marry you."

"You would never."

She eyed him with disdain. "Would you care to call me on that?"

He thought. Finally, he said: "No. I'd better not. I have no idea how you would respond."

She smiled, closing her eyes. "Wise choice."

Like this, they sat. The fire grew stronger. After a moment, the entire room was ablaze with motion as the light from the flames danced about the room. Slowly, gently, Philip leaned his trim, uniformed body down against the supine figure in the bed. For the briefest moment, his lips touched hers.

As he pulled from her, she startled him with: "You call that a kiss?"

He laughed. "For now. Do you feel hungry? Mrs. Kennison said -- "

"And what has she been telling you? That I haven't eaten? What?"

"Yes. She said your breakfast was left to get cold, untouched. That you refused to allow her to bring up your lunch tray. What's wrong? You need to eat to regain your strength."

"At the time, *doctor*," she paused to draw emphasis to the sarcasm, "I felt unable to eat. Now, however, I'm famished."

"Shall I get you something?"

She thought. "If you help me," she said calmly. "I think I can go downstairs. We'll eat there."

"No. You stay here. I'll -- "

"Philip," she said, forcing her shoulders up from the bed. "I need to get around, to walk. I'm sick of this room. I'll be all right if you help me." She glared deeply into his eyes. It was a dare to argue with her.

He acquiesced. "Fine. What do I do?"

Slowly, one motion at a time, Carole instructed Philip to help her move first her upper body, then each arm, then her legs from the bed. She stood, wobbly. After each movement she paused, insuring her strength. To her surprise, she stood well enough to not need Philip's strength. But it would be a different matter as she challenged the stairs.

She walked, unassisted, to the door and out onto the landing. Philip moved into place and, draping her arm around his shoulders, helped her take the first step down the stairs. One by one, the steps disappeared behind them. She managed them all in short order. Into the living room she walked, by herself. But her strength ebbed. Knowing she could not finish the journey, she decided they would dine on the living room sofa. "Ask cook to bring some fruit and cheese into the living room. We'll eat here." She shifted her body to the back of the sofa, reclining to one side.

"Anything else? The duck perhaps?"

Carole smiled. "Of course. And anything else left from last night's dinner. Especially some of the peach cobbler." The thought of all that food revolted her. She knew, however, such an order would please Philip and thrill Mrs. Kennison. After a few minutes, Philip returned, both hands laden with trays of food for their cold supper. He set the trays onto the large, flat table in front of the sofa. He moved to the fire, added a few logs. Carole watched his lean figure cross the room toward the wall of tall windows. With a flick of one hand he sent the curtains flying open to either side of the doors, exposing the terrace, covered in snow and bathed with the light of a waxing moon. As he returned to the sofa, he clicked off the two lamps, creating a breathtaking setting for their meal.

"Now," he said, his voice almost cryptic. "Let's celebrate the Christmas you missed." He moved closer to her and touched his lips to hers. She responded by moving closer to him, reaching for his warm mouth, his sweet kiss. They remained in this embrace for a long moment, neither wanting to pull away, neither wanting the moment to end.

Philip pulled back his head. Carole's eyes sought out his, pleading for more. Philip smiled. His hand reached into his uniform jacket, pulling out a small black box; the moonlight catching the gold-edged tips of the box, making it come alive. "To my wife to be," he said and handed the box to her. Carole's hand clasped it.

With great wonder she opened it slowly, to make this moment last. Inside, a star glowed into life; a bright burst came from within the box. She looked closer and saw a brilliant diamond surrounded by a handful of smaller diamonds, rubies, sapphires, emeralds; all combined to make a star and its rays. Nothing Carole had ever seen was more brilliant than this star. She removed the ring, and handed it to Philip. "Put it on me."

He gently placed the ring on her finger and brought her hand to him, turning it over, palm up, and kissed her palm, gently, lingeringly. He looked up to her, still holding her hand. "I will love you as long as the diamond on this ring exists in this world. Wherever I am, I will always have you by my side. For as long as I live, you will live within me. Until the sun itself turns cold, I will love you and then, even longer."

The moonlight from the terrace caught the ring, each movement creating a starburst. Carole could not hold back the tears welling in her eyes. For her part, she was willing to give the rest of her life to this man; willing to live the rest of her life trying to earn the right to wear the ring she now wore.

Philip spoke. "Carole."

"Yes?"

"I must --" he stopped.

She reached her hand to wipe away the single tear which flowed down his cheek. As it lowered, he grabbed it, kissed it again. Held it.

"I must go," he blurted out.

"I know."

"I've been ordered to report tomorrow to the airport. I leave for England in the morning."

She nodded her head.

"They need me, Carole. I must go."

"I understand," she said.

There was much more he wanted to say to her. Much more that needed to be said. Carole's eyes told him no explanation was needed. "Listen to me. I understand and I'm proud of you. I love you for the fact you can go over there and fight for our country. If I could, I would stand with you, over there, fighting by your side, because I love you and nothing could ever make me feel otherwise. Wherever you are, for however long you must be away from me, I will hold you in my heart. Nothing can ever come between us: no distance, no length of time. When this war is over, when this damned war is finally over, you will return to me, and I shall be waiting for you, to become your wife. We will live our lives together. Each star I see in the sky will remind me of this ring and I will tell each and every star how much I love you, every night, for as long as you are away, for as long as it takes you to come back. Now go, go as you have come: quietly. Leave me as you found me: alone, wanting you, waiting for you." She turned and looked out onto the terrace.

Philip rose from the sofa. He walked through the living room, through the foyer, up to the front door. He stood watching the silhouetted figure of the woman he would always love. He watched her, then turned and walked through the door. Refusing to look back. Carole sat on the sofa. She waited until long after the sound of the door closing. Hours passed and she sat there, staring out onto the terrace, her robe wet with tears. Finally, exhausted from crying, she fell into a deep sleep, her hand with the ring clenched into a strong fist, buried deep under her robe, held near to her heart.

Wednesday Morning

"What is this dreadful mess?"

"What do you think it is?"

"Well," she pondered, looking warily at the heap of pink meat on her plate. "I'm not quite sure." She lifted her fork from the linen place setting and poked the edge of the heap. "I'm not even sure," she said, warily, "that it's even dead!"

Irene laughed. She could not help but to. Carole's face was wrinkled like a prune and she made the most impolite sound. "Carole," she scolded through fits of laughter. "You'd better stop that, or Mrs. Kennison might -- "

It was too late. The burly woman stood in the doorway of the dining room, her feet planted squarely apart, her arms crossed, her mood sour. "Miss!" she shrieked.

Carole leaned across the table to Irene and whispered. "Oops! Looks as if we've been found out." With a wink she added: "Act innocent." She smiled at Mrs. Kennison. It was the most awful looking, sincerely insincere smile Irene had ever seen. To the angry, red-faced woman she said, simply, "Yes?"

The cook did not budge. "What do you think you be doin', poking at my good cooking like it was some kind of dead animal?"

"What do you mean, Mrs. Kennison?" Carole purred, sweetly.

"Don't play innocent with me." She walked toward the table pointing and waving an angry finger at the young woman. "I suppose I should be grateful you're better; but, I swear you aggravate me something awful. Sometimes to the point of -- well," she stopped. "Being a good christian woman, I'll keep my words to myself."

Carole blinked, exaggeratedly, at the woman while Irene snickered uncontrollably, holding her serviette up to her face. "But, Mrs. Kennison," Carole inquired gently, her head tilting in the direction of the unknown entree. "Whatever is it?"

"It's poached salmon!"

"No it isn't," Carole replied. She eyed the heap once again. It could not be fish, she concluded.

"Yes it is!" the woman replied. Irene thought, one more second and Mrs. Kennison would be stomping her huge feet to punctuate her claim.

Carole poked it again. She tried, but failed, to get it to flake. "But it isn't."

"It is so," the cook insisted. "I opened the can myself, and -- "

Irene stopped laughing, her eyes wide; Carole's head whipped around to look at the cook. In perfect unison, they both said, "The can?!"

Caught, Mrs. Kennison said nothing. She cast her eyes downward, awaiting her reprimand.

"Well?" Carole pushed.

"The market didn't have any fresh salmon. For some reason Mr. Thompson tried to explain but I didn't understand there is a shortage of fresh fish this week. I heard tell that it's gonna get worse!"

"Worse?" Carole asked. "What do you mean, worse?"

"Don't you read the papers, Miss?"

"No," Carole replied, picking again at the pseudo salmon. "I haven't the time." She turned from the woman and grinned mischievously at Irene.

"Well," the cook began, righteously, her arms folded across her ample bosom. "There was a shortage of meat and fish for the holidays. On the first of the year, butter goes up to 34 ration points, asparagus and green beans are gonna be hard to come by." She shifted a glare to Carole. "I was very lucky to get the ducks we had for dinner Christmas.

"Good thing Mr. Thompson and I is good friends from back in Scotland. The best I could do was canned salmon. I even fixed it the way you like it. So," she said, stomping from the dining room, "you had best enjoy it!"

The two women were apoplectic with laughter, spurred on by the image of the woman waddling from the table. Irene, desperately trying to be serious, broke the laughter first. "It really isn't funny, you know."

"Whyever not?"

Irene poked the salmon. "Things are getting worse every day, Carole. We've felt a big shortage in the factory. Parts are getting harder and harder to come by, and I hear the women complaining about trouble getting sugar, shoes -- all sorts of things. I don't know when or where it will stop."

Realizing Irene's point, Carole stopped laughing, began to eat her breakfast. "Yes," was all she said. The women ate in silence. "You know Philip left last night," Carole said, trying to ease the moment.

"I do," Irene replied. She had been afraid to raise the subject first, but was glad Carole did voluntarily.

Carole looked up. "You do?"

Irene nodded. "He called me at the plant yesterday. He told me he wanted to be alone with you and asked if I would come home late. So, I had dinner with some girlfriends from the plant and we went to the Blue Panther afterward for drinks. I came home and saw you asleep on the sofa in the living room. I didn't want to wake you, so I just went into my room."

"Thank you," Carole said with a smile of gratitude.

"Do you know anything?..." Irene asked, trailing off.

"He wouldn't tell me anything. He did give me this, though." Carole lifted her left hand which she had been desperately trying to keep hidden all morning. As sunlight reflected off the great diamond, Irene gasped. The room came alive with points of light.

Irene inhaled. "Carole!"

Carole could not help but to smile at her friend's reaction. She returned to her food, playing down the excitement of the moment.

"And?..." Irene insisted, wanting to hear more.

"And what?"

"Didn't he say anything?"

She shook her head and slowly drank her orange juice. "He just left? Like that?"

Carole nodded.

The two ate in silence. When Carole finished she rang the silver bell which sat at the corner of the table. Shortly, Mrs. Kennison walked in. "Mrs. Kennison, please take this away and bring me some muffins and jam."

Mrs. Kennison turned her head slightly and peered at Carole.

Carole slammed her fork onto the table, uttering something under her breath. She stood up, forcefully, and walked toward the woman. "Don't tell me. No jam?"

The cook could only nod.

"But why?" Carole demanded.

"None in the stores, Miss. There's not been any since late last week."

Carole paced around the table for a moment, turned to the cook, her finger pointing accusingly. "Are you sure, Mrs. Kennison, that you are not hoarding our coupons so that you can stock up on chocolates?"

Mrs. Kennison, shocked at such an accusation, replied, a look of hurt in her eyes. "I would never!"

"No?" Carole cut her off. Irene noticed Carole's actions changing, her demeanor becoming more gruff. She now resembled, Irene thought, that radio lawyer, Perry Mason. "Just how do you explain that empty box of Barricini Candies I saw on the butcher block last week?" Carole pressed.

"They don't require points, Miss. They were a gift!"

"A gift," she spat out, mockingly. She leaned her hands on the table separating her from the cook as if it were the railing of a witness box. "A gift from whom, Mrs. Kennison?"

"Well, I...."

"I submit, your Honor," Carole said to Irene, laughter beginning to break through her words. "That this woman and her alleged accomplice have been clipping ration coupons so that they, and they alone, could benefit from the chocolates they could buy. As we all know, coupons cannot be accepted if they have already been removed from the ration booklet, so I further submit, your Honor, these chocolates have been purchased on the *black market*!" Sure of her victory, Carole turned on her heel, her back now to the cook, and strode back to her chair.

Finally grasping the put on, Mrs. Kennison turned, shaking her head. "I'm calling the doctor, Miss. I'm sure you're suffering a relapse of sorts."

The women collapsed into laughter. It had long been a trademark of the relationship between these two friends that they could laugh in the face of adversity. Where others might become depressed these two women could find solace in their laughter. Outsiders often thought them odd.

Irene folded her serviette, placed it next to the empty plate, and rose. "It's late, dear, and I have got to get to the plant. I'm the new crane operator," she added, with pride.

"Really? Irene, how marvelous for you!" Carole paused. "What's a crane operator?"

"Ah," Irene said. "It's a very important and glamorous job. I get to take huge wings and body parts from one side of the plant to the other so that they can be assembled to make the huge flying aircraft we affectionately call the B26G Marauder. If not for my dedicated work, the war would be lost." She laughed as she walked through the foyer and grabbed her jacket from the hook. "Will you meet me for lunch, Carole?"

Carole walked across the tiled flooring, following her friend, her pumps clicking; the sound echoed through the empty hallway. "I don't know," she sighed. She raised her hand and replaced a wisp of hair which had fallen across her face. "I'm not sure whether I want to stay home or go out. The doctor said it would be good for me to take a drive into the city if I wanted, but...." The but was that she wanted Philip to return.

"Carole," Irene started, her coat draped over her shoulders. "You'll have to continue your life until Philip returns. The sooner you begin to do that the healthier it will be for you." She opened the front door, stepped out. "I have lunch at twelve and I expect you there in time. I'll send my car for you at 11:30. Be ready." Irene walked through the doors to her awaiting car. Carole dropped her head, an empty feeling flooding her body.

"This is the operator. Your number please." The soft voice on the other end of the line crackled through to Carole's ear.

"Yes, operator. VErnon 71340, please."

"Yes, ma'am." The phone went silent for several moments, followed by several short clicks and two short buzzes.

"Hello?"

Carole paused for a moment, afraid to speak.

"Hello?" The voice asked again.

"Mrs. Craig?" Carole asked, hesitantly.

The old woman's voice replied, "Carole? Dear, is this you?"

"Yes, Mrs. Craig. It is."

"Dear!" The voice was cheerful and young despite the woman's true age. "It is so good to hear from you. Philip showed his father and me the ring. Do you like it?"

Carole looked at the ring. "Of course," she replied quietly. "It's the most beautiful thing I have ever seen."

"Yes, my dear. It is. And how are you?"

"I'm fine, Mrs. Craig. I -- " she stopped. She wanted so much to speak with Philip, but was unsure whether he was even still home.

"Yes?"

"I was wondering," she spoke softly. "Has Philip left yet?"

"You miss him already, don't you? Well, I'm afraid he caught the first train out this morning for New York. He leaves from there later this afternoon. Did he not tell you he was leaving?"

"He did, but I didn't know that he would leave this morning. I just wanted to talk with him for another moment. I guess it's too late."

"I am sorry dear," the soft voice cooed. "He said he would call me this evening. Is there a message you would like me to give to him?"

Carole thought for a moment. What could she say? She wanted to thank him again for the ring. She had so much to say, but couldn't leave it all in one long message. "No, Mrs. Craig," she finally spoke, defeated. "Do you know his mailing address?"

"Dear, I am afraid he is to be moving around quite a lot. I think your best chance for reaching him would be to write to him here and we will forward it if we get an address. I could, of course, have him call you."

"No." Carole blurted. "I, uh, think I will just wait for him to call me when he gets settled. Wherever he's going."

The woman's voice became soothing. "I know how hard this is for you, my dear. Remember that we will always be here, if ever you are in need of us."

"I know, Mrs. Craig. I know. Maybe father and I could have you over for dinner one night. Maybe something over the New Year? That would be nice, wouldn't it?"

"Oh, yes, Carole. I think that would be lovely. Please let us know."

"Of course. Thank you, Mrs. Craig, for everything. My

best to your husband."

"Yes, dear. Goodbye."

The line went dead. Carole stood, the phone in her hand, unable to replace the receiver on the cradle. A heavy sigh escaped her. She replaced the receiver in a quick motion then walked to the sofa in the living room. Restlessly, she reached into the magazine holder and dug around for something to read. She passed the newest *Vogue*, several old issues of *Screenland*, and settled on the current issue of *Time*, featuring Norway's Bishop Berggrav and the legend: "Peace is won by accompanying god into the battle." She sighed again, not pleased with the prospects of finding anything of interest in this issue. She turned to the table of contents, located the cover story on page 53 and began reading.

She realized quickly that this would not take her mind off Philip. Frustrated, she flung the magazine across the room where it landed squarely on the fire in the fireplace. The pages blackened quickly, crinkled and turned into ashes. She stood with a violent force and began pacing around the living room, her hands pulling through her hair. She walked into the dining room. Unsatisfied, she stalked into the kitchen wanting anything that would take Philip from her mind. She would have gladly welcomed an argument about dinner with Mrs. Kennison or a talk with the gardener about next spring's planting. Anything. The kitchen, Carole soon realized, was deserted.

Carole felt a sudden pain in her stomach, a pounding in her head. She steadied herself by leaning against the huge butcher-block table in the center of the kitchen. Her legs went watery. She lowered her suddenly exhausted body onto the floor as around her the room went black.

The impatient sound of the telephone broke through her silence. Carole opened her eyes slowly, feeling pain from the harsh sunlight filtering into the room. With hesitation, she raised herself onto her knees, then feet. She walked carefully into the living room to answer the telephone. "Hello?" she asked, groggily.

"Carole? It's Irene, dear. What's wrong with you? Did I catch you napping?"

"Actually, yes," Carole said, hopefully covering her momentary lapse. She grabbed the telephone's base with her free hand and walked to the sofa where she reclined, waves of exhaustion feeding on her strength. "Yes, that's it. I had laid down to take a nap, and you woke me."

"Well, you had better get dressed. It's already after eleven. My driver is on his way to get you. You didn't forget about lunch, did you?"

"Irene, I don't -- "

"Yes, you do," Irene interrupted. Get dressed and get over there. My break's over. I gotta run."

Carole attempted to protest again, but the line went dead. She returned the receiver, resigned to her fate. She rose from the sofa, walked toward her bedroom, thinking about what Irene had said. "It's already after eleven...." Carole had lain on the kitchen floor more than three hours and could not remember why.

Wednesday Afternoon

The lunch crowd at the Blue Panther grew considerably in size in only a few minutes. Irene looked to her watch and saw five more minutes had gone by without sign of Carole. She turned to the bank of telephone booths, the thought of calling her again. The double doors opened with a *whoosh*!

As if nothing was wrong, Carole strolled in. She stopped inside the doors allowing her eyes to adjust to the dim light inside the club. She looked around quickly, spotted Irene immediately. Hurriedly, she strode to her.

"I'm sorry to be late, Irene dear."

Irene greeted her friend with a smile. "Not to worry. Our

table's not quite ready anyway. I'll tell you," she began, raising her voice to cope with a rowdy crowd which had just entered the club. "Giving soldiers first dibs on the good tables is a nice idea but a real pain in the -- " she stopped, smiled at Carole. "You know what I mean."

Carole smiled. She rummaged through her clutch purse, trying to locate her powder. Finding it, she looked around for the ladies lounge. Not finding it, she stopped a passing waiter, who was dressed in a light blue waist coat and black pants. "Excuse me, boy," she said. The waiter stopped quickly, his face indicating his eagerness to be of assistance.

"Yes, ma'am?"

"The ladies' lounge, please."

The handsome young man, probably all of sixteen years old, turned his face and pointed across the expanse of foyer. His blond hair peeked from under his light blue cap. "Through there, ma'am." His green eyes twinkled as they reflected the candlelight in the room. Handing him a quarter, Carole thanked the boy.

The young man turned and walked in the direction he had been going, as if nothing had interrupted his original journey. The smile never left his young face.

Carole stepped closer to Irene, excused herself and moved through the foyer toward the lounge. She walked past the wall light which threw a dim cone of light upward from its opening to cover some of the black wall surrounding it. She passed the white and black lined walls, her hand reaching for the brass doorknob on the door to the lounge. The door opened quietly, smoothly. Carole noticed the workmanship of the inlaid onyx and gold curves framing the door, blending smoothly with the motif of the club. She walked with confidence into the room, smiling at the Negro attendant who demurely smiled in reply; a half smile crossed her face -- she did not want to seem too familiar, yet wanted to acknowledge the friendly smile. Carole walked quickly past her, through the inner door to the toilets.

After a few minutes, Carole emerged through the inner door, smiled again at the maid, accepting the proffered towel. She sat in front of the mirror and set about retouching her makeup.

She sat there in the quiet din of the room, looking herself in the eye. She noticed how tired she seemed, how drawn and pale. She dumped the contents from her purse, searching for her rouge, the powder, the eye lining pencil. One or two strokes, a pat here and there, and she felt more like herself. She could not shake that tired feeling within her body. A heavy sigh escaped her as she replaced the contents of her purse, making sure to forget nothing. She walked from the lounge handing the attendant a quarter. The woman, who needed the job more for distraction than for income while her husband served overseas, curtsied in thanks.

"Good thing you came back quickly," Irene said as Carole approached. "Our table just came open. Let's grab it before that sailor elbows his way in." Irene looked quickly over her shoulder at the uniformed sailor who had come through the double doors only moments before, a cheap-looking woman hanging on his arm. Carole followed Irene's lead as the two women stepped carefully down the lighted steps into the dining area which served double duty as a dance floor at night. Their table, much too small, Irene noted with disgust, was set with a small cloth, a proper silver setting, two glasses each and a small white-milk vase with a single rose. The waiter handed each a menu after assisting them into their chairs. He excused himself.

"This place has become so popular in the last couple years," Irene noted.

"I wouldn't know," Carole replied. "I don't get out here as much as you."

"Trust me," Irene smiled, looking over her menu. "It used to be only someone with money could get in here; but with the war it seems like everyone has clout these days."

Carole did not reply; she looked over the menu. She did not feel the least bit hungry; in fact, she felt more ill than anything; but wanted to avoid a scene with Irene on that subject. From the waiter, who silently returned, she ordered some soup, a small salad, and a tall glass of orange juice. Irene, always hungry after a rough morning in the factory, ordered a huge steak ignoring the hefty $5.00 price, a large baked potato, a loaf of bread, a large glass of milk and another of orange juice. Carole paled at the huge amount of food.

"I'm still a growing girl, Carole. They have us working so damned hard at the factory. I need all the energy I can get in an hour's lunch. And today," she continued. "I'm taking the whole hour." Carole understood: most of the women who worked in the plant took half lunches or less and usually refused their breaks. The men resented it. Although it was supposedly detrimental to the war effort to take a long lunch, most of the men did; and Irene was determined to spend some time with Carole in order to keep an eye on her recovery.

You know," Irene said, brightly, folding her hands in front of her. "There was a big problem with absenteeism over this last holiday. Can you believe it? I felt bad taking Christmas Day off, but some of those people -- mostly men, I might add -- took two or three days off. My lead man says it could put us all behind schedule. He got some communiqué from Washington telling him and all the supervisors to prevent a recurrence over the New Year's holiday."

"I see," Carole said, picking at the salad which arrived during Irene's comments.

"Carole, what's wrong with you?" Irene said. "You sounded so tired this morning when I called. And you looked so pale when you came in today. Are you feeling all right?"

Carole looked surprised. She did not realize others could tell she was not looking well. "But, I'm fine," she offered.

"Really?"

"Well, no actually," Carole confessed. "I'm afraid I fell asleep right after you left, and only woke up with your call."

"You did? You were that tired?"

"No. I actually fell asleep in the kitchen."

"The kitchen?"

"Yes." Carole began to laugh, trying to make light of the situation. "I felt dizzy of a sudden and lowered myself to the floor to rest. Before I knew what happened, you called."

"Carole, that's not like you. I don't think you have ever taken a nap during the day for all the years I've known you. Have you told the doctor this?"

"Oh, Irene," Carole said, jabbing a hunk of salad. "Why should I? You're treating me like a child."

"But, Carole -- " Irene was alarmed. Being so tired after only just getting up was not usual even with a recent injury. She felt something had to be done.

"You're being silly, Irene. I'm perfectly fine. I even know what it is."

"You do, Carole? What?"

"Oh, it's those little pills the doctor gave me. They haven't worn off yet -- that's why I've felt so tired. Be all right in a couple days. You'll see. After all, it was your idea to drag me out in such weather for lunch," she smiled over her fork at Irene, who laughed with Carole; but she knew that something was wrong.

Lunch finished, Irene departed with a wave to Carole as she walked down the sidewalk in the direction of the factory. Carole returned to the car, exhausted. She fell asleep in the back seat before the car even pulled away from the curb.

Wednesday Evening

"So," she continued between sips of hot chocolate toying with one of her stud earrings. "I decided to close up the house for the rest of the winter. I'll give the staff a couple month's paid leave and move in here for a while. There's no reason for me to stay in that huge house -- and you, what with Philip away and all, I'm sure you could use someone around to talk with -- if you need it, I mean." She sipped more chocolate, and smiled at

Carole across the table. "So? Any complaints?"

Carole reached across the table, serviette in hand, and wiped away Irene's chocolate moustache. Irene laughed. Carole turned and looked at the fire, contemplating the offer. She lifted a hand, moved a strand of hair from her forehead. "You know," she said. "There's no real reason for you to do that."

After dinner, the two women retired into the music room to listen to their favorite radio shows. During dinner, Carole's father had phoned to say he would be detained in Washington for a few days. The house was, then, fully staffed for only two: Carole and Irene. The house was much too quiet; much too big.

"You don't like my idea?" Irene asked, nestling her mug of chocolate between her hands on her lap.

Carole shook her head. "It isn't that I am not pleased with the idea. In fact, I am. I think it would be wonderful having you here for a while."

"Then, what's the problem?"

"There is no problem, Irene," Carole said. "I just want you to do this for the right reasons. I don't need a babysitter and if that was the reason you offered, then, thanks, but no."

"You know better than that, Carole."

"Yes, I'm sure I do. But I wanted you to make sure you knew that, too. I'm fine, really. I can cope with Philip being away for a while. And Father being away, for a while."

"Then, it's settled."

Carole looked across the expanse of table between the overstuffed peach-colored chairs on which they were seated. "Yes," she smiled. "It's settled. Thank you for offering." She reached her hand across the distance, grasped Irene's and gave it a small squeeze.

"Good!" Irene said. "Now, we have to plan just what we will be doing over the holidays. We could take a drive to New York, or got to -- "

Carole interrupted. "Wait a minute. I said I could live life without Philip here, but do remember, Irene, that I'm still convalescing. I don't think I'm up to traveling, yet."

"Of course you are, Carole. I called the doctor this afternoon after work because I wanted to ask you to go on the trip with me. I needed to know if it was okay before I asked you and maybe got your hopes up."

"A trip?"

"Yes," Irene smiled, mischievously.

"But, where can we go over a weekend? New York? Connecticut? Virginia? What do you have in mind?"

"Canada...."

"Of course," Carole said, drinking more hot chocolate. "We fly out Friday night, come home in time for your return to work bright and early Monday."

"Well," Irene began. She had thought out this conversation on her ride home. "We wouldn't have to be back Sunday."

"What happened? You quit?"

"No. I haven't taken any vacation time for two years so I have quite a lot built up. So, I talked with my lead man, told him you were sick and he said I could have two weeks off," Irene's voice reached fever pitch. "Isn't that great?"

"You? Taking time off your job? You? Rosie the Riveter? Something happened. Didn't you get a promotion only yesterday?"

"Yes, but you would never believe the luck. The plant is slowing production because of the shortage of parts. As a matter of fact they've begun laying off some of the workers. Because of my new job, I am safe from the layoff, but they don't need a fulltime crane operator during the day shift, so.... It worked out very well, I would say."

"It would appear so."

"Oh, Carole. Don't look so glum!" Irene leaned forward, put her mug on the table, resting her elbows on her knees. "Carole. This is absolutely the best thing for both of us. Philip is away, overseas, Father on business in Washington. I have no one to help me celebrate the arrival of 1945, so, why not us?"

"I don't know." Carole let her mind wander back to the fire roaring in the place across the room.

"Oh, sure you do." Irene reclined in the chair, trying to remain calm. She wanted this trip for them so badly. She was afraid her eagerness might put off Carole. "I have tickets on the first flight out Saturday. We'll be in Canada in time to shop there all day New Year's Eve. We'll celebrate at some special place that night, then start the year off right: shopping for two weeks! Can you imagine the fun we'll have? Come on, Carole. We deserve the break."

If not for her quick reflexes, Carole's mug would have crashed onto the table as she bolted up from her chair, ignoring the pain in her neck. "Get a hold of yourself, Irene. What's all this talk about traveling and shopping? There's a war on! I could no more go to Canada and drop a bundle shopping than cheat on shoe ration stamps. There's plenty to do here, in the states." She walked around the piano, lifted the cover, and sat down to play.

Irene, reproved but undaunted, walked to the piano, rested against the polished top. She stood, caressing the mug in her hand, listening to the music. "Of course you're right, dear. I'm sorry. I don't know what got into me. This whole war thing has gotten to me. I guess I just panicked at the thought of two whole weeks away from nuts, bolts, and airplane wings. Forgive me?"

Carole looked up, but continued to play. It was Beethoven's *Moonlight Sonata*. "How could I not? You are my dearest and best friend. So what if you get a little tipsy over the thought of a few extra sugar coupons?" She chuckled to herself. "But, I do know what we can do."

Irene turned toward her, intrigued. "What?"

"Well, I've been wanting for some time to see that new Broadway show called "Oklahoma!" If we act fast we might be able to get a pair of tickets for this weekend."

"Never," Irene scowled. "It's only a few days away from the holiday. How could we get tickets for a show which must have been sold out for months?"

Carole looked up as she finished the piece of music. "I have friends at the St. James," she replied, mysteriously, referring to the theater where "Oklahoma!" was playing. "I could get us a pair of good house seats."

Irene's smile turned into a girlish grin. "No."

Carole looked up and smirked. "Yes." She lowered the piano cover, walked to the fire, basking in the warmth which gave her a feeling of comfort and safety. She stood there, quietly. "You know," she finally said, turning away from the fire, seeing Irene seated by the table. "As nice as it sounds, I can't help but think of those poor boys sitting in trenches overseas, cold, hungry, scared." She moved across the room to the windows beyond the piano. She watched the trees, illuminated by the moon's rays, blowing in the breeze. "Here we are, two very lucky women, planning a holiday for New Year's. We drink our hot chocolate, our stomachs filled with roast beef and snuggle up to the warmth of a fireplace. Where is the fairness of it all?" she asked, turning back to Irene. She walked back to the fire, standing too close, hoping its heat would sear her face, make her feel the pain she knew she should feel but could not.

"There's nothing you can do for them," Irene said, her voice soft. "Nothing you can do for Philip by feeling so down about the whole thing." She rose, walked to Carole, placed her hand on her shoulder. "I lost the only two relatives I had because of this damned war. I'm not about to lose you, Philip, or anyone else. As long as we have each other we can last this thing out. We buy bonds, we help the boys overseas. We give scrap paper and tin foil to the war effort, our old pots and pans to the war effort, our old shoes, old coats, whatever, it helps the war effort." She turned her face to her friend's. "You and I, even though we are not over there blowing up the Germans, we are here doing our part. We are winning the war here, on the home front."

Carole looked at the fire reflected in her friend's eyes and knew the truth in those words. She smiled. "I'll call and get those tickets for us first thing tomorrow morning. I'll make the reservations for us in the best hotel and the best restaurants and we'll have a damn fine time. And each bite of food, each dance we dance, we'll do for our boys, over there."

They turned to face the fire, and stood there for a long time. After a while, Carole left the room and went to her bedroom; Irene followed toward hers.

In her room, the door closed to the world outside, the fire roaring, Carole sat at her writing desk. She wrote:

My dearest Philip:

Twenty-four hours ago, I saw you for the last time until this horrible war ends. I don't know where you are or what you are doing, but I know you are safe. I spoke to your mother this morning. She said I could write letters to you in care of your parents, and they would be sure you got them. So, here's the first.

I'll try to write you every day until I know how you're doing, and where you are. Irene and I are planning a holiday in New York. We'll catch a show or two, and think of you. Father is still in Washington. I guess the government just can't get enough of him. I wish you were here. Take care of yourself and write me when you have the chance.

Love, Carole.

She addressed the letter, placed a stamp on it, and sealed the envelope. She left the letter on her table as she moved to her closet, began to undress, her thoughts never leaving Philip. She climbed into bed, turned on her small radio, listening, hoping to hear something interesting, something which would take her mind off Philip. She turned the knob, found a station of music, and closed her eyes.

Strains of *Moonlight Serenade* filled Carole's mind, blended with the crackle of the flames in the fireplace as her thoughts began to wander. She could not stop thinking of the news reports about the disappearance of bandleader Glenn Miller whose music she was now listening to. Two weeks, no news. Her favorite bandleader gone. She remembered back to that last performance of the band at the Central Theatre in Passaic, New Jersey two years before. It was to be Miller's last performance before he went into the service. Carole's father, who knew Miller well, had been invited to the event and took Carole with him. She could remember, as if it were only yesterday, that night in September 1942. The band played all her favorites. All her favorite singers performed. She could feel that electric moment when Harry James himself walked onto the stage, placed his trumpet to his lips and played. She cried at the excitement of the moment; she never could have imagined such a thrilling feeling! She listened to the words Miller spoke, not knowing those would be his last public words.

Her mind gave up the last, tenuous hold on the waking world as she drifted into a smooth sleep, the warmth of the fire covering her body. In her mind was Philip's face, his mouth moved. She knew they were words of farewell, but could hear nothing.

Thursday Afternoon

After a quickly downed breakfast with Irene, Carole decided it was time to ride again. After Irene departed for work, she dressed and walked the distance to the stables. The day was beautiful. There had been a heavy snowfall during the night, making it a chore to trudge through the two-feet-deep, snow-covered path.

She tried to focus her mind on things to do today, of the weekend coming, and the trip to New York; the point of the exercise to keep thoughts of Philip from filtering in, taking over. It was not working. She wanted to speak to him again, tell him not to go. Her fear of his leaving was heavy; she could not shake the fear.

The stables rose in the distance over a rise in the path.

She greeted Clifton who was grooming the horses with obvious care and pride. "Good Morning, Miss Trent. Decided to give it a try again?"

"Yes, Clifton. The doctor says I'm fine and ready to ride again. Is Monterey ready?"

A look of apprehension crossed the boy's face. "Don't you know? Monterey was injured when you fell." Carole recoiled, shocked. In the excitement and concern for her, no one told her her horse had been hurt.

The young man reached out his hand, grabbed her forearm, briefly forgetting his station. His warm, green eyes held her with more force than his strong hand. "Don't you fret about it, Miss Carole. It wasn't too bad. When you slipped off her, she ran into a branch. It took a chunk off her flank and she had to be bandaged a bit. That's all. She'll be okay, better than new, actually; but she can't take any riders just yet, not until that nasty wound heals."

Carole returned his concern with a smile. "Thank you, Clifton. If you say she'll be fine, then I'll not worry more about it. Which horse is ready?"

"Colter is ready," the stable boy replied. "She looks mighty fine today, if I say so myself."

"Fine then. Bring her out, would you?"

Clifton excused himself, dashing to the stable where Colter was waiting. Carole adjusted her gloves. The ring she now wore snagged in the gloves; she made a mental note to have a few pairs done up when she was in New York. After a few moments, Clifton reappeared leading Colter by the reigns. The sight of this beautiful, pure white horse sent chills through Carole's stomach as it always had. Colter was the only pure white horse in the stables; the horse had been her father's.

Carole mounted the horse, took the lead from Clifton. "Thank you," she said, as she kicked Colter into motion.

They walked slowly, at first, the blackout still fresh in Carole's mind. The two sauntered through the snow-covered forest. She stopped Colter and just sat, watching the forest activity around her. She saw a small rabbit hopcrawl over the path, looking for a few bugs, or twigs of grass. She caught herself marveling at the beauty of nature around her. It was not something she did often if ever before. She had been so busy living her life that she never took the time to notice it. She inhaled deeply, the cold air bringing a chill to her lungs. It was a welcomed chill. She felt so good to be alive, away from the war, from the stuffiness of her house, from worries of -- She stopped herself.

She began to feel light-headed; she turned the horse and headed back to the stables. She secured Colter and took a slow walk back to the house, right into her bedroom, still brushing snow from her black jacket. She felt the warmth of the logs burning in the fire. They cracked and popped at her entrance as if welcoming her.

She undressed slowly, her eye caught the unmailed envelope sitting on the small table in front of the window. She had intended to give the letter to Irene to mail in the city, but had forgotten. Now she would have to ask someone to take the letter to the box at the end of the drive. But she didn't want anyone to know she had already written a letter to Philip. She slipped on a pair of wool slacks and a blue silk blouse. She wore expensive clothes casually as if their expense did not concern her. Even recovering from her accident, Carole had a natural beauty which came not from her stunning looks; it came from her casual air of indifference to what surrounded her.

She decided to wait until tonight, when she would give the letter to Irene to mail the next day. She grabbed an advance copy of the novel "Forever Amber" -- a book that had not been released yet. But, Carole's father knew a man at the publishing house -- her father knew everyone, it seemed -- who had given him an advance copy to give to his daughter. Everyone knew of her accident. It was a nice of him, she thought to herself as she walked from the room, down the stairs, into the living room lit by the glow of the raging fire.

The Christmas tree still stood in that one special corner

looking forlorn without presents under it. Carole sat on the couch, immersed in the 17th-century romance. On occasion, she would catch the faint glitter of a reflection that irritated her. She placed the book down onto the couch, got up, and tried to find the source of that glittering image. Finally, she saw it was the reflection from one small present which had gotten pushed back behind some of the tree's branches. She crawled on her hands and knees, reached far back under the tree for it. She immediately recognized it as one of the gifts she had gotten for Philip. With all that had happened, she had forgotten to give it to him.

She walked back to the couch, tucked her legs beneath her as she sat and held the small box in her hands. She carefully undid one end of the wrapping paper, slid a black velvet box from its cocoon and opened the lid. The gold medal inside shined brilliantly. She withdrew a Saint Christopher's medal and wished she had remembered to give it to Philip.

She replaced the medal, rewrapped the box, and placed it back under the tree where it could be seen prominently and easily. There it would wait, Carole knew, until Philip returned safely.

Thursday, Early Evening

The door to the library opened. Irene walked in. "Hello!"

Carole looked up from the book, moving a handful of hair which blocked her vision, and smiled. "Home so early?"

Irene looked at her watch as she entered the library. She removed her jacket, tossed it onto the back of a small sofa where she sat, heavily. "Early? It's after six o'clock. Have you been here all day?"

Carole stretched her arms, made a small, primitive sound of pleasure. "No," she yawned, trying to hide the action. "Only for a while, but longer than I thought." She marked her place in the book, looked at Irene and rose from her comfortable position on the large couch. "Mrs. Kennison made a wonderful lunch for me and I decided to come in here and read." She motioned for Irene to move over, making room for her on the sofa. "I went riding today."

Irene brightened. "Good for you! How did Monterey run?"

Carole turned her head, tilting it slightly. "Didn't you know Monterey had been hurt?"

"Oh, dear me, yes," Irene said, looking down. "I had forgotten. How is she?"

"Clifton insisted she was fine, only a few days of rest, that's all. I took out Colter. We had a fine ride."

Irene patted Carole's leg. "I'm glad," she said, adding: "You did take it easy, didn't you?"

Angered, Carole rose, walked to the window, threw open the drapes. "Yes, Irene, dear. I was a good girl."

"Carole, why are you so sensitive? Have I done something to upset you?"

Carole turned her back to the window, perching lightly upon the ledge, crossing her legs at the ankles. "No," she said, looking down at her black pumps. "I can't seem to get Philip from my mind, I'm afraid." She lurched from the window, began to pace. "It's so silly, really. I am afraid of going away this weekend because he might call me. There I would be, in New York, having this great time and he would be hanging on the other end of the telephone line waiting for me to answer, wondering where I was." She laughed, adding, "Can you imagine?" She fixed Irene with a determined stare. "Am I so silly as to feel like this?"

Irene, too tired to rise from the comfortable sofa, spoke. "Of course, Carole, you aren't. When Matt and father left for the war, I stuck by that telephone each and every moment. I waited home for the mail every day, knowing that if I left the house for even one moment, I would miss a call, or letter. It was several months before I decided I had to live my own life. I just had to, I was driving myself so crazy. I couldn't plan my life around a telephone call or the mail delivery. Then, several months later...." She turned away from Carole, tears forming in her eyes. She didn't want to cry again. Finally, Irene continued. "Of course, you're feeling just what every mother, daughter, wife, or girlfriend is feeling: lonely helplessness."

Carole returned to her spot on the sofa next to Irene. "Well," she started, the sentence stopping there. "Well!" she said again, in conclusion.

"Did you get the tickets?" Irene asked, eagerly.

Carole dug into the pocket of her blouse, pulled a small piece of paper from it. "Yes," she said, joining in Irene's eagerness. "We have seats on the floor, orchestra section, along the aisle," she added, reading from the paper.

Irene forgot her tiredness for a moment, jumped from the sofa, hugged Carole. "See, I told you we could still get good seats, if only we put our minds to it!" Irene continued hugging Carole.

"You told me?" Carole asked. "I seem to remember it being the other way around, Irene."

Irene looked at her "Really?"

They both laughed, Irene falling back to the sofa, spasms of laughter sending tears down her face.

From outside the library doors, the women heard a few discrete knocks. Slowly, the door opened. Mrs. Kennison entered.

"Yes, Mrs. Kennison?" Carole could not stop laughing. Irene had begun a tickle attack and Carole was having little success defending herself.

"If'n it's all right with you, I have some dinner waiting for you and Miss Irene. Its getting cold."

"Stop it, Irene!" Carole said, rising from the sofa to escape the assault. She adjusted her blouse, tucked it back into her blue slacks and turned to face the cook. "Fine, Mrs. Kennison. Irene and I will be right out just as soon as she grows up!"

Looking at the two disheveled women as one would look

at two mischievous children, Mrs. Kennison disappeared behind the library door, closed it silently.

"So," Carole said, continuing her answer to Irene's question. "I sat in the living room, read for an hour or so, but when it became so damned quiet around here, I went into the library. Then you came home."

Irene sipped her cold cucumber soup. She had taken time to change and wash up. Not wanting to hold up dinner, she did not do up her hair, pulling it instead into a loose ponytail; the thick, brunette hair looking deeper and darker because it was still damp. She looked young and radiant. "Well, I'm so happy you rode today. That's the first step to getting over this."

"I am over it, Irene. I would have gladly remounted Monterey the day I blacked out if that rotten old doctor hadn't pumped me full of his voodoo medicine. I blacked out. Neither Monterey nor I were responsible. It was just one of those odd things."

Carole finished her soup, rang for Mrs. Kennison. The cook emerged from the kitchen, her hands laden with the next course. Outside, the sun had set, a snow storm beginning to gather force. As the wind blew outside, the snow began to fall. Carole glanced outside and shivered, although perfectly warm inside. There was a heavy fire raging only a few feet away, yet she felt cold. "Looks like it's going to be a big one, this time."

Irene looked up, the almost-full moon barely lighting the storm outside. "I hope it's fine tomorrow night. There will be a full moon. You know how I love a nighttime walk with a full moon."

"Yes," Carole nodded, eating. "We'll go. But we can't stay out too late. Our train tickets are for early Saturday morning. You know what a grump you are without nine hours of sleep." In response, Irene tossed a dinner roll at Carole, missing the target. It hit the crystal bud vase, tipped it over, and continued rolling along the floor to the French doors at the end of the dining room.

"Rotten shot," Carole laughed.

Her words were lost to a loud, ear-crashing thud as the two middle French doors blew open. Carole turned at the commotion behind her in time to see the other doors slam open, the glass panels shattering, scattering onto the floor. She dropped her fork in astonishment, quickly lurching from her chair. She knew she had to get away from the noise and the glass. Another loud crash; the lights went black: quickly, noiselessly. Irene screamed. The wind howled, the flurries of snow rushed through the open wall of doors. Mrs. Kennison rushed in, faced with a torrent of snow and wind.

"Miss Trent!" she shouted, trying to be heard over the loud whooshing of the wind. "Where are you?" A tree crashed onto the terrace outside, a rush of leaves poured into the dining room; the sound of the crash cut off Carole's reply.

Irene, who had leaped to the floor at the first crash, grabbed Carole's arm, pulling her under the dining table. The two women crawled under to the other side toward the safety of the kitchen.

"Mrs. Kennison!" she yelled, unsure she could be heard through the storm. "Get back into the kitchen!"

A whirl of sound came through the doors, followed by a fresh onslaught of snow and debris. Wet rain coated everything in the dining room, the full force of the storm upon them. Through the howl of the wind, Irene could hear the other doors slam open, their glass panels shattering at the impact; the entire house a cacophony of wind, breaking glass, crashing doors; the Christmas tree tugged and pulled by the force of the wind. Finally, unable to stand, it tipped, one whole side falling into the open fireplace.

Irene tugged Carole into the kitchen; Carole turned to see the violent red fire as the tree burst into flames. She tore away from Irene's grip.

"Irene!" she cried, stumbling to her feet. "The house is

on fire!"

Irene, unable to hear Carole's plea, watched as Carole ran back into the dining room, back into danger. Irene's gaze finally spotted the horrid yellow and red glow in the living room and realized the meaning of Carole's words. "Mrs. Kennison!" she yelled to the cook. "Get the others! Call the fire department! The house is on fire!" Frozen in fear, Mrs. Kennison could not move. "Now, Mrs. Kennison! Call them in here or we'll lose the house!" She turned away from the frightened woman and returned against the storm's fury to follow her friend. Irene followed the path Carole had taken, stumbling through the dark room lit now only by the fire's bright tongues of flame, lashing out and touching all parts of the room. Most of the tree had been consumed; the remnants of its progeny lapping at drapes, couches, shelves. She saw the hand-carved wood paneling darken under the force of the flames, curl as it pulled from the wall; she saw flames leap the distance from floor to ceiling along the curtains, then from one side of the room to the other along the ceiling's beams. Carole, for the brilliant light, could not be seen. "Carole!" Irene called, not knowing where she was. Behind her, Irene saw the cook; John, the houseman; Clifton, the stable boy and the other servants as they hurried into the room, stopped in shock at the inferno raging in front of their eyes. She quickly began shouting orders and instructions to the group.

"Grab the poker from the fireplace," she commanded John. "Use your jacket, it might be hot. Knock down the curtains over the French doors, try to pull the unburned ones far from the fire!" The old man moved quickly, removing his jacket, heading toward the fireplace.

To the cook and the other servants Irene barked orders to fill pots or buckets with water, then dump it onto the base of the flames and onto the still untouched areas to prevent to fire from spreading until the fire department arrived.

Irene suddenly panicked at no sight of Carole. She rushed through the eerily lit room, looking for her, afraid of what she might find. Finally, she found Carole on her hands and knees on the outside terrace shoveling snow with bare hands onto the base of one side of the flames, attempting her best to put out the fire. As Irene lowered herself to assist, throwing handfuls of moist snow onto the fire, the wail of sirens broke through the wind's howl.

Thursday, Late Evening

Carole walked around the still smoldering rubble of the living room. She shuffled her feet through pieces of wood, metal, stone; looking for anything salvageable. The fire had raged through the living room, dining room, and one bedroom, leaving charred ruins in its wake. One of the cook's assistants suffered slight burns when he was felled by a huge beam from the ceiling. Otherwise, members of the household emerged unscathed.

In the rubble, Carole found a small porcelain owl in nearly perfect condition; a lump which was all that was left of a silver spoon; a pewter frame, the photograph burned away. It once held a photograph of her and Philip.

Carole turned at the sound of a crunch of footsteps behind her. It was Irene, her clothes smudged and charred. "If you planned this as a way to keep my mind off Philip," she joked, "it worked!"

Irene forced herself to join in Carole's laughter. She approached Carole, wrapped an arm around her shoulders. "Of course, dear. What are friends for?"

The two exhausted women stood there, gazed at the ruined rooms illuminated by the light of the full moon. "I wanted for us to go for a walk through the forest under a full moon," Irene said, quietly. "This is not what I had in mind."

The fire trucks had arrived within minutes of Mrs. Kennison's call. They extinguished the fire quickly. The fire's spread had been limited through Irene's quick thinking and the actions of Carole and the house staff. The fury of the storm passed almost as the fire was put out. The air around them was calm, eerily quiet.

"Well, Carole. Tomorrow is Friday. Do you think we can get someone out here so close to a holiday to clean up this mess?"

Carole picked at a smoking piece of wood with her shoe, pushed some snow on top of it to insure it was out. "I'm sure we can. Father has a lot of friends. We should have no problem." She turned toward Irene. "Still on for New York?"

"Still want to go? What about the house?"

Carole turned, walked over the rubble into the house. "Father is due back in a day or two. John and Mrs. Kennison can watch the house. We'll get a carpenter, or whomever, to start work tomorrow. This is even more reason for us to be out of everyone's way, don't you think? We'll pack tomorrow and leave first thing Saturday." She smiled at how easily the situation worked itself out.

Irene, unable to argue with logic, smiled and followed Carole into the living room. She walked, staring at the remains of the Christmas tree laying still half in the fireplace. As she stepped over the tree's trunk, crunching on the burned rubble beneath her, she thought, "What a shame."

Carole, too, concentrated on the remains of the tree. Earlier, she had searched the ashes around it for that one very important something she knew should be there; she did not find it. It, too, had been consumed in the flames.

Saturday Morning

The sleekly designed flooring in front of the long, white, cosmetic counter was a symphony of colors. The richly crafted linoleum tiles fitted together with a perfection that betrayed the many long man hours of the skilled craftsman. A brilliant splash of geometric designs, an influence of the recent explosion of styles from the French *Exposition des Arts Decoratifs et Industriels*

Modernes in Paris, the tiles glistened in the bright, reflected sunlight from outside the store.

Two exactly fitted, black patent pumps clicked heavily across the tiles in long, precise strides denoting a woman of obvious purpose; her strides long, confident, proud. The legs stretched for one step and then another down the long expanse of flooring, the arms swinging strongly in opposition. Underneath the light black veil which rimmed the ebony-felt hat, her hazel eyes surveyed the other shoppers coming and going around her. Steady with intent, she hunted her quarry.

Behind her, another equally stunning pair of jet grey Italian shoes clicked along the tiles in a futile effort to keep up with the pair in front. The legs moved hurriedly, frantically, strangled by the tight-fitting black wool skirt. The arms resembled a pendulum gone awry as if due to a heavy earthquake. Ahead, the quarry lay, unprotected; within sight if not yet within reach.

"For goodness sake, Carole. Can't you please slow down?" Irene, breathless, called after her friend while trying to keep up. This was not the first store they had visited since their arrival in New York City this morning. Carole showed no sign of abating; her search relentless.

The strong strides took her past the Hazel Bishop cosmetic counter, the Helena Rubenstein display and the Chen Yu counter.

"Irene, you know how it upsets me when I cannot find what I want. This is the fourth department store we've been in and none of the others had it. If this store doesn't, well, we'll just have to go somewhere else!"

Silently, Irene hoped this store would be the one. The thought of another mad hunt like this was almost too much for her weary body to bear. Suddenly, it loomed ahead. The object of their search: the Revlon counter. Clicking hurriedly past the small intersection between counters, Carole almost ran to the display. Grabbing the attention of the closest sales girl, Carole requested the previously unfound: a bottle of Revlon's Pink

Lightning nail enamel.

Smiling, the sales girl gave the dread reply. "Sorry, Ma'am. We've been sold out for a week. Holiday rush, I'm afraid."

She stood there, stunned, breathing heavily, motionless. She moved only enough to turn her head at Irene's approach.

"Please, let there be some in stock," Irene gasped, barely enough air in her lungs to support the words.

Carole turned a weary eye toward her friend. She shook her head from side to side.

Irene's eyes rolled to the ceiling of the store, her mouth opened. "Oh, no." She felt faint, weak. "All right then," Irene said, recovering her strength. "Why don't you just slice out my heart?"

"You obviously don't seem to understand the importance of this. I cannot go to the theater without my nail enamel. It just cannot be done!"

"But," Irene said, turning to face the cosmetic counter, almost paralyzed with frustration. "Look!" She swept her arms in a gesture which captured the entire store. "The whole store is filled with nail enamel. There has to be something here you like. The odds are on our side!"

If a single glance could ignite fire, Carole's gaze at her friend would have started the inferno. "But not," she said, her words steady, controlled. "Pink Lightning."

There was a heavy silence between them. The sounds in the store had all but ceased. Suddenly, Carole smiled and began to laugh, heartily, from the stomach, her eyes brimming with tears. "You should have seen yourself running in that tight skirt," she said, gasping for breath. "It was too much, really."

Irene parried: "And you! If you stepped any harder on these tiles, the whole store would have been able to hear you. It was as if you were a woman possessed!"

Their laughter died down. Carole removed a light blue handkerchief from her clutch purse, wiped her eyes gently. "How about stopping for lunch? This running about has gotten the best of me."

"I am so glad you finally asked," Irene replied. "But what about -- and I know I'll regret asking this -- the nail enamel?"

"There's a beauty salon at the Plaza. I'll just go there and have them do my nails before the show. I think I can live that long." The two women walked along the same tiled flooring, away from the cosmetics department and out the front entrance, Irene sighing, quietly, in relief.

The conversations of the other diners in the room surrounded Carole and Irene as they ordered their lunch. Shortly, they began feasting on salads.

"Boy, am I beat!" Irene said, mouthfuls of salad hiding her words. "I swear, every time I shop with you, I lose ten pounds!"

Carole chuckled, her mouth filled with salad.

Irene looked at Carole with suspicion. "Don't you ever eat anything other than soup and salad when you dine out? Honestly, Carole, you must learn to try new foods, experience the unusual."

"I do experience the unusual: every time Mrs. Kennison cooks." Carole said. "I only trust her when I try new foods."

They finished lunch, light conversation punctuating the courses. Carole wiped the edges of her mouth with her serviette, gathered her purse and hat from the table. "I'm dashing into the ladies for a quick touch up. Will you excuse me?" She rose from the table, pushing her chair back silently. As she reached her full height, Irene noticed a strange look on Carole's face. It seemed as if Carole's mind went completely blank, she looked down at Irene, frightened. Before she could react, Carole's face grew deathly pale. Her body slumped to the floor in one swift movement.

"Carole!" Irene gasped as her friend hit the richly carpeted floor. She rose from her chair, moving quickly around the table. Irene arrived at the body of her friend as the waiter came around the table, alarmed by Irene's scream. Carole's face was drawn, white, pale. Irene grabbed Carole's shoulders, shook them.

She screamed in frustration as the waiter moved to the telephone to call the doctor. Irene looked around her at the faces in the room, trying to divine some hidden knowledge from them, something that would allow her to help her friend. All seemed lost, when a gentleman moved in silently behind Irene.

"Excuse me. May I be of assistance here?" The old man bent down beside Irene.

"Yes, please," Irene spoke. "She was recently hurt in a riding accident. The doctor said it was all right for her to come out, and...." Irene knew words were tumbling out with little organization; she could not force her mouth to cease working and wait until her mind could catch up.

The old man looked under each closed eyelid, a small light pen in his hand. "It will be all right, Miss," he finally said. "I'm a doctor. I believe she has just fainted." He checked her pulse, loosened the knotted bow of the blouse, his hands moving with a deft skill.

The waiter returned, smelling salts in his hand from the house doctor. He handed them toward the old man. "Yes! Good man," the doctor said, pleased at the young waiter whose face was red from the excitement.

Uncapping the small vial, he moved the bottle of odiferous salts under Carole's nose, their pungent smell wafting from the motion. With a small choke and a swift side-to-side motion of her head, Carole's eyes flashed open. She looked around her, panic in her eyes. She spotted Irene's face; her arm reached up to grab Irene's arm. "Irene! What happened? Who are all these people?"

The doctor reassured her. "Calm down, Miss. You just fainted, that's all. I'm a doctor. You'll be fine." He rose from the floor, motioned with his eyes for Irene to move back, to follow him. When they had moved several feet away from the crowd assisting Carole to her chair, he spoke. "What happened to her?"

Irene didn't know where to start. "She was in an accident, just last Monday. She had a blackout while riding her horse. The doctor, her family doctor, said it was all right to travel."

"I see," he said, almost to himself.

Irene's eyes went dark with fear. "She will be all right, won't she?"

"Yes," the old man said. "She will be all right for now. Once she has had the opportunity to rest a while. I'm sure that's all it is. What activities have you two engaged in today?"

"We spent all day shopping."

"That shouldn't have -- "

"No, doctor. She was racing from store to store. I was exhausted just trying to keep up with her. It was madness."

"Well then," the old man said, pulling a piece of paper from inside his coat pocket. He scribbled on the paper, handed it to Irene. "Take this to the hotel pharmacist. Have him fill it. It's just something to help her relax. No need to worry. What plans have you for your stay here?"

"Well, we're going to see a show tomorrow and do more shopping. Sightseeing. Is that all right?" She folded the paper, placed it into her handbag.

"Yes. That should be all right. But don't do any running around. Have her take her time, rest a lot. She should be fine. But I do think she should see her doctor again when you return home. When will that be?"

"We had intended a two week stay; but, if you think -- "

"No. That will be fine. See to it she rests. Don't allow her to get too excited. Have her see her doctor in two weeks. She'll be fine."

Irene smiled, reassured. "Thank you, doctor. To whom should we send payment?" Irene reached into her handbag, removed a slip of paper and a small, gold pen.

The doctor laughed as he removed his wire spectacles,

wiped them gently with an obviously fine-linen handkerchief. "What have I done that deserves payment, my dear? I'm just an old man who helped out when help was needed. I, too, am vacationing with my dear wife. I have no time to worry with paperwork, bookkeeping." He replaced his spectacles, smiled. He reached his hand for Irene's. "Just take care of her, and have yourself a happy New Year, dear. That will be payment enough for me." He turned from her, walked back to the table where an elegantly dressed, older woman sat swathed in a fur jacket, pearls and diamonds around her neck, adorning her ears.

Irene returned to the table where Carole waited.

"Where have you been, Irene? And who was that old codger you were conferring with?"

Irene smiled, thinking, "Same old Carole." "That old codger was a doctor," she said. "He told me you shouldn't be running around like a mad woman anymore. You aren't strong enough, yet, for this much excitement."

"No? Just watch."

Irene adopted a serious tone. "Really, Carole. You've only had a few days to recover from that awful accident. You should take things a bit more easily until you have had more time to heal." She opened her handbag, removed the piece of paper given her by the doctor.

"What's that?" Carole asked, spying the paper. "Some voodoo medicine?" She laughed, took a sip from her glass of water. "He looked like a witch doctor."

"Carole! Be still," Irene scolded. "It's a prescription, something to help you rest, he said. And we're going to get it filled as soon as we leave here. There will be no more shopping today. I'm tired and need to rest as do you." She rose, taking command, pushing her chair back slowly.

Carole looked up at her, opening her mouth as if to begin an argument. Irene maintained her stance, glaring at Carole, saying without words that no argument would be accepted, demanding the subject be closed without further discussion. Resignedly, Carole grabbed her purse, hat and followed Irene out of the restaurant with a quick wave to the doctor and his wife.

In reply, the old man watched her, clinically, looking for another sign, another symptom. In the short time he had to observe, he noticed nothing else.

New Year's Eve, 1944

As the large, sweep second hand moved slowly across the giant clock's face, moving ever nearer to the moment the assembled guests had been awaiting, the richly attired men and women began echoing the traditional chant: "Four... three... two... one...."

New Year's Day, 1945

The black hour hand, the black minute hand and the glittering gold second hand all pointed upward, reaching for the stylized numeral "12" on the face of the bronze and black clock. From all corners of the filled-to-capacity ballroom cheers and music rose to fill the air, thick with cigarette smoke, with a deafening din. Those with noisemakers or horns put them to their use; those without shouted and clapped their hands at their joy at the entrance of a new year. Through every mind went one simple thought: "Maybe this year, the war will end."

Carole remained seated at the table in the giant ballroom of the Plaza Hotel. Irene, towering over her, stood, cheering, waving multicolored streamers she clutched in her hand. Carole tried to show the gaiety she did not feel. Irene nudged her, shouting over the noise. "Come on! Join in the fun. Don't just sit there. This was your idea, Carole!"

Carole glanced up from the champagne glass she had been nursing, shot a cool look at her friend. Not wanting to spoil Irene's fun, she added a fake smile to her face, turned back to the shimmering liquid. From there, her gaze traveled across to a small, potted palm positioned next to her table. "Should I drink this crap, or should I dump it?" she asked herself. With one swift movement of her hand Carole dumped the warm liquid into the dirt of the palm. She eyed the plant, sure it would wilt and die at any moment from the onslaught of the foul liquid. When the fronds did not curl up, when the palm did not die, Carole turned away, disappointed.

She sat there, patiently, waiting for the cheery din to subside. She frowned as the raucous noise continued unabated. Finally, after what seemed an hour, the band picked up the beat and began to play a happy, cheery tune. Exhausted from the activity, Irene plopped into the leather-covered chair, a great sigh escaping her lungs.

"Whew!" she said "That was fun. Look, Carole, if you aren't having any fun, why are we still here? You were a grouch during the matinee and dinner. Even when we ran into the Murphys you couldn't loosen up." Gerald and Sara Murphy, the famous expatriates, had been friends with Carole's family for years.

Carole shifted in her seat, uncomfortable. "Irene, how can you be having so much fun? I'm worried sick about Philip. I haven't gotten a letter from him since he left. His mother has told me about every phone call but insists Philip is too involved in his 'top secret' mission to call me or write. I could just scream." As she said the last word, shouting to be heard over the band's tune, the music ended, suddenly, leaving her word alone to punctuate the sudden silence. She looked around her, self conscious, while Irene smirked, her face hidden behind her serviette.

"Stop it, Irene," said Carole, quietly, not pleased with Irene's reaction. "You're acting like a spoiled child and I won't stand for it any longer!" Carole bolted from her chair, knocking it over. She stalked through the crowd, rudely pushing aside people in her way. Through the bouncy strains of *Juke Box Saturday Night*, Carole elbowed her way to the ladies' lounge,

Irene in close pursuit. Carole stormed into the lounge, raging at no one in particular. "I can't stand this not knowing any more!" she raged. She threw her purse onto the vanity, sending the small courtesy bottles of perfume scattering in all directions. She turned to Irene and fumed. The young, Negro attendant, intrigued by the excitement, watched discretely. Carole's face was red with anger. "All of you! It just makes me sick. Those kids singing and dancing this afternoon, without any thought in their mind that there is a war on! For all I know, Philip could be dead, for what I've heard from him personally -- which is nothing! And you! You have lost two people to this damned war. Don't you have any respect?"

Irene, not accepting this, yelled back. "Of course I have respect, Carole! You're not the only person affected by this war! We're all suffering. Just because they are over there and we are here does not mean we're all having a gay time. I am sick of your carrying on like a martyr. Philip is fine. Believe me, if he wasn't you would know! And for once, could you try to enjoy yourself? If you feel so damned guilty about being in New York and going to shows, dinner, then just think of this as our USO. The boys have breaks from the fighting and they get to ogle the stars, laugh at Bob Hope, listen to them sing, watch them act, forget their troubles. This," she continued, her arm sweeping across the lounge, reaching beyond the confines of the wall to include the ballroom and all of New York itself. "This is our USO." She paused to regain her breath. "Don't you think I'm sick of this, too? If I see one more short film about buying War Bonds, if I again see Bugs Bunny dancing around pushing War Stamps, I'll just stand up in the theater and scream. I promise! I am sick of saving my newspaper, turning in one empty tube of toothpaste just so I can buy another. Coupons, ration stamps, points, excise tax on clothing. I hate it all. This dress cost me an extra 25% just because of the damned federal excise tax! It was almost one hundred dollars. Can you imagine that? Me? I have more money than I know what to do with and I'm all upset about an extra twenty-five dollars! I'm just sick of this whole affair!"

Irene got up from her chair, walked over to the table next to the wide-eyed attendant, grabbed a cigarette and waited for the young woman to light it. She inhaled and began choking (she did not smoke). She returned to Carole and stubbed out the cigarette in a huge crystal ashtray next to her arm. Then, with a grand sweep of her hand, she whisked the ashtray off the vanity, sending it flying across the lounge, nearly winging the attendant, to crash into tiny bits against the brass railing on the opposite wall. The attendant inhaled silently at the sound of the fragments showering the tiled floor.

Irene smiled at Carole and said in a deep, husky voice. "This place stinks. Let's blow this dump, doll face!" Carole, amazed at her friend's actions, burst into laughter, her face turning red. Irene placed her hand firmly on her hip, turned on her heel, stalked past the attendant handing her a crisp five dollar bill. "For the mess. And keep the change for yourself." Irene threw open the door, turned, smiled at Carole. Carole retrieved her purse, still laughing, and followed out the door.

The two women left the hotel, emerging onto Fifth Avenue; it was a beautiful sight, with a fresh covering of snow. Here and there the snow was trampled into a black soup; but mostly the snow lay there, untouched, unspoiled. On the buildings all ornamental lighting was out, due to brown-out restrictions in effect during the war. The lack of lighting cast an almost gloomy eeriness over the bright city which lay in front of them. Irene and Carole linked arms, walked casually through the snow, down the streets.

The city was quiet, unusual for New York at the start of a New Year. Somehow, there was a calmness about the city which permeated the air, made its impression upon Carole and Irene. Yes, there was an occasional siren piercing the quiet, the frantic cries of a reveler; but basically a silent hum enveloped them.

"It's so beautiful, here, Irene. I can't think of any place I would rather be than here by your side. It would be nice for Philip to be here also. And someone for you. But for now, thank you."

Irene smiled, turned to Carole. The snow had begun to fall again. Both faces were flecked with small flakes of white. "I'm glad you're happy now, Carole. I know it's hard, but we must make the best of this bad situation. It could be worse, always remember that." They walked in silence for some many blocks in a circular route, ending in front of the Plaza. They walked through the glass doors and were immediately assaulted by the warmth which permeated the lobby. Carole shrugged her mink jacket off her shoulders; Irene kept her white lynx jacket on. They strode confidently across the foyer, stopping in front of the elevators.

Arriving on their floor the two women emerged from the elevator, bid the elevator operator a happy New Year, and walked to their suite of two rooms. They changed, washed. Carole joined Irene in her room. Irene was sprawled across the large bed, in a pleated white dressing gown, thumbing through a copy of the *New York Times*.

"Anything of note?" Carole asked, jumping onto the bed across from her friend.

"Not too much," Irene said, almost to herself, her hand flipping pages, stopping here and there to read a headline. "No, not much. "Here's something about those German prisoners who escaped from the Papago Park Prison in Arizona a few days back during that big rainstorm. It says the authorities are still trying to figure out how they managed to escape and wind up at the Mexican border. Only six have been caught so far." Irene shivered in fear, thinking about the enemy loose on our soil.

"Nothing more cheery?"

Irene continued looking through the paper. Suddenly, she shrieked in joy, startling Carole.

"What is it?"

Irene struggled into a sitting position, her legs crossed, and folded the paper back onto itself. "Look!" She thrust the paper to Carole, who took it, carefully.

"What am I looking for?"

Irene leaned forward, peered over the paper's top. "There!" she said, pointing with her finger over the paper. "Jay Thorpe is having a January sale of natural mink coats. Ooh! Let's go first thing tomorrow!"

Carole read the advertisement which was the source of so much excitement, made a disgusted sound, returned the paper to Irene.

"What's wrong?

"If you had read further, you would have seen the fine print about the 20 percent excise tax."

Irene slumped, defeated, like a child whose balloon broke at the same time her ice cream slipped off the cone. "Rats!" she said plopping backwards onto the soft bed. "Well, then. What shall we do?"

Carole rose from the bed. "I don't know about you, friend. I'm going to get some sleep. This revelry has all but worn me out!" She walked across Irene's room, toward her own, flicking off Irene's bedroom light. "Goodnight!" she called as she walked through the door separating the two suites.

"Goodnight," she heard, in reply.

Carole crept to the bed in darkness; crawled under the heavy covers, her head resting gently on the pillow, her eyes closed; she did not dream that night. When she awoke she was in a hospital.

PART TWO
Thursday Afternoon, 11 January 1945

It seemed like it had been only minutes after she closed her eyes that Carole reopened them and found herself blinded by a piercing white light. She flinched as she opened her eyes, the glare from the white walls startled her. She tried to open them once again. When they opened this second time she was able to focus on her surroundings. A screened window, a small end table which served as the base for a glistening steel pitcher and a small glass. Her eyes roamed around the room. A wooden door (to where?), a framed painting on the wall. Her gaze continued around the room, stopping on a weary looking, tired, bedraggled image which, if one used enough imagination, would almost resemble -- "Irene?" her voice asked, barely audible. Her throat felt parched, dry. Her voice was one she did not recognize.

Carole watched as the small figure, slumped asleep in a stiff wooden chair, stirred awake, the eyes squinty in the bright glare of the afternoon sun piercing the screen covering the window, throwing a spike of sun into her eyes. Slowly, the figure roused itself awake, spotted her on the bed. "Carole!" the voice called in excitement. "My god, you're awake!"

Carole watched the sloppy figure jump from the chair, run to the door and shout for someone to come quickly. In moments, the room was filled with a team of white-robed men and women racing about, shouting and talking rapidly amongst themselves. She tried to ask a question but was rudely shushed by a woman who instructed her to lay back, keep still. Again, she tried to call for Irene, but was ordered to remain silent.

Carole complied with the orders of these strangers; but only as long as Irene remained in the room. After an eternity of whispered comments, wild rushing about, the white-robed men and women left the room except one, older man on one side of the bed and Irene, looking so old and tired, on the other.

Looking sternly at the older man, Carole spoke. "May I

ask you something, sir?"

"Of course you may, Carole," the doctor replied.

Wondering how he knew her name, she said: "Firstly, I wish to know why you and that woman have been so insolent with me. How dare you speak to me in that manner!"

Irene laughed to herself, looked at the doctor. "She seems all right to me, doctor."

Carole's eyes lit up in surprise. "You're a doctor," she stated.

The old man smiled, nodded his head. "Yes, I am, Carole."

Carole looked at him, sternly. "Then, someone had better teach you some bedside manners, sir."

Acting petulant, the doctor smiled, spoke softly. "I'm very sorry, Carole. I hope you will forgive me. It's just that we were all so surprised, that -- "

"Surprised? Why are you so damned surprised that I woke up? I assure you, doctor, it's something I've been doing every day for many years."

Irene spoke, softly. "That's just it, dear. You haven't awakened for many days. Ten, I think."

Carole turned to Irene, disbelief playing across her face. "Ten days? You had too much to drink last night, dear. I told you we shouldn't have stayed at that party so long."

Irene looked up to the doctor, pain evident in her eyes.

"New Year's was last week," the doctor said, quietly. "Today is the eleventh of January."

"What do you mean?" she asked, looking at the old man. She turned to look at Irene. "Tell me what he means!"

"Carole," Irene began. "You went to bed New Year's morning, but did not wake up when I came into your room later that day. You've been," she paused, trying to find the proper words. "You've been asleep since then. This is the first time you have awakened. We were so scared you might never -- " Irene broke off, her words choked.

Carole turned to the old man. "Is this true, Doc?" He

nodded his head. Carole felt frightened now, like a deer that had been shot but lay mortally wounded, not yet dead. "What happened to me? I didn't drink that much. I promise!"

The doctor smiled. "You had a blackout a couple weeks ago. You remember that, don't you?" Afraid to move, Carole nodded. "Something happened in your head. We still aren't sure what. We think it made you," he paused, "sleep. It made you sleep for a long time."

Tears began to roll down the side of Carole's face, dampening the pillow. "What's wrong?" she pleaded.

"Well, the doctors don't know," Irene volunteered. "They want to do some tests, to find out."

Carole's eyes widened, her head shaking from side to side. "No! No tests. No!" she shrieked, her words punctuated by sobs from her throat.

Irene reached down, stroked her forehead softly, tried to calm her. The doctor spoke again.

"Now, then. It'll be all right, Carole. These tests are quite simple, but they will tell us -- "

Carole refused to allow the old man to finish. She shrieked again and again the single word "no" until the doctor had no choice but to call for a nurse who entered, in her hand a hypodermic needle filled with a cloudy liquid. Carole shrieked through the injection of the sedative; a few moments later, she calmed down.

Irene stood by the bed, holding Carole's hand. "Carole dear, there's nothing to be afraid of. It's all right, really."

Carole, feeling light and hazy, turned her tear-streaked face toward Irene. "That's the last thing my mother said to me."

Irene looked at the doctor, not understanding her words. "What did your mother say, Carole?"

"When mother was in the hospital, she held my hand when Father and I came to visit her. She told me to be a brave little girl, that there was nothing to be afraid of, that it would be all right." She began to cry, again.

Irene urged her to continue. "What's wrong with that?"

Carole closed her eyes, remembering. "I never saw her again. She died on the operating table when the doctors were doing *tests*!" Carole's head tilted down, onto the pillow. She was fully sedated now.

Irene, shocked, looked to the doctor. "I knew her mother was dead. She never told me how it happened. We never spoke of it. I never knew."

"Come, Irene," the doctor said, reaching around the bed. Taking her arm, he led her from the room. "Let her sleep for now. When she awakens tomorrow, we'll talk further with her; but, for now, you must get some rest. And tomorrow, you must talk her into getting these tests done. They are crucial."

She walked through the door, stealing one last look at her sleeping friend. Irene turned to the doctor. "But, are they really necessary, doctor?"

They walked a few feet down the white, sterile-smelling hall. The doctor nodded solemnly. "I'm afraid they are very necessary."

Friday, Early Evening, 19 January 1945

The slightly frayed, yellowed photograph rested lightly in her hand. The scalloped edges worn. In the photograph, a woman stood. She was youngish, about twenty, holding a spray of short-stemmed roses tied with a ribbon. The bride -- for that's what the woman was -- smiled a slightly cockeyed smile which brought small crinkles to the sides of her eyes, emphasizing the bright dimples on either side of her lips. She stood on a mat of newspaper so as to protect the shimmering satin gown; even without a train it trailed into little folds on the ground. The veil blew sideways in a strange way, speaking of a wind which must have been blowing outside the building which served as the backdrop for the photograph. Behind her, a shoulder-high brick wall topped with louvered windows through which other members of the wedding party peered.

They had a dull, almost bored look on their faces as if this were but one of many photographs they had taken that day. But, she was smiling.

The photograph slid, then tipped onto the ground as Carole's hand moved slightly. It was the only photograph she still had of her mother. It seemed so long ago, that day when her mother told her everything would be all right. Yet, even now that Carole was a grown woman, she could not shake that hollow, empty feeling deep inside of her. She rarely thought about the woman in the photograph.

She looked across the desk in the library to the clock resting upon the mantle above the dying fire. One more hour and Irene would return. She rose from the heavy leather chair, walked slowly, exactly, to the fireplace shifting her jacket closer around her neck. It had been snowing nonstop for days; even when the fire roared, the air had a bitter cold edge to it. Nothing she did could remove it. Crouching at the fender, she grasped the poker. A slight movement of her hand and the last of the unburnt logs shifted, catching. They flared, briefly, into life, then died out. She glanced to the empty wood carrier, made a mental note to remind John to keep it filled.

Resigning herself to the fact she would not get any warmer by staying where she was, she rose, walked from the library. The living room was different since the fire. Somehow, there was still the smell of burnt wood in the air, different from the familiar smell of burning firewood. The couch was new, no longer the inviting peach colored, lush sofa where Philip had spoken his last words to her. In its place, a bright, sky-blue arched-back sofa which looked too new, alien. In fact, the entire room looked as if it belonged in another house. The only familiar feature was the dark marble fireplace. The mantle was new, it had been damaged by falling ceiling timbers. But, the room looked complete, finished. How quickly the damage had been erased. When she and Irene returned from New York, after the stay in the hospital, almost the entire house had been put back in order. A few odds and ends on order, or delayed due to war shortages; but, for the most part, the house was complete.

Carole avoided the new living room since her return. It held so many memories of good times which were no more and bad times she would never forget. She fingered the diamond ring on her hand, feeling the cool, slick metal. She moved into the large room, sat hesitantly on the sofa. She pulled the stack of newspapers from their cradle, thumbed through them not looking for anything in particular. She looked up from the paper long enough to search out the clock on the mantle. Only a few minutes had passed. It was going to be a long wait.

Bits and pieces of the news caught her attention. A lot had happened since she left. One headline heralded "96,369 planes of all types were made in the U.S. in 1944, with a total airframe weight of 1,112,000,000 pounds, the War Production Board announced today." Another indicated General MacArthur in the Philippines, and that America was 107 miles from Manila. She read some of the president's speech to the nation as printed in the *New York Times*, Sunday, January 7; another event missed. Two weeks pass quickly in a person's life; she never realized just how much happened from day to day. She scanned the remainder of the text, flipped through to a crossword puzzle. She returned to the puzzle she had begun earlier that day, having completed half before she grew bored. She remained stuck on number 42 across which read "Ancient town of Osci, Italy -- 6 letters." She pondered the clue when suddenly the front door flew open and a white-tipped, fur-covered creature ran in, dropping bundles and packages in its wake.

"Aaaaaggghh!" cried the creature, as Carole stared at it.

She rose slowly from the couch, stood at the end, and observed Irene stopped in the midst of the foyer as she shrugged her silver-and-white dyed mink to the floor. Irene stood there, surrounded by small and large boxes, snow, and a dead animal.

"Nice entrance, dear." Carole said, smiling. "If ever there

was a time I wish I had a camera...."

Irene "humphed" with irritation in reply, stalked down the few steps separating the foyer from the living room. She stopped in front of the landing, removed her soiled red pumps, stood erect. As she began to walk to Carole, she sent the shoes flying from her hands to "thump, thump" against the solid front door behind her. "My new shoes are a mess," she complained. "My hosiery got two runs in them and some fool bumped into me with a full cup of hot chocolate, spilling it all over the bottom of my new dress. The guy's lucky my fur was at my table or I would have beaned him. I did give him a swift kick to the shin though," she added with a grin. "It was the least he deserved. Then, he had the nerve to glare at me as if I had done something wrong. People!" she said, crossing the landing. She walked to Carole, embraced her, asked how her day had been, then walked to the new dark-blue divan. She sat.

Carole smiled, turned, and followed the conquering hero fresh from another conquest. "Shall I have Mrs. Kennison get you some java, or chocolate?"

"No, thanks," Irene replied, her voice breathy from the dash to the house through the storm outside. She ran both hands through her brunette hair. For a moment, Carole envied her friend her beautiful face, stunning when her hair was pulled back. "I just want to rest for a few minutes. How much time do I have until we leave for the hospital?"

"Do we really have to talk about it? I want to see what you bought. I hope you found everything I wanted." She rose, walked to the foyer and, grabbing the bundles, brought them into the living room, setting them in front of Irene. She sat on the floor and rummaged through the boxes.

"Boy, did I," Irene laughed. "I found everything on your list. I found the most beautiful nightgown for you to wear instead of that nasty hospital gown they'll inevitably insist on. It's all peachy color, has a pretty lace trim, and -- " She continued a run down of the items she purchased while in the city; Carole's mind began to wander. It was Irene's mention of the color peach bringing her mind to the burned sofa and that night Philip opened the velvet box....

" -- and, Carole. Carole? You haven't heard a word I said. What's the matter?"

Carole returned. "Nothing. I just miss the old living room. That's all."

"Yeh, isn't it the most? I can't believe there was ever a fire here, though. It seems like normal except the color."

A pause filled the air, the silence broken only by an occasional sound of the wind outside and an occasional crackle from the fireplace.

"You still miss him, don't you," Irene ventured, reaching down to stroke Carole's hair.

Carole turned, looked through the French doors. The new drapes were still to arrive, another victim of the war shortages, leaving the view of terrace exposed, open. "No," she finally said. "I don't think it's that."

"Are you feeling all right?"

Carole turned, looked at Irene. "Yes," she said, smiling, placing her hand on Irene's knee. "I'm fine, really."

"Then, what -- "

"I don't know, Irene," Carole said, a sigh filling the pause. "You know, it's the funniest thing. Right after Philip left, I felt so, so, hollow, I guess. I'm not really sure. But, now that weeks have passed, it's almost as if he had never been here. I mean, I do miss him, but I don't." She laughed. "Do you understand?"

"Yes, actually."

"I pulled out my old photograph, the one of -- " she paused, thinking, "mother. I tried to feel what I felt inside about her. I haven't thought of her, really thought of her for a long time. Not until..." her voice became low, a whisper, "that awful day in the hospital. She left me so early. I had to live my whole life without her. I knew she was gone, but I didn't feel abandoned. I'm not making any sense, am I?"

Irene didn't reply.

"I got out the photograph, but before I looked at it, I sat in Dad's chair. I closed my eyes. I sat there, in the dark, and tried to make mother's face come to me, in my mind. I sat there, thought about her eyes, her hair," she turned to Irene. "She had hair like yours, you know." She paused. "I couldn't do it, Irene. I couldn't make her face come to my mind. I tried and tried and couldn't. When I finally looked at her photograph, I remembered, it all came back to me. I'm so glad I still have that photograph." She looked away. "Is that going to happen with Philip?"

"No, Carole. It won't. Sometimes, when I'm lonely, I do just what you did, sit in a chair, close my eyes and try to remember my father, or Matt. Sometimes, they come to me, really quickly. When I remember learning to ride a bike, my dad running beside me, pushing me, yelling 'Steer it! Steer it!' Or Matt helping me learn to throw a baseball. It's when I remember us, them and me, together that they come to me. Just remember Philip and you dancing, or when you went fishing, or, we -- you know."

"One thing I do remember is what you said in the lounge in New York, about that being our USO."

Irene suddenly laughed, a refreshing, alive laugh which soothed Carole. "Oh, boy! Did you see that girl's eyes when the ashtray went flying against the wall?"

"It was pretty funny. But, more than entertaining, you made me realize something. I'm not sure just what, but you made me feel unguilty."

"What?"

"Yes. Before, I felt so guilty that Philip was off somewhere fighting for us, me. I drove by the Craig house late one evening. I saw that service flag with the one blue star on it hanging in their front window. It was late, there was a full moon. For the briefest moment, I thought the star was gold. My heart, leapt, froze. 'Philip dead!' I thought. But, as I drove closer to the house, I realized it was only the moon's light reflected on the glass that made the blue star appear gold. I cried, I was so glad. I had never been so happy to see a blue star in my life!"

"That explains your boundless energy during New York."

"Exactly," Carole said, sitting upright, suddenly glad Irene understood what she was talking about. "Yes, that's why. I had to keep running, always moving, because then I wouldn't have time to think about Philip, and -- "

"And what, dear?"

"And the fact he could die at any time, that someday the Craig's blue star would really be gold. I couldn't handle it." A log fell from the grate, plunked into the ashes below. A flare rose, lit both women. Carole's eyes glistened as she spoke again about Philip. "So, then, when I thought about mother dying in that hospital, I just fell apart. But when I took time to think about the whole situation, those extra days in the hospital, I decided I would not die there like mother did, that I would come through those stupid tests and begin to plan for my wedding."

Irene was startled by the words. She turned, watched Carole's face.

"There's a lot to be planned, you know, and the sooner I start, the sooner I'll become Mrs. Philip Craig." Carole looked out at the terrace and the snow falling onto the railing.

Irene moved her hand from Carole, rose from the divan. "I'm going to grab a glass of juice before we go. Are you all packed?"

Carole spoke to her retreating figure. "Yes, all ready." She lifted her body from the floor, walked down the hall to her rooms, her mind lost on satin, lace and roses.

Irene turned the corner, walking into the darkened kitchen. A flick of her hand brought light to the room. As she poured a glass of juice from the pitcher her mind, too, was on satin and lace. From somewhere deep within her came a dull ache, a foreboding, a feeling that the wedding would never occur; that maybe a gold star would one day hang proudly in the front window of the Craig home.

Friday Evening

The long, black car pulled through the snowbound roads with a slow movement, like an animal stalking its prey. Some drifts had blown above tire height along one side of the road and roof height along the opposite side. Carole peered out the frosted window, searching for any sign of life along the path. She found none. For some reason, she was saddened by this. The thick coppice of trees in the distance beckoned to her; the limbs of snow-kissed trees waved to her in a come-hither way. She sighed. Irene was looking at the broad expanse on her side of the car, the coldness of the scenery biting at her mind. She moved a finger against the condensation-covered glass, cleared away a small round viewing hole, and sighed, her frosted breath closing her window to the outside world.

"It's all so beautiful out there. Yet, at the same time, so lonely," Carole whispered.

Irene did not reply, the silence broken only by the crunching of the snow underneath the car's tires.

"Aren't you worried about taking time off from work? What about your promotion?" Carole faced Irene, gazing through, rather than at, her.

"I told my lead man about your situation, that your father was in Washington on important war business. I told him there was no one else to take care of you. He said I could take off all the time I needed. You know, I think he was rather glad I wanted the time off."

"Why?"

"There's been a lot of talk about laying off all the women when the war is over. I mean, the minute the war ends, we're to be given our walking papers."

Carole's eyes shifted to meet Irene's.

"Why would they do that?" she asked, skeptically. "I just read how war production in all plants with women was up, that the supervisors said you all worked better, more efficiently, and -- "

Irene laughed. "That's true, at least as far as I can tell. There was this stupid article in *Life* magazine a couple months back. I think it was sometime in September. It said how great it would be when the veterans came back because they had all that military training. They would be trained in radar, chemistry, engineering, all the rest. It was the talk of the plant. There was some poll in the article about some survey done by the Women's Auxiliary of the American Legion. It said about 54% of the women wanted to quit! Well, no one asked me, but I know that isn't true. At least not any more. We like the work! A lot of those women, and a lot of the women in other plants, came to the cities because they couldn't find any work where they lived. A lot of them came from farm families. And they sure like the money they're earning! Can you blame them? I mean, the $1.25 an hour I'm now making doesn't mean too much to me, but to some of them, well, I know most of them began at 75 cents an hour. It's like inheriting big bucks. They wouldn't go back home to the drudgery of dishes, cleaning, kids. Who would?"

"But, if you do so well, and you like your jobs, why would they want you out?"

Irene laughed again. "The guys, you should have seen their faces when women started to take over some of the vacant jobs held only, and I mean exclusively, by the men. They were frantic. It was like they had been found out. They would play tricks on us, make things rough on us. The creeps. They didn't stop to think we were all working for the same goal, to beat the hell out of the enemy, to bring them to their Japaknees!" Irene laughed at the lyrics from the song. "But men are like that," she continued. "Aren't they? See, it started a couple years back with that article in *Time* magazine. It was about what awful workers women were. One of the big plants, Douglas Aircraft, in fact, had to close because of women smoking, women wearing tight sweaters, women gossiping, women not showing up for work. It's all a bunch of bull. And, this is the worst, it said women were fooling around with the guys during the lunch breaks.

Well, it takes two to fool around, you know? The guys were just as much to blame as were the women. And I think the guys made up all this crap because the gals *wouldn't* mess around with them. They're just like little children, the men. They're so afraid about us taking their jobs because we're so much better than they are -- with the facts to back us up." She sighed. "So, my supervisor welcomed my request for a leave. Anyway, you are far more important that any old job," she said, grasping Carole's gloved hand. "You're my best pal, after all."

"Thank you."

They had been talking for so long that they were both surprised when the car suddenly crunched to a halt. Irene looked through the frosted window and saw the lights and walls of the hospital. "We're here," she said.

Carole only nodded.

"Will you be all right?"

Carole looked at Irene, her eyes glistening. She nodded. "Yes, I think so."

Irene's door opened, the driver reached in to help her from the car. "You go in, dear," she said to Carole. "I'll get your things from the back. Be careful with those steps." Irene emerged from the car, the sudden sting of the bitter cold bringing a flush to her face. She helped Carole, motioned for the driver to assist with the luggage from the trunk.

Carole held the hospital door while Irene walked up the drive and the steps toward the building. Once in the lobby, the doctor met them.

"Miss Davis, Miss Trent," he said. "You're right on time. If you will just follow me, I'll show you your room, Miss Trent."

They followed behind the youngish doctor who led them through the halls and to a large room. He held open the door for them. "Here you are. I hope it'll be to your satisfaction."

Carole walked past him, removed her heavy coat. "Nothing in this whole affair is to my satisfaction, doctor. When will I meet the doctor who has been assigned to my case?" She tossed the coat onto the bed, motioned for Irene to place both suitcases onto the floor by the window. Irene sat in the chair in the corner without removing her jacket.

The doctor, suddenly embarrassed, smiled. "Miss Trent, I have been assigned your case. I'll be doing the tests over the next few days and anything else that might need to be done."

Carole eyed him, suspiciously. "What do you mean, and anything else?"

The young man moved toward her. "Now, I didn't mean to suggest anything. You might need treatment, or medication after we discover what's wrong with you. Why you keep fainting, having headaches. I'll be the one to oversee any such treatment."

Carole rose from the bed, walked toward the doctor, confronted him. "Aren't you rather young to be given so much responsibility, Doctor... Doctor?..."

He quickly thrust out his hand. "Forgive me, Miss Trent. I took for granted that you must already know who I am. I'm Doctor Fischer. And I appreciate your compliment."

"Oh?"

"Yes," he chuckled. "About my being too young. I assure you, I do not look my age; but I have many years of experience with this. I have received training from the very best."

"Experience with what, Doctor Fischer?"

"Oh," he began, sitting half on and half off the bed. "People fainting, having headaches. That sort of thing."

"Well, Doctor Fischer, I'm sure I am nothing like those people. I'm just a bit... oh, I don't know. They're only innocent headaches, that's all."

"Well, I'm sure they are. But wouldn't it be nice to know for sure?"

"Are you trying to suggest they're not?"

"Not at all, Miss Trent. But, that's what these tests are for, after all. We want to make sure that they are just innocent headaches."

"Well," Carole said, walking to the door. "I assure you, they are." She stood at the door for a beat, hoping her subtle signal would be understood. Finally, it was.

"Of course, I'm sure you would like to talk. I'll have a nurse check back with you in a couple of minutes. You'll find your dressing gown in the closet."

"But, doctor. Do I have to wear that ugly thing? I have the nicest nightgown which I got just to wear here."

"Well, I don't know -- regulations being what they are."

Irene added. "Please, doctor," she said, throwing her thick, east-coast accent into the words. "She did get it for the stay and wouldn't it be just awful to make such a beautiful woman wear an ugly hospital garment? Do you think, just this once?..."

He smiled. "Yes. Of course it'll be fine. I'll have the nurse come in and take that ugly thing away. I'll see you in the morning if that meets with your satisfaction."

"Yes it does, doctor. Thank you." Carole smiled as the doctor left the room, closing the door behind him, softly. Carole walked across the room, took Irene by the hands.

"You had better go, dear. I'll be fine. I have the rest of "Forever Amber" to get through, and the other books you bought for me. Will I see you in the morning?"

Irene rose, hugged Carole, pushed her away to an arm's length, her hands grasping Carole's forearms. "Of course you will, my dear. Of course. Is there anything else you need? Something I can bring you tomorrow morning?"

"No, thank you. Doc and his regulations...."

They both laughed. "All right then, until tomorrow."

"Yes, until then." Carole leaned forward, kissed Irene on the cheek. "Thank you for everything, dear."

Irene left the room, walked down the hall, out of the hospital toward the waiting car.

Carole leaned onto the bed and looked around the room: cold, aloof, forbidding. She rose, began to unpack her things. The first item from her suitcase, which went right onto her pillow, was a notebook. On the cover were the words "Wedding Plans."

Saturday Morning

The cold of the tiled hospital floor seemed to permeate the soles of his shoes as he walked around the corner, toward the nurse's station on the ground floor of the giant hospital. He pulled her chart from the holder, read through it as he ran his hand through his heavy, thick, black hair. A sigh escaped his lungs as he closed the file, strode the distance to her room.

Doctor Fischer stood at the door to room 113, remembering his younger days as a boy in Paris. "How times have changed," he thought to himself with a sigh. He remembered his father, his mother, and the German S.S. that tracked them down, into France after their nighttime escape through the German countryside. He was too young, then, to understand the importance of the resistance -- too young. Now, as he stood safely on American soil, at the door to a hospital room in Maryland, he knew he had a past. He knew his parents had died at the hands of the Nazis for a reason. Now, with the end of the war so close, he might actually begin to rest more easily. He might actually sleep an entire night without dreaming of his father's face when the soldier's knife sliced through his throat; his mother's scream, the bright smile on the young soldier's face. He might now begin to feel some ease when he walked alone at night, no longer fearing that, from behind some tree, might come that same German soldier, finally having tracked him down. He might be able to marry, settle. Put his past behind him.

Roughly, his hand pushed against the door which slid silently open. His smile greeted the smile he saw inside.

"Good morning, Doctor," Carole said, looking up from her wedding plan book. "I was wondering when you would come say hello."

"Miss Trent. I thought I should wait until after breakfast before coming to confer with you."

"That was nice of you."

"Was everything to your satisfaction?"

"Surprisingly, yes."

"Good." He looked at the small notebook in her hand, resting lightly by her side. "What have we here?"

Carole brightened. "I'm getting married."

"Oh? When?"

"Well," she paused. "When my fiancé returns."

"Congratulations. Overseas?"

"Yes, that is, I -- "

"They haven't told you where he is."

"No," she replied, honestly glad he understood. "But, he'll be coming home soon and then we'll marry."

"We'll try and have you all fixed up and ready to walk down the aisle in short order."

Carole smiled in reply.

The doctor began to outline the tests that had been planned over the course of the next four days. He spoke slowly, carefully, as not to alarm her. He already had an idea of the cause of her complaints. The files from the hospital in New York and the original doctor's report had given him conclusive evidence. As would any doctor, he had to have results from a battery of tests before he could safely voice his diagnosis. As he spoke, there came a sharp rap at the door. They turned as it opened slowly.

"Ooh, my. But don't we look serious today." Irene strode into the room, her jacket dusted with snow from the light fall this morning. She held a huge potted plant in her arms. "You would never know how hard it was to find a healthy potted plant this time of year. Sorry I'm so late."

She plopped the plant onto the window sill, dropped her jacket onto the chair in the corner and planted a big kiss on Carole's forehead. "Good morning. Are they treating you well?"

"Yes," Carole offered. "The good doctor and I have been getting along swimmingly."

"Sorry to interrupt, Doc. I've been running around all morning, I guess my manners just went out the window. Good morning, and how are you?"

Doctor Fischer laughed, extended his hand in response to hers. "Think nothing of it. I understand."

There was a moment of uncomfortable silence as Irene, the doctor, and Carole all looked at each other. Irene suddenly realized the cause. "Oh, my. You must think decorum is not within the realm of my understanding, don't you, doctor? I'll leave the two of you alone to finish all this doctor-patient stuff."

"No, that's all right. I was almost finished, anyway. I know you two have a lot to talk about."

Irene smiled. She noticed something different in this young man, a familiarity, a warmth that had not been there before, and one she had only rarely sensed in another man. She knew nothing of him, not even his first name; but, somehow, she felt completely at ease with him. She looked at him, quizzically, almost as if studying a blueprint at work. She extended her hand, warmly. "Thank you, doctor. Will I be out of your way in this chair?"

"Yes. I only need another minute or two."

Irene seated herself, folding her jacket over her lap. She crossed her legs at her ankles and busied herself with a perfunctory examination of the lining of her jacket, wanting to be seen to be doing something other than eavesdropping into the conversation. The doctor quickly finished his run down with Carole, omitting a few minor details which would have only taken up time. He left the room with a quick goodbye to Irene.

There was a pause. Carole's first words startled Irene. "You're in love with him, aren't you?"

Irene choked, began to cough. Carole laughed at her accurate guess. "I thought so," she said.

Irene spoke, "Goodness! How could you have come to that conclusion? I only just met him, just yesterday."

"Yes," Carole said. "But, I couldn't miss that look on your face, dear. You were about a subtle as a truck smashing through a maternity ward. You are one, love-sick woman."

Irene could only laugh. Could that something she felt have been affection? No, she assured herself, it doesn't happen that quickly.

The young doctor stood at the nurse's station, documenting his visit with his patient. As he replaced the file, he thought about his life. Born in Berlin, in 1918, the twenty-six-year-old doctor was now an American citizen, glad to have his past life behind him. As he walked back to the small cubbyhole which served as his office he thought of living in Baltimore, of American food, of the distance, in time and miles, between him and what he remembered. But more, he thought of the woman he had only just met. The feeling in his heart, the flush through his face, the weakness in his knees. Was it love, this thing that made his stomach tingle? Not this quickly, he assured himself. No. He opened the door to his office and thought of the small notebook in her hand. Will I know I love her before she gets married? he thought. Will she die before she knows she loves me?

Wednesday Afternoon

"Doctor Fischer, I'm afraid the facts speak for themselves. Your diagnosis is, unfortunately, accurate." The grayed old man placed his hand on the young doctor's shoulder. He gave a small, but firm squeeze. "I'm sorry, son."

Doctor Fischer stopped walking, turned, looked at the old man. "So you agree with the prognosis?"

"There is no doubt, Doctor. I agree with a six-month prognosis although, personally, I would give her less. Probably two or three months; but that's only my opinion. The facts bear out your report."

He turned away, his face burning with frustration.

They walked the length of the brightly lit hallway, no words were spoken. "Bretaigne," the older man said. "There is only so much we can do. We are doctors, not magicians. I know that does little to lighten the load you feel you must carry. Is this the first time you've had to tell a patient she was dying?"

"It is. I never imagined it would be like this."

The sagacious man sighed heavily. "Death, my son, is very hard to accept, whomever it is."

"So, she insisted I bring this along!" Irene hoisted a heavy wicker basket onto the bed with a hollow-sounding thump. "Mrs. Kennison said she didn't want you to suffer with hospital food any longer."

Carole raised her body upright, her nose twitching at the smells of freshly baked bread and chicken. "Goodness! What all did she put in there?"

"Oh, there's fruit, cakes, a couple slices of her gooseberry pie left over from last evening. All sorts of goodies." She lifted the two halved tops, digging out the items as they were mentioned. "And, she included two complete settings of your Limoges, plus crystal, silver. And, if that weren't enough, she insisted I bring napery enough for an army. I think she doesn't think hospitals have napkins or towels."

Carole could not restrain herself. She imitated Mrs. Kennison's instructions to Irene: "Miss Irene. I am sure the hospital has no napkins or towels, so take these. There are enough here for an army." The two women broke into fits of laughter, broken only by the sound of the opening door. It was Doctor Fischer. He saw the two women laughing. It made his heart sink. It was going to be so hard to explain his findings to Carole. He envisioned a dark, somber room, Carole patiently awaiting him. Instead, he found her so alive.

"Laughter? Not at my expense, I hope." He smiled, walking into the room, commanding attention.

Irene howled. "No, no, no. Goodness, but you did miss an excellent imitation!" She laughed, unable to stop.

"Of me?" he said.

Carole broke in, barely able to speak. "No. It's our cook. Look at all this!" she said, indicating the feast laid out on her bed, covering nearly all of it.

"I see," he said, pushing his hand through his heavy black hair. "Does your cook not know that the ten-dollars-a-day you pay for your room includes meals?"

"Oh, of course," Irene offered.

"Yes," Carole added. "But, she worries an awful lot about me. Apparently someone told her I've lost a few pounds, and Mrs. Kennison -- that's our cook -- would not allow it."

"Well, I'm sure she'll be happy that your prison stay will end in a few hours, after your lunch, that is. I would however, like to speak to Miss Davis before you dig in, if that's all right?"

The two women laughed again. Irene laughed half heartedly; for, in the eyes of this young man she saw a pain, a hurt. She knew instantly that something was not right. "Of course, Doctor." She turned to Carole. "Touch none of this," she instructed. "I'll be right back and I expect both pieces of pie to be here when I return." She smirked at Carole, walked around the bed, through the door being held open by the doctor.

He smiled at Carole, turned, and followed Irene. The door *whooshed* close.

She walked through the door and felt a chill finger touch her spine. She and the doctor stood in the hall, down from room 113, silence between them. Irene's legs trembled. She had never felt such a dull, empty feeling like the one which gripped her now. She lifted her eyes to his, rested her fingers lightly upon his arm. She could not make the words she wished to speak come from her mouth. She exhaled, frustrated, her eyes never leaving his.

He knew she was in shock. One that would pass, or, at least, become stable in a few moments. He rested his hand on her fingers. He waited.

Words came to her. "She is," she said, inhaling deeply, tears forming in her eyes. "Going to...." He nodded. She knew it was true. Tears began to course down her cheeks, her breathing was labored. She doubled over from a sudden pain so forceful as if struck in the stomach by an unseen adversary. The doctor said nothing.

Moments passed. They had to; Irene needed time. She regained her composure, wiped her face streaked with mascara, forced herself to control the breathing. "How..." she sobbed, speaking slowly. "How long?"

"Six months," he said softly, knowing no words would make the truth more easy to understand.

"Six?"

He interjected. "Maybe less; maybe more. These things are impossible to know for certain."

Suddenly, the implications struck her; another blow from the unseen foe. She looked at him, her eyes boring through him. "You cannot tell her," she said, firmly. He protested; his words quickly bitten off. "No!" Irene demanded. "I absolutely forbid it! She must never know!" Again, he tried to protest. He spoke no words. "Damnit, no! I'll tell her when the time is right. She's happy now. You saw that face, you heard that laugh. Do you think it's fair to end that happiness now?" She paused. "That's what will happen, you know, if you tell her. I have never seen her more happy than she was a few moments ago. If she has, only.... If she has six months to live, as you say she does, doesn't she deserve them to be months filled with happiness? Would you rather she spend each and every minute of the next six months waiting, wondering which moment would be her last? Would you?"

"No."

"Then don't tell her. Don't tell her father. Give it to me, anything I need to sign that will absolve you from any responsibility. I'll take full responsibility. I've known her my entire life. I'll know when the proper time has come." He said nothing. Irene grasped his forearm, her nails digging through his jacket into the flesh of his arm. "Promise it!"

He exhaled, nodded. "Yes. All right."

Irene smiled, the triumph hers. "Thank you doctor. You have just done the most difficult thing in your life." He looked at her knowing that statement was not true, for she would never know the difficult things he has done in his life, could never understand. "I think you and I should meet within the week to discuss the details, But, if there is no reason for her to stay, I would like to take her with me when we finish lunch. Is this all right?"

"Of course."

Irene walked slowly, resolutely, toward room 113. Bretaigne Fischer stood in the cold hospital hallway, slumped against the wall which provided the only force to hold his body upright. His figure created a lone image in the shadow between the bright, illuminating cones of light marking even distances down the length of the deserted hall. Alone he stood, weeping.

PART THREE
Wednesday Evening, 14 February 1945

Carole hired an orchestra for the evening. It played mostly standards for the assembled group. The melodies filled the entire house, even though the music came from the living room. From the far bedrooms to the kitchen the house lived and breathed music. Always the perfect hostess, Carole moved from small group to small group, her smile ever present, sincere. Her flowing red hostess gown vibrantly set off her blonde hair, her hazel eyes. It was small matter, but she noted with pride she was the only woman wearing the country's most controversial nail enamel color: Fatal Apple Red, which she had received as a promotional sample from Revlon's founder Charles Revson himself. She had, in fact, chosen the dress to match the sample. As she walked through the living room, the rustle of her heavy silk dress wooed her, called to her. It was a dress she had purchased during a trip to California last year. She was traveling with her father on business and allowed herself a side trip to Beverly Hills where she stumbled upon the impressive couture salon of Adrian on Wilshire Boulevard.

Adrian, whom Carole had admired from a very early age, was world famous for designing costumes worn by Greta Garbo in her Hollywood days; he was also known for his striking shoulder pads for the glamorous Joan Crawford. She entered the building, the outside wall of white adorned with Adrian's distinctive signature in a towering bronze script. She had an initial fitting done on one dress she liked, extending her stay in California until the final fitting could be finished.

She walked up to Irene who was talking with a small group. She smiled brightly, suddenly the focus of attention. "Happy Valentine's Day, Irene, dear." She lifted her glass, sipped of the champagne lightly, her eyes twinkled brightly. Her hand lowered.

"And to you, dear." They kissed cheeks.

The others in Irene's group echoed the sentiments of the

day, smiled, praised their hostess for yet another stunning party for Maryland's privileged. Carole enjoyed these soirees, but was less than enthusiastic about those in attendance. Most of these well-heeled men and women she had known since childhood; as she matured and came to appreciate her privileged life, they only became more stuffy, staid. They were, in short, no longer any fun. She waited a slight moment, not to seem rude, grasped Irene's elbow, motioning toward the library. It was the one small area of the house which had not been opened to the gathered throngs; it would be their only safe haven. Irene nodded, understanding Carole's code. Carole turned, walked through the crowd, disappeared into the room. Waiting a moment or so, Irene followed, smiling to those she passed, disappearing through the door to the library.

Through the door, Irene breathed an exaggerated sigh of relief at having a moment's respite from the pressures and responsibilities of the crowd. "Goodness! I can't remember another party of yours with such a huge turnout."

Carole had taken refuge against the side of the desk, her gown too constricting to allow her the comfort of actually sitting down. She laughed, downed the rest of her drink. Setting the glass onto the desk, she walked slowly to Irene, leaning on the arm of the sofa. "Yes," she began. "They've all heard about my illness and wanted to see the body before it was laid out."

"Oh, really," Irene said with disgust. "You shouldn't talk like that."

"Irene, try not to be so serious for just one minute. How much do I have to do before you will realize I'm just fine? And, for the last time, do please be a bit more cheery, would you? For me?"

Irene sipped from her glass, looked out the window of the library. She cast her eyes down, then around the room, finally resting on Carole. She looked at her beautiful skin, her blonde hair pulled back into a chignon, her hazel eyes. She felt sad. She didn't realize her lack of happiness was so obvious and made a note to keep up her guard whenever around Carole.

"How can I keep this up?" she asked herself. She thought of all those years they had spent together; the time they found the abandoned fawn in the woods behind the old tree; the time they snuck into the kitchen late one night when Irene had stayed over and ate the entire chocolate cake Mrs. Kennison had baked for Mr. Trent's birthday the next day; how they both got so sick from the cake they had to stay home from school for the next two days. Irene sighed, turned away from her friend. She was no longer able to hold the gaze.

"Carole, dear," she began, a heavy feeling thick in her throat.

"Yes, Irene?"

Irene looked at her, then away. "Carole, there is something which I really think I should have told you. I -- " She stopped, rose from the sofa. A heavy pause filled the room. The silence broken only by the strains of music from outside the door. Irene walked to the window, leaned against the sill, her head turned toward the beauty outside.

Carole followed, silently. She rested her hand on Irene's shoulder.

"I, um...."

"What is it Irene?"

She turned, looked at her friend, the outside light reflected onto her face, beautifully illuminated her features. "How can I ruin this?" she thought. "How can I say anything to dampen this beauty?" A tear flowed from her eye. Carole wiped it away with her thumb. "I am very,..." Irene said, swallowing. "I just wanted to tell you how very happy I am that everything is all right with you," she lied.

Carole began to laugh. "Is that what all this silence and sadness was about? I thought you had something terribly important to tell me."

Irene laughed, too. "It was just," she wiped her face, laughed. "I was so scared when you went into the hospital, I mean -- " Her laughter broke off her words.

"You were so calm, Irene. I would never have imagined."

"Yes, well. That's me: Cool Irene."

Carole walked from the window, once more reclining against the desk. "Irene, you might eventually show some interest in why I asked you here."

Irene stood. "Goodness! I almost forgot you wanted me in here, not the other way around. Yes, Carole. What did you want to talk with me about?"

"I thought you might want to know," she began, a smile trying desperately to break through her lips. "I took it upon myself to invite a friend of yours tonight. One that you somehow forgot on the invitation list you gave me."

Irene smiled at the adventure, the mystery. She walked around the desk, faced Carole. She busied herself, trying not to look too anxious. She smoothed the peplum of her blue-silk jacket, picked off a piece of lint only she could see. She turned her head, her heavy brunette hair falling off to one side. She looked at Carole. "One of my friends?"

Carole would only smile as she turned away.

"Which friend could that be, I wonder?" Irene asked.

Irene lifted her gloved hand, straightened the diamond necklace which adorned her throat. She lifted her hand to the diamond studs in her ears. Finally, not able to stand the suspense, she crossed her arms against her chest, lowering her voice. "Carole!"

Carole would not reply.

"Carole Marie Trent! If you don't tell me what you've done, I'll -- " The implied threat was enough.

"The doctor."

Irene's eyebrows slanted downward; she was stunned. "Which doctor?"

Carole laughed in reply. She rose from the desk, walked to the library door in response to the sharp double knock she had heard. "The doctor." She turned from Irene. "Excuse me, while I get this," she said, mysteriously; obviously enjoying each and every torturous minute.

Irene slumped against the desk, knowing full well Carole

was in control. She waited impatiently for Carole to finish.

Carole opened the door a crack, listened as something was whispered, replied in a whisper, listened again, smiled and closed the door. Turning, Carole motioned for Irene to join her. Irene and Carole emerged from the library. Irene's face belied her sense of apprehension at the adventure about to unfold. Carole's face was distorted with a Cheshire-cat-like grin.

"Carole," Irene whispered nervously. "What's going on?"

Carole would say nothing. They continued to walk through the crowd, toward the foyer, smiling, tossing casual words to the guests they passed. The foyer lay in front of them. There, Irene saw a snow tipped man dressed resplendently in a black dinner jacket and pants, his back to them. Irene watched, intently, as this man handed his snow-covered overcoat to the maid. He brushed snow from his shoulders, straightened.

Carole left Irene, approached the man whose heavy black hair glistened in the bright lights in the foyer. She bent his head down to her mouth, whispered something softly into his ear, gesturing in the direction of Irene. She laughed.

The man turned, following Carole's outstretched arm. His eyes met Irene's. He smiled.

Irene gasped.

In the summer of 1939, the two young women had been enjoying their break from school. Carole had finished her second year of college while Irene was preparing to begin her first. They had spent the early summer months traveling through New England as they had every summer since they were young. Matt, Irene's brother, was along for the trip as was Carole's father and Irene's. As a group, they traveled by train for several weeks enjoying the beauty of the east coast. Quite suddenly, Carole's father had received notice of a supply problem with a certain chemical which his company imported from England. It forced them to cut short their trip. Undaunted, her father insisted they all join him for what would be the children's first trip overseas. Enjoying the adventure, they took the train to New York where they were scheduled to join the British liner *Athenia* en route from Montreal to Liverpool.

It was a marvelous trip for the children -- especially Irene and Carole. They immersed themselves in the separate world of the liner. They attended the dances, enjoyed the social whirl, lounged lazily in the sun along the ship's first-class deck. It was within this fantasy world where Irene and Carole met Joe Elliott, a pre-med student studying at Harvard.

The young man, not much older than the two women, cut a lithe swath when he walked the deck of the lounge past where the two women sunned. Carole saw him first, nudged the half-asleep Irene. When she lifted her sleep-heavy eyelids, she inhaled deeply at the sight of this golden-skinned, black-haired young man standing directly over her chaise, his white smile slashing his golden face.

"Excuse me," he said, tipping his straw hat slightly. He was six feet tall, even, and his light blue eyes twinkled in the reflected sun. He had on a light-cream colored, fine linen suit which intensified his natural coloring. His jacket parted to one side as he lifted his hat, revealing a pair of dark suspenders clinging to a muscled torso, along with his sweat-dampened shirt through which Irene could see his twitching chest muscles. Irene was sure she had stopped breathing.

She sat there, the hot sun beating directly onto her, smelling the heavy salt air of the sea. The light breeze did little to cool her excitement as she was no longer listening to the lulling sound of the ocean's waves, lapping against the ship's hull several feet below. She blinked her eyes against the glare of the sun, unable to completely make out his face.

Noticing this, he tilted his body slightly to his right, blocking the sun from her eyes.

Smiling, she thanked him.

"You are most welcomed," he said, his manner not patronizing. She was immediately taken by his soft yet firm voice. She quickly reviewed the accent, trying to determine in her mind where he was from. He continued. "I'm sorry to have awakened you, but it seems that my pocket watch was left in my room. Would you have the time?"

Irene looked to Carole who fumbled with her pendant watch. "It has just gone past two o'clock." Irene noticed the look of disappointment crossing his strongly formed, perfectly smooth face.

"Then I am late," he scolded himself. "I knew I was cutting it close, but I didn't realize I was so tardy."

"What is it you have missed, if you don't mind my inquiry?" Carole asked.

Removing his hat, he smiled again. "Forgive me talking to myself. There was a lecture to begin at two o'clock in the ship's smaller ballroom. It was about the plant and animal life to be found in England. As I fancy myself an amateur naturalist, I was interested in attending."

Carole, shading her eyes from the sun with her left hand, said, "But, it's only a few minutes past. You could still make it -- if you hurry."

Irene shot Carole a deadly look.

He sat on the chaise lounge next to Irene. It had just been vacated by an older woman who had been watching the interchange and didn't mind aiding the course of true love. She relocated to another chaise. The man answered. "Yes, but I have this definite rule against being tardy to anything I wish to attend. If I am late, I do not allow myself to go, thereby teaching me to not be late. It is not, I'm afraid, working very well. It has given my father and mother untold hours of grief." Dropping his head in mock shame, he added, "I guess I shall never please my father."

Irene, more compassionate than naive, raised her body to a seated position on the chaise, letting her issue of *Collier's* drop onto the deck. Her hand reached to his arm, grasped it lightly in support. "You poor dear."

He lifted his head, smiled again. "I know that this is to be considered horribly rude of me," he began, slowly. "But, if you have not made plans for supper this evening, I would so very much enjoy the pleasure of your company at my father's table." As a second thought, he quickly added, "And, of course, please bring your friend. She would be most welcomed." Adding, "Unless she had made *other* plans."

Irene could hardly contain her excitement at the invitation. She turned to Carole for approval. Reluctantly, Carole nodded, lifted her issue of *Vogue* pretending to resume reading, thereby dismissing herself from further consideration. "Things are moving too fast on this cruise," she thought to herself.

"It's set then," the young man said brightly. "We shall see you at seven, at table twenty-four."

"Right," Irene replied, unsure she wanted the conversation to end just yet.

He rose from the chaise, replaced his hat, gave Irene's hand a slight squeeze. "Until tonight."

As he turned to leave, Irene bolted from her chaise, calling after him. "Wait!" she shouted, attracting the attention of the others on the deck.

He stopped, turned his body to face her.

Irene stopped short, directly in front of him. "I don't -- " she stammered. "We have not been introduced."

Blushing with embarrassment he again removed his hat. "I am sorry." He extended his hand. "I would like you to meet a very good friend of mine: Mr. soon-to-be Doctor Joe Elliott, from the Bronx." He smiled brightly, nearly blinding Irene.

Irene extended her hand to meet his. "And I would like you to meet a very good, lifelong friend of mine, Miss Irene Davis, Maryland."

He took her hand in his, turned it, bent forward to brush his lips against it. He stood there, looking at her. "So, you're an American?"

"Yes," she replied, thrown by the question. "Why?"

"I thought you must be a wealthy heiress from Canada or Europe spending her leisure time on this liner -- unlike we poor working stiffs who are en route to a medical convention and whose personal accounts have been severely tapped by the high cost of this trip."

Irene could only laugh. She pulled back her hand. "Will you tell me more of this pitiful story after dinner tonight, Sir?"

"Yes. I shall." Joe turned lightly on his heel, walked the length of the deck, a spry lift to his gait. Irene returned to her chaise and her magazine certain she had heard him whistling as he walked away.

It was her first "big girl's" dress. As a gift, Carole had insisted on purchasing it for her in New York before they caught the *Athenia*. Carole was not sure if there would be any need for such a sophisticated dress as the blue silk Irene now wore, but felt it best to be prepared for a situation like the one they both found themselves in now. Down the spiral staircase she walked, her dark hair pulled into an upswept style, her blue eyes glittering much like the sapphires around her neck. Her knees trembled slightly as her soft blue slippers took her lower, step by step. Even with Carole's faithful presence at her side, Irene still felt nervous as she heard the soft strains of the orchestra in the dining room below. She had trouble keeping her mouth moist and felt a thick, cottony feeling as she licked her lips. She turned and smiled shyly at Carole, who was much more calm, reserved in her striking black organza dress with a neckline only slightly less than approvable. But, with the carefree recklessness of a nineteen year old, Carole pressed onward, against her father's stern reproval. She lifted her hand to the choker-length strand of black pearls pulled across her lightly tanned skin and twisted the catch to its proper position in back of her neck.

She smiled back to Irene. "You're doing just fine," she whispered to her friend. "Just breathe deeply, don't think about it."

Irene chuckled, nervously, and stumbled over the next

step. She grabbed the balustrade, steadying herself then continued, hesitatingly. They had seen the dining room before, but never dressed as magnificently as it was now, on this last night before reaching England. Flowers were everywhere, silk hangings affixed to the walls in bright colors, swells of music synchronizing perfectly with the gentle sways of the huge liner providing a serenity that neither woman had quite felt before.

Joe rose from his seat at the table, quickly wiped the edge of his mouth with the pink serviette. He saw the women descend the stairs, reach the landing. Irene and Carole made their way quickly to the table, smiling all the way. "Good evening, ladies. May I introduce my father, William Elliott, my mother Patricia, sister Monique and her friend Robert. This is my new friend, Irene Davis, and her friend -- " He stopped, nonplussed, realizing he had not been introduced to Carole. Noticing this, she quickly saved the moment.

"Carole Marie Trent. And it is a pleasure to meet you all. I'm sorry to be arriving late to dinner; we ran into a small problem while preparing."

William Elliott, an older, stately man with a full head of white hair, rose as the two women found their places on either side of his son. With a congenial smile, he began the conversation. "We ordered a cheese tray; we decided to await your arrival. Your timing is to be commended." He turned his gaze to Carole. "Tell me Miss Trent -- "

"Please, sir, call me Carole," she interrupted, never one for formality.

"Of course," he smiled. "And you will please call me William?"

Carole smiled her reply.

"As I was saying, Carole, are you a member of the Maryland Trent family?"

"Yes," she said, smiling at his formality. "Perfectly a gentleman," she thought to herself.

"Ah, I thought you might be. It seems your father and I have known each other for some many years now. We are both in the chemical industry."

Carole was surprised, as were Irene and Joe. "Really?" Carole asked. "Then you must be going to Europe for the same reason as my father."

"Yes," he laughed. "It is quite the sticky business, as it were. Tell me, would your father care to join us for dinner? I could send a porter to his room."

"I'm sure he would enjoy that, William, but Father does not take well to ocean cruises. He is on this liner out of necessity, not desire."

William laughed. "I know the situation well. Please, then, send our wishes for his speedy recovery and our regrets at not having known he was on board. As it was, it was quite fortuitous for us to have met at all. If my son had not forgotten his watch, as he is prone to do, then -- "

"Father, please. You're embarrassing Carole." Joe cut in with mock indignation; his mother laughed. This topic was brought up often in the family; they all knew there was no resolution to the conflict.

"But father," Monique chimed in, apparently part of the routine. "You know future veterinarians have no need for the civilities which we so often take for granted. Why, Joe moves as the winds command." She looked toward her friend, Robert, for approval. Irene quickly classified him as more than just a friend. Monique laughed, drank a sip of juice.

"Monique!" Joe reproved. He turned his attention to his two dinner guests. "I'm afraid this repartee is going to impart to you an unfair portrayal of me. Please do not listen. They are quick to jest and it's sometimes misunderstood by others."

Irene smiled. "I think it's very witty, Joe. I'm enjoying myself." Then, she smiled at him. It was a smile she had never felt before. As her gaze fixed on his ice blue eyes, she felt a warm, burning sensation in her chest. This was an alien feeling, yet, at the same time, welcomed. Around her, the sounds and smells of the dining room and the diners disappeared as her world revolved around his eyes, his smile, his face. Never before had she felt this way about any person, let alone feeling this for a man. Until this very moment, men were merely boys. They were the objects of consternation, play, ridicule: never the objects of such desire. She now wanted to throw herself at Joe, to hold him, touch him, be with him forever. But, she merely sat at the table, politely, her hands folded on her lap, her gaze fixed on his face; nothing belied her true feelings. Returning to the world of the liner's dining room, she turned and cast a quick glance at Carole. She felt her face burn with blood. She felt warm all over and a bit more nervous than a few minutes ago.

Dinner progressed slowly, uneventfully. At the end, Joe nudged Irene's leg, whispering, "Care to join me for the dance in the ballroom?"

Irene looked into his eyes once again. She responded. "I would love to."

It was later, as they stood against the ship's railing, that Irene received her first kiss. It was a small, almost too quick kiss, but it sent her heart reeling. There were more kisses, these more fervent than the first but none had the same effect on her as that first one.

Time was against them as the *Athenia* was scheduled for a morning arrival in Liverpool. It was here they would part. Joe and his family, as well as Carole's father and Irene's father and brother, were to continue to London; Carole and Irene to take a side trip to France, to visit family in Paris.

Irene did not want to go. Carole wanted to visit Paris, the fashion capital of the world; Irene knew she could not disappoint her friend. Their stay in France was scheduled to last two weeks; the meeting being attended by Joe's and Carole's fathers was to last only one. Mr. Trent was to join the girls in Paris, with Matt. Irene knew the Elliott's were returning to America on the *Athenia*, when it sailed on September 2. They made plans to meet in New York several weeks after, and parted company in Liverpool the next day.

Paris was filled with excitement and life; but rumblings of war were heard everywhere. After settling in with the Trent relatives, Carole and Irene set out to explore the grand city. It was on one excursion that they stumbled upon Madison Chanel and met the designer herself. Gabrielle "Coco" Chanel, by now a queen of fashion, was preparing to retire after decades of fashion designing. She had come to this decision due, in part, to the death of her lover in a car accident a few years earlier.

Always a lover of the young and the beautiful, Coco took to the two women immediately. By the time Carole's father joined them in Paris, the two had seen little else other than the inside of the Chanel atelier, where they had been introduced to every aspect of couture fashion. Carole did not escape the Chanel influence. Upon seeing this elegant woman who, in a fit of rage over the man she loved, had cut her long hair into a bob, Carole instructed Irene to help her do the same. Mr. Trent, livid at the sight, quickly swept the two girls onto the first liner out of Europe.

Mr. Trent's anger saved their lives; for France had just declared war on Germany after that country invaded Poland. Suddenly, Paris was no longer a safe haven. Safely aboard the *Ile de France* they heard confirmation of France's declaration of war on Germany. The *Ile de France's* sister ship, the *Normandy*, had only just docked in New York and would not be allowed to return. Irene feared for Joe and his family, but was reassured by Carole the *Athenia* had departed as scheduled and was now safely steaming its way to Montreal.

That evening, as Carole and Irene sat quietly, introspectively, at the table in the glorious dining room of the *Ile de France*, Mr. Trent arrived, a solemn look across his face. "Irene dear," he began, hands trembling as he held a piece of paper which rattled as he lifted it. Carole looked up at her father, noticed something was wrong.

Without addressing the young women directly, Mr. Trent looked down at the paper in his hand, reading: "At 9 p.m. yesterday, the third of September, the British liner, *Athenia*, sank, with a loss of one-hundred and twelve. There were survivors, but it is known that twenty eight of the Americans on board were lost." He looked at Irene. "Dear, I am so sorry." He folded the paper, placed it in his jacket pocket, took a seat at the table. He looked at Carole. "It seems that another world war has begun. God help us all."

The music of the orchestra filtered out of Irene's mind as she stood there, watching the snow-covered man turn around, running his hand nervously through his hair. The eyes were the same. The golden tan in place and the bright white smile slashed across his face as it had five years before.

With assured poise and confidence, he walked the few steps from the foyer into the living room. Extending his hand, he stopped directly in front of Irene. "I must say, Miss Davis, that five years have done nothing but make my memories of you seem pale, indeed."

As if those years had never passed, Irene felt the same warmth in her heart that had been there only once before. She extended her hand which he took gently. Lifting it, his lips brushed the back of her hand. He lifted his eyes to hers. The world around them seemed to stop, completely.

"Mr. Elliott -- "

"It's Doctor Elliott, now."

Irene laughed, nervously. "Yes, of course. Doctor Elliott, how... how -- "

"I was sure you would be filled with as many questions as Carole when we ran into each other last week in Baltimore. She said she wouldn't tell you anything before I could surprise you myself. Did it work?"

Irene smiled, "Yes," and promptly fainted.

"... when she walked down the street! I couldn't believe it. She was running, trudging through the snow with the heavy coat of hers yelling, 'Doctor! Doctor! Wait!' She didn't realize I wasn't *that* doctor. What's his name? Fischer. Anyway, the look on her face when I realized I was the person she was making all the fuss over and turned around. Like she had seen a ghost. She reacted, somewhat, like you did. She didn't take it all the way to the floor, like you, but she did turn this deathly white. I knew it was Carole the moment I saw her. I guess she knew it was me. She did ramble on about how you all thought we had died in the *Athenia* in '39. It was really all so innocent. We were supposed to be on that ship to go back to Montreal, but your tales of France, Italy, and the rest of Europe convinced Father to extend the business trip and go sight seeing. As you probably guessed, that put us in France the day they declared war on Germany. We had a terrible time getting safe passage home. We all snuck onto a ship to England, another to Ireland, then a tramp steamer to America! It was all the excitement you had promised."

Joe tilted his head back and let out a quick puff of cigarette smoke, allowing his hand to remain near his face. He thrust his free hand into his pants pocket and laughed. "You should have seen my mother. I rather fancy she shall never forgive my father, as if it were all his doing." He took another long drag of his cigarette, then stubbed it out in the bronze ashtray on the coffee table.

Irene sat on the couch, across from the coffee table, in the library where they had gone for peace and quiet from the party. When she regained consciousness, she was again startled by the man standing over her. "It sounds so simple," she said, sipping hot tea. "But why didn't you contact us? Your father knew Carole's, and -- "

"That's just it. We tried. We all tried, but in the months that followed when we were trying to escape from Europe all sorts of things happened. I mean, the war broke out in earnest, they were more concerned with fighting Nazis than in two young -- " He stopped short of the word "lovers." It was what he felt, but he did not know his standing with Irene. " -- people who met by accident aboard a ship. Then, years went by, I had my medical training, and, well...." There was a pause. It was a heavy pause hardly lightened by the melodious strains of the music playing beyond the doors. Finally, Joe spoke. "I finished school, just last year started my veterinary practice. I was in Baltimore last week, Wednesday, I think, for another of those conferences which seem to always take me away from my work and was doing some window shopping between lectures when I heard Carole. Well, there it is. The story's gone full circle."

"Yes, it has. I cannot get over the resemblance to Carole's doctor. You could be brothers."

"As Carole said." He took another drag on his cigarette. "Is he here tonight?"

"No. He had some other commitment and couldn't make it."

"A shame."

The door to the library opened. Carole peered around the corner. "Aha!" she screamed, loudly, her face brightly lit. Then, seeing that nothing was going on, she walked into the room, clearly disappointed. "Why are you two just standing there?"

Joe answered with a blank look.

"Well," Carole said, whirling into the room, sitting next to Irene. "I thought with this privacy, you two would be -- "

"Carole!" Irene gasped, shocked.

Joe laughed. "We've only just met, Miss Trent. Surely some appropriate time must pass before -- "

"Piddle!"

Irene turned at Carole's uncharacteristic outburst and laughed.

"If you're not going to," she paused, "*get to know each other better*, then you had best rejoin the party, because everyone out there is thinking that everyone in here -- I guess that includes me -- is getting to know one another quite well." All three laughed at the innuendo as they made their way back to the gathered crowd.

Although it was late, the party was showing no signs of

waning. Through the party's last hours, well into the beginning of the new day, Joe and Irene kept company with one another. Occasionally, they held hands, whispered something to the other, chuckled politely, looked at each other, or stood together at the French doors, overlooking the new morning.

Carole kept a firm eye on them, never neglecting the other guests who, noticing the late hour, were beginning to depart to their responsibilities in the real world.

One by one they filed out, still resplendent in their finery, but none outshining Carole and her red dress. No other couple seemed more romantic than Irene and Joe, who were now huddled together, glasses in hand, in front of the raging fire in the living room.

Carole looked at them, her heart aching for Philip.

As she busied herself supervising Mrs. Kennison and crew cleaning up the house, she touched the vase that would hold the flowers Philip would bring; the leather chair which was his favorite, spared in the fire; twirled the ring on her hand. She sank into the blue sofa, her hands covering her face and cried. She cried many tears in the weeks since he left, not receiving one word, one letter from him. His mother had told her "I am sorry, dear; but his is a most secret mission. It is one where no communications are allowed, in or out. We have only received the barest of word from him as it is." She inhaled, lifted her face, scanned the room.

Irene and Joe were walking toward her, Irene looking concerned. "Carole, dear. Are you all right? Shall I phone the doctor?" She quickly checked herself, realizing suddenly that such concern for a person who was supposed to be well was unwarranted. She thought quickly. She grabbed Joe's arm and pushed him forward. "Here he is!" she laughed. "How's that for efficient service?"

Carole laughed, Joe seemed perplexed. "No, Irene. I was just thinking... about Philip. I'll be fine. I guess seeing the two of you, together again, brought back all those happy moments we had."

Irene sat next to her, wrapped an arm around her. "Of course. I'm sorry. I should have thought."

Carole squeezed Irene's hand. "It's not anything you did, or you Joe," she said, looking up to him. "I am so very happy for you both." She smiled. "I think I'll go to bed now. If you'll excuse me?" She turned to Joe. "I cannot tell you, Joe, just how glad I am you are back. Please feel free to stay here as long as you wish. If there is anything you need, please just let me know."

"Thank you," he said, as Carole retreated up the stairs. He turned to Irene. "Philip?"

"It's a story for another day, dear," she said, smiling, squeezing his hand. "Now, I am very tired. Do you want to stay here? There are plenty of extra rooms."

"No, thank you," he said. "I have meetings to go to and people to see. This evening was, I'll admit, rather unexpected."

"All right. Well, telephone me around lunch time. Perhaps I'll let you take me to dinner, weather permitting."

Joe smiled, leaned forward to kiss her. Irene's hand abruptly shot up, blocking their lips.

"Not now," she teased. "Maybe later."

Joe laughed, hugged her, then walked her, hand in hand, to the foyer. Opening the door, she stopped him as he walked through. "Joe?"

"Yes?" He turned.

Impetuously, she leaned forward, planted a brief kiss on his mouth, then stepped back. "A sneak preview," she laughed and slammed the door in his face as his mouth opened to speak. She laughed to herself as she hurried up the stairs toward her bedroom.

Thursday Afternoon

The telephone rang, waking Irene. "Hello?" she said, her voice thick with sleep.

"Miss Trent?"

"No. This is Miss Davis, sound asleep."

"I'm glad I got you, Miss Davis," said the voice, thick with static through the line. "This is doctor -- "

Irene cut the voice short, jumping to a seated position on the bed, flinging her heavy hair back from her face with her left hand. "But, aren't we being formal this morning or whatever time it is. Did you have fun last night? I still can't believe I've found you again."

The voice on the other end cut Irene short. "Miss Davis, I'm afraid you have me confused with another person. This is Bretaigne Fischer, Carole's doctor. Although I can honestly say I wish I were the person with whom you seem to have had such fun last night, in truth, I'm not."

Irene slumped back onto her pillows. "Goodness, Doctor. I knew it was you all along. I thought you might enjoy my little joke," Irene said frantically, covering with an excuse which she hoped didn't seem as feeble to him as it did coming from her mouth.

There was a pause, before the crackling voice continued. "Yes, of course. And quite the good joke it was, too."

Irene, suddenly realizing who was on the telephone with her, quickly asked: "Doctor Fischer! Is something wrong?"

"Yes and no, Miss Davis," the dark voice began. "I would like to see you this afternoon, if that will be possible. Could you come by my office around three. Would that be convenient? It's just gone one o'clock now."

"Yes, Doctor," Irene replied. "See you at three."

She laid in her bed, the bed linens crumpled up under her chin, cursing her inability to sleep, having spent the entire night tossing and turning. Carole, now wide awake, was in a foul mood, her mind filled with never-ending thoughts of Philip. Angrily, she thrust aside the bed sheets, laid there shivering in the cold of the morning. With growing anger, she gathered up the comforter and sheets and pulled them up to her neck.

After several more fits, she finally thrust aside the bed linens with such a force they left the bed in a flowing heap, crumpling onto the floor several feet away. Carole rose, wandered to the fireplace and its dying embers. She paced back and forth, going from the snowy morning outside and thoughts of Irene and Joe, to the fireplace and worries about Philip, alternately cursing herself for bringing them together and letting Philip go. Her frustration and confusion finally got the best of her. She threw her body across the bed and wept.

The door to the outer office opened quietly, Irene noticing just how alike the two doctors were as Bretaigne stepped around the edge of the door. She sat there, on an uncomfortable chair, thumbing through months-old issues of magazines she had already read. The light wool skirt and jacket she wore made her feel self conscious: it was too dressy for a doctor's office, she felt. She had tossed on the first thing she could find, including a grey blouse and a single strand of pearls, dressing hurriedly so she could leave the house before Carole came downstairs, avoiding the questions the encounter would bring. She phoned for her car to be brought around, telling Mrs. Kennison she had an appointment in town. The drive into town was swift, Irene constantly instructing her driver to drive faster. She finally arrived at the hospital with a half hour to spare.

"Miss Davis, you're early," Bretaigne said, admiring the image of Irene: at once a young girl in a doctor's waiting room and a mature woman elegantly attired, sure of herself. He smiled. "I must apologize for maybe sounding too emphatic when we spoke this morning. I didn't mean to alarm you; but I felt, in light of some new information, you and I should speak."

"Of course, doctor. But, what is it? Is Carole all right? Has she gotten better?"

He walked further into the room, sat down in a chair next to Irene. He carried a manila folder. Irene could not help but notice the strength in his hands, how they looked to belong to someone twice his age. She smelled his strong masculine smell, felt something like that warmth she had felt in her heart only twice before. She sat where she was, unmoving, as he seated himself mere inches from her. His closeness suddenly made her feel uneasy. That this stranger could so remind her of another man unnerved her. "Why didn't I notice this resemblance before?" she asked herself, watching the young doctor settle into the chair. She watched the veins on the back of his hands, watched as they pulsed with his heartbeat. In her ears, she could feel the synchronized beating of her heart with his.

"No, I didn't mean to give you the impression her condition had improved. She is, I'm afraid, still quite ill. But, I've reviewed recently published works on conditions similar to hers. We, the other doctors and I, now believe she may have as much as an additional six months to one year, not as I originally felt. It isn't much, in the way of good news; but, I hope you see why I told you."

"Yes. But, if she has more time than you originally thought, couldn't you be mistaken about some other aspect of her illness? Isn't there a chance, even an outside chance, you could be wrong?"

Doctor Fischer placed his hand on her shoulder. "Miss Davis, there has been no mistake, as far as diagnosis and prognosis are concerned. I double checked everything long before I ever told you. We are not wrong about this. She is dying. The question is not whether, only when. I'm sorry."

Irene sat, examining a thin layer of dust on the linoleum flooring illuminated by rays of sunlight piercing the blinds of the office and felt a heavy feeling replace the warmth in her heart. Wearily, she lifted herself from the chair, walked to the window, stood there, her hand against the sill for support. Bretaigne watched as she moved. "So," she said, finally. "It's true then, isn't it?"

"What, Miss Davis?"

Irene sighed heavily, watching the world outside the window. She ran her hand over the sill, nervously. "Until this very moment," she breathed, "I never truly believed what you had told me. I thought, maybe, there was a chance you were wrong. I always hoped Carole would survive this. But now, now...." She dropped her head, suddenly enveloped by hopelessness. Bretaigne knew she was crying and respected that she did not want him to see her do it. Irene thought of the war, the toll it was taking on her. She thought of the father she had loved, the brother she had admired, and, now, her best friend: all struck down too soon, too young. The toll had been heavy, even after Joe's return; she felt nothing but the pain. After a time, she felt his hand on her shoulder again, opened her eyes to see a crisp, white handkerchief held in front of her face. She took it. "Thank you," she said, her back still to him. "I'm sorry."

"I want you to know, Miss Davis, that I understand. I know this is hard, but I thought you should know. I also think it's time we spoke to Miss Trent about this. She has a right to know. The other doctors and I think it's time."

She whirled around, furiously, to face him. "Never!" She spat out the words, her face red with anger. "I told you I would take care of that. I will not have you interfering with our lives!"

He held her by her elbows. "Miss Davis, you must listen to me. She must know the truth. If she has a year to live, she must be allowed to make plans for her future. If she wishes to travel, she must be allowed that choice."

"I can take her anywhere if she wishes to travel. She does not need to know!"

"But, it's not up to you to decide what she wishes to do. She must be allowed to choose."

Irene struggled to free herself from the doctor's firm grip. He would not allow her to be free. He had to make his point clear. "No!" she screamed, struggling. She pulled and tugged, writhing against his firm grip. She felt hot blood rushing to her face and a warmth filling her chest. She struggled, then looked into his eyes. Suddenly, she stopped fighting him, felt her knees give under her. He held her.

Trembling, she stood there, looked at this stranger, this man she hardly knew who wanted to destroy her life. They stood there, their faces mere inches apart. She could see the small beads of perspiration which formed over his skin, on his upper lip.

She leaned closer to this man, her lips brushing against his. She looked at him, closed her eyes, then kissed him again, hard, brutally. Her eyes flashed open. She pulled away from him, confused, and ran through the door, slamming it after her.

Bretaigne stood there, trembling. His mind raced as he thought about this woman, the friend of the woman he knew he loved. What had he done, what had he allowed her to do? The sun moved behind the clouds that dotted the sky, making the outer office dark. He walked through the door to his office and sat in the leather chair behind his desk. He leaned back into the comfort of the chair and covered his face with his hands.

Irene raced through the halls of the hospital. She ran blindly, her eyes filled with tears, her face streaked. Her sobs echoed through the silent, sterile atmosphere; her image attracted attention from the others around her. Down the steps of the hospital she ran, into the waiting car which quickly sped away. Irene, sheltered from the curious onlookers, sat inside, alone, terrified.

The estate on West Lake loomed nearer, the sound of gravel crunching under the car's tires signaled her return. Irene bolted from the car, ran through the freshly fallen snow, through the large doors of the house.

Carole, alerted by the commotion, looked up as her friend rushed into the foyer. "Irene, dear. What's happened to you?" she asked, joyfully. She then understood the look on Irene's face. It was one of intense pain.

"Carole!" she gasped. "I thought you would still be asleep. I didn't -- "

"Yes, I can see that, Irene." Carole replaced the magazine she had been reading. "That doesn't explain what's wrong. Why have you been crying? Have you and Joe had a fight, already?"

Frantically, Irene wiped her face, but did not move from the foyer. "No, it isn't that. I allowed myself to think of father and Matt again," she lied, "and, well you know how I get...."

She stood there, her arms hanging by her side, hoping her quick explanation would end the discussion. Suddenly, she bent forward, made the actions of brushing from her hair newly fallen snow. "Whew!" she said, trying to move the discussion as far from the truth as possible. She stood, removing her overcoat, allowing it to drop onto the floor. She smiled, walked into the room, joined Carole on the blue sofa.

"You know how I can get myself worked up over them. I'm all right now, really."

Carole hesitated, knowing there was more to the story than Irene protested. "Are you sure?" she asked. "It isn't anything you've heard about Philip, is it?"

Relieved at being able to speak the truth, Irene reached out, touched Carole's arm. "Heavens no! I told you, Carole. It's my annual crying jag over Dad and Matt. Really." Irene rose, moving toward the kitchen. Carole followed.

Irene entered the kitchen, smiled at Mrs. Kennison. Carole walked through the door a step behind her. She busied herself at the icebox, the pantry, pulling out ingredients to make a sandwich, trying to keep active to keep Carole off the subject.

"Irene," Carole insisted. "I know you're not telling me the truth. At least, not the whole truth. I've known you too long. If I can help, please let me."

It was too much. Irene whirled on Carole. "Listen!" she shouted, startling the cook and the kitchen staff. "I'm just fine. I just got to thinking about how I have lost the two people closest to me. It happens from time to time, which you know full well. All right? Now," she said, turning to the cutting table where she was assembling her sandwich, "will you please just leave me alone?"

Carole knew something else troubled Irene. Of course, there were occasions when Irene would allow herself to get upset over her family; but, she always came to Carole about it, and together they worked through it. Irene had never shown anger toward Carole when upset by the loss of her family. She stood, watching her back as Irene assembled her meal, wondering why Irene would be thinking of that now, when she was so happy. She had found a man she thought lost forever. She should be thinking of the future instead of the past. After Irene left carrying a meal tray, Carole tidied up, helping Mrs. Kennison. She didn't want the cook to get upset by Irene's sudden hurricane attack on the serenity of the kitchen. Then she left, nibbling on a roll, and returned to the sofa and the magazine she had been reading. She knew there was much more to the events of the last few minutes and she aimed to find out what.

Thursday Morning, 01 March 1945

Yesterday afternoon, without even so much as a "Thank you so much for all of your hard work," Irene was given her notice at the Glenn L. Martin Company. She received a small severance check as well as a perfunctory pat on her behind from one of the men who apparently felt some sorrow at seeing her dispatched with so little appreciation. Angered more at the fact she had been summarily dismissed than at the outright injustice of being denied her right to continue doing not only a job she did well, but one she loved, she felt her face grow red hot with anger as she turned from her boss's office and stormed from the plant, slamming as many doors as she could.

Now, much of the initial anger abated, but still feeling the sting of the unfairness of the deed, she sat, slumped, in an easy chair next to the fireplace in her bedroom, watching the shadows play against the newly fallen snow.

She had gotten the fury from her system, racing home, yelling and screaming her story to anyone who would listen. It was a moment when she actually saw red. After annoying Carole for untold hours last evening, she locked herself in her room, refusing to speak further with anyone. Even when Joe telephoned her, she refused to take the call. She looked carefully out the window to see which first signs of spring were emerging. She was disappointed at seeing none. Frustrated, she dressed in a hurry, slumped down the stairs, joined Carole at the table for breakfast.

"You're sure a grump this morning," Carole said, adding a smile before downing a full glass of orange juice.

Irene did not reply; but called into the kitchen for Mrs. Kennison who came promptly, unhappy at being summoned in so unnatural a manner.

"Miss Irene, getting your voice all up like that will do neither of us any good, will it? We're all sorry about what they did to you, but we are your friends, after all. Don't let's forget that." She crossed her arms over her bosom. Her smile was filled with compassion and authority.

"Yes, I know, Mrs. Kennison. Please don't think me ungrateful for your words of kindness. You just have no idea how this angers me. It's so damned unfair that I was fired solely because I'm a woman. I was only just promoted and was one of the best workers in the plant with the documentation to prove it!" She again pleaded her case to Mrs. Kennison, finishing her display with a sorrowful look on her face.

Mrs. Kennison laid her hand on Irene's drooped shoulder. "Well, Miss. It might surprise you that I know just what you're going through. Perhaps it's for the best. Now you can go with Miss Carole this afternoon, when she goes into town to begin planning and arranging her wedding."

Irene, a look of shock belying her lack of knowledge about this turn of events, looked across the table to Carole, who was busily finishing off three scrambled eggs. "Carole. So soon? Why, you two haven't even set a date. As it is, you don't even know when Philip will return."

"I'm well aware of that, dear. But, I'm planning for autumn, the war will be over by autumn and Philip will want us to get married with the beauty of the turning leaves to surround us. Besides, one can never plan too soon for something like this. A wedding is a woman's most precious memory." She downed her tea and continued. "And, you might just as well begin to plan, too, you know. You and Joe will surely be tying the knot soon." She smiled, wiping the corners of her mouth with her serviette, replacing it on the table. She rose. "Dear, finish you breakfast while I get ready. The car will be around at eleven, then we can be off. I understand the weather will be glorious today!" She turned, walked up the stairs, entered her rooms, getting ready for the trip.

Irene gave orders for the day to Mrs. Kennison and relaxed with the newspaper, her mind thinking seriously about Carole's words. "You and Joe will surely be tying the knot soon...." As well as the two of them had been getting along, Irene had never really given much thought to the subject of marriage before now. She wasn't sure if Joe had, either.

Since her moment of weakness in Doctor's Fischer's office, she had not seen him. This is not to say he had not been in the forefront of her mind many times. She was unable to explain to herself why she had not resisted the urge, why she had given in to that presence of his. She had discarded the fact of his resemblance to Joe as the reason for her weakness; but with all the other reasons discarded as well, she was unable to explain her actions. She mulled over the situation as she ate her breakfast of one scrambled egg, some fried potatoes, some fruit, a glass of apple juice and hot tea.

Breakfast completed, she awaited Carole's return to the living room, aimlessly watching the fire dart and lick in the fireplace. Presently, Carole returned. "Sorry to have kept you waiting, dear. How was your breakfast?"

Irene nodded. "Fine," she said, rising to meet Carole on the foyer landing.

Carole tugged on her gloves, noticed Irene's preoccupied look. "Cheer up, Irene. Mrs. Kennison is right: now we can both spend the needed time planning our weddings!" Carole threw open the door, walked across the drive to the waiting car, Irene in tow.

The day was bright and sunny. Carole and Irene made the rounds of the finer shops collecting ideas for flowers, fashions, catering. Armed with the newly published "Blue Book of Social Usage" by Emily Post, Carole happily paraded around the town, almost a different woman. But it was as she looked at the pictures of wedding dresses that her loneliness finally hit.

"Irene," she said, suddenly quiet. "I think it best we go home now." To Irene's questioning look, she continued. "I'm all right, just sad and feeling alone, again. The longer Philip is away the more I think he will never return." She looked at Irene, then away. "I think," she said, almost inaudible. "I think I'm losing all hope."

Irene wrapped an arm around Carole's shoulders, hugging her. "I know, dear. What do you say the two of us go somewhere stunning for lunch and drown ourselves in our sorrow?"

Carole could only laugh. Here she was, maudlin, Irene upset over losing her job. A more perfect match could probably never be made.

"Okay," Carole said with a smile. "Where do you suggest?"

"Well," Irene began, a mischievous gleam in her eyes. "Anywhere but the Plaza Hotel. I don't think enough time has passed for them to have forgotten our little scene."

"I agree."

"Blue Panther, then?"

Carole smiled.

With no more consideration, they closed the book of wedding dresses and trouped off down the street, sending the car ahead to await them. Carole was not sure, but she would almost say they skipped down the sidewalk.

Lunch over, plates removed, their troubles were almost completely forgotten. "Let's decide between us," Carole ventured, "to not dwell on those things which have been bothering us so much lately. All right?"

Irene smiled, laid her hand across the table. Carole took it in hers, held it. "Do you think we can?" Irene said

"And why not? Goodness, Irene. Look at how much we have gotten through just since Christmas. Since the war began. I mean, really."

"Yes." Irene felt compelled to agree.

"We barely got out of Europe, safely, and I barely escaped Father's wrath over my bobbed hair. You've gotten Joe back, I've gotten back my health. We are both young and wealthy," she said, giggling. "So what if Philip is away? He's fine, I'm sure. No telegram has arrived." She stopped short.

Irene looked to her. "It's all right, Carole. Like you said, let's forget about the past. Live today and tomorrow." She squeezed Carole's hand hard, almost too hard. Carole placed her hands firmly on the table, pushed her chair back, rose. Reaching down, she grabbed a spoon left from lunch and tapped her tea cup, loudly, its ring resounding through the large room. "Ladies and gentlemen!" she shouted. "May I have the attention of all of you?" The room grew quiet, faces turned to see the source of the commotion. "I would like to announce the rebirth of two very lovely young women. Miss Irene Davis and her best friend, Miss Carole Trent. Happy birthday to us both!"

The other diners, most having only heard the "happy birthday" part, responded with half-hearted applause. It was when the entire restaurant burst into a spontaneous chorus of the "Happy Birthday" song that Carole smiled, looked at Irene, tears glistening in her eyes.

Irene looked around at the strangers wishing them a happy birthday and could only smile, still not sure if she should be embarrassed or thrilled. As tears filled her eyes, she laughed, grabbed her cup of tea and, in response to Carole, drank a silent toast to their newfound lives.

Minutes later, things having returned to their normal state, Irene and Carole signed their tab and walked out of the Blue Panther. They passed the sign which read "Ladies Lounge" and, remembering their escapades at the Plaza in New York, burst into laughter once again.

Friday Evening

"Want a smoke?" he said, reaching into his dinner jacket for a pack of Camels and his lighter.

"No," she laughed. "You know I don't smoke. It's a nasty habit. But, if you have a piece of Clove gum, maybe I might let you offer some of that to me."

"By Jove, buy Clove?"

She laughed again.

He ran his hand over the balustrade turning to overlook the gardens below. The smell of the gardenias from the house forgave the lack of scent from the snow-dusted grounds below. He inhaled slowly on his cigarette, then exhaled, his head tossed back. "I know something."

"Yes?" she asked casually. She turned away from the house and the dinner guests inside, looked over the neatly trimmed gardens below. She had so enjoyed dinner with the Waites, for she always made the habit of touring their balcony, looking at the gardens below, snow or not. It was a beautiful house, one which she visited often. This occasion was their 30th wedding anniversary. Her invitation had specifically instructed her to "bring a guest," the Waits knowing of her romance. She moved her body closer to his.

"Well," he began. "I know how much I cared for you five years ago on the *Athenia*."

"Yes," she said, moving closer.

He turned sideways to meet her, his body leaning against the balustrade. His eyes sought hers in the light reflected from the house inside. "And I know how happy I was to see you at

Carole's party." She turned sideways, facing him, her eyes seeking his. He took one last drag on his cigarette, tossed it to the ground, stubbed it with the toe of his shoe. He exhaled toward the floor. He lifted his hand to Irene's shoulder, stroked her arm. He smiled. "And I know how good you make me feel right this very instant." She moved her body as close to his as discretion would allow, her eyes fixed on his.

Without further words, they kissed. It was not two separate motions, but one as together their bodies met. After a moment, they pulled apart. "I would like to ask you a question, Irene."

"Yes?" she asked, looking up.

"Would you marry -- " before he could finish his question, she stopped him, pulling from his embrace.

"No!" she shrieked, loud enough to be heard inside. "Don't ask me that." She stepped away from him, turned, looked back over the garden.

"What's wrong?" He moved toward her; but, at each step, Irene stepped back.

"No," she pleaded, tears cascading down her face. "Please."

He walked forward again. This time, she stood her ground. "Why Irene? Did I say something wrong? Did I do something?"

She turned to face him, her head held up against the strong desire to look away. "No, Joe," she began calmly. "It isn't anything you did or didn't do. It's just... it's me."

"I don't understand."

She turned from the balustrade, paced the balcony. She was thankful the music inside had begun again, shielding this conversation from the others. "I..." she began. She stopped.

Joe turned in place, following her with his eyes.

Throwing down her arms in frustration, she turned, looked at him. "How long will it be before I lose you, too?"

"What? You'll never lose me, Irene. Why would you worry about that?"

She stepped forward. "Because everyone I care for I lose. My father. Matt. You know about them. I thought I lost you as well. I grieved for you once. I don't think I could grieve for you a second time. It would be just too much."

"That's silly, Irene. I understand about your father and brother, but nothing you did or didn't do caused their deaths." He lowered his voice, stepped toward her. "It was this damned war, Irene. A lot of people have died. What about Carole? She's your best friend. Someone you care about very deeply and she's all right."

Irene looked at him, her eyes holding his. "But, she isn't. She's...." Her hand flew to her mouth, her eyes flared open. She gasped.

"She's what?"

Irene turned from his piercing gaze. "Nothing. I was just so worried after her accident. Every once in a while I think about how close she came to death, and...."

Joe closed the distance between them, took her in his arms again. "Irene, are you sure that's all it is? Is there something you're not telling me?"

She laughed in that way one does after receiving a terrible scare then realizing it was something innocent, like the cat. "No, Joe. I'm telling you everything there is to tell. Really."

"Why won't you marry me then, if everything is all right?"

She struggled to pull free from his grasp, but could not. "Please," she pleaded. "If you love me, you will let me go."

Joe tightened his grip on her shoulders, moved his face closer for a kiss. More and more like a caged animal, Irene fought against his strength, turning her head side to side. "Please. Joe. Don't." She looked into his face and saw the face of Bretaigne that day in his office. Her shouts of protest attracted a few of the dinner guests, assembling to see the cause of the commotion. Seeing their approach, Joe loosened his grip. Irene turned and fled from the balcony, lost in the sea of people inside the house. Frustrated, Joe looked from face to face of the assembled guests and smiled. "It's okay. We only had a disagreement about wedding plans, that's all." He ran his hand through his hair, walked through the group, laughing to himself at just how accurate his comment really was.

Tuesday Morning, 27 March 1945

With a fire roaring and her legs curled beneath her, Carole snuggled onto the sofa to read the newest issue of *Time* magazine which had arrived with the morning's mail. As was her habit, she quickly flipped through the opening pages, to the "U.S. At War" section. She read the caption under one photo "Dead Marine on Iwo Jima Beach." It was a grim picture of one lone body slumped against a sand dune, the Navy's ships on the water in the distance. As she moved down through the rest of the article, under the heading of "The Nation" she read:

"No stopping:

"The Navy did not say who she was, whether aging mother or young wife. But it thought her letter typical of several received recently, and therefore made it public. Somewhere in the U.S. an American woman had written:

" 'Please, for god's sake, stop sending our finest youth to be murdered on places like Iwo Jima. It is too much for boys to stand, too much for mothers and homes to take. It is driving some mothers crazy. Why can't objectives be accomplished some other way? It is most inhuman and awful stop, stop!' "

Carole continued to read, stopping at the sound of the door chime across the room and the sounds of John answering the door. Presently, the door clicked softly and John appeared across the foyer landing, down the stairs. He stopped a few steps from Carole.

"I'm sorry, ma'am," he said.

Carole looked up from her magazine. "Yes?"

"There's a gentleman at the door"

Her heart leapt, thinking it might be Philip. "Is it?"

"I'm afraid it's a telegram, ma'am. He says he must speak with you directly."

Her heart suddenly sank. She allowed the magazine to drop onto the floor as she felt her face grow hot. John recoiled, as if struck a blow, at the fear in her eyes. The room around her grew dark as she tried to force her body from the sofa. It was as if her legs weighed hundreds of pounds, her arms weighted down with lead; for every move she made required so much effort, so much strength that the fight exhausted her within moments. All around her disappeared as the front door became the focal point of her life; the door seemed to be framed with the light from the morning sun, shining into the living room. It was an icon of her defeat. She found the ability to force her body from the sofa, to begin the miles-long trek to the front door, to the telegram waiting for her on the other side. Each step was laborious, as if she were walking through mud several feet deep. She felt her face grow wet as the tears flowed from her eyes down her cold cheeks. She lifted a hand, wiped her face. Sobs escaped her clenched lungs, words hurriedly formed in her cluttered mind. "He's dead," she said to herself over and over as if a refrain. "I knew it. I knew he would die," she thought. The sobs came more frequently and with more force as the steps to the landing loomed desperately in front of her. One step after another she forced her tired weary legs to walk up, to finally reach the landing. Only a few steps more to the door and the end of her life. Only a few steps more. As if it were a massive stone, Carole had to summon the strength from both of her hands to move the front door open. On the other side, she saw a young man, a boy, really. "It's not supposed to be like this," she said in her mind. She had heard the stories of telegrams being delivered. She knew well Irene's stories. Always the facts had differed, but one thing remained the same: each time a telegram had been delivered, it had been by an older man. Why was this a boy now? Why had she not been forced to see an older man remove his hat as she peered around the door? Why was this different?

She opened her mouth to speak but only breath came forth. She closed her mouth, swallowed heavily, ran her tongue over her suddenly parched lips, tried again. "Yes?"

The boy, seventeen years old, looked impatient as he chomped rudely upon the thick wad of gum in his mouth. His breath shot out in front of him with each loud chomp. His eyes did not seem to focus on her, but more on the telegram he held and the receipt book which Carole would have to sign. He hated his job. Especially now during the war. Each time he went to deliver a simple telegram to a woman she would answer the door just like this; so afraid it would be news from the government. He found himself laughing at how pitiful the situation was. Didn't people receive telegrams every day? "These dames sure make a big deal over nothing," he thought to himself. "Telegram, ma'am," he said, hating to have to be polite after she had kept him waiting so long.

He looked at her eyes, saw she had been crying. For a moment, he felt pity for this woman then let his mind wander from her eyes to what was under the two matching pockets on her wool sweater. A smile crossed his face as he took a real good look at her. "Not a bad looker," he thought. "To bad it isn't a telegram from the government. Maybe then I could offer to console her." He wiped his mouth with the back of his gloved hand, thrust the telegram out with the other. "Yeh," he thought. "Too bad."

Carole looked at him. "Who is it from, boy?"

"Here we go with the twenty questions," he thought. "It's out of New York, ma'am. Overseas wire from England. Sent through New York." He pushed the telegram farther toward her, pushed the receipt book toward her right hand. "Sign here, ma'am."

Slowly, Carole reached for the telegram, then took the receipt book with the pen pointing at the line she had to sign. "Right there, ma'am," he said, trying to hurry things up.

She took the telegram, signed the book, turned and began her journey back to the living room. Shifting back and forth on his feet, the boy cleared his throat. Carole turned, saw the boy waiting. "Yes? Was there something else?"

He stood there, tried to seem polite but wishing she would just dole out the two bits so he could get out of there. She gave him the creeps, the way she acted so odd. It finally hit her why he was waiting. She reached into her pants pockets and found a dollar bill. Not wanting a fight over change she handed the note to him, turning away.

Jumping on the balls of his feet, the boy smiled. "Hey, lady. Thanks. And -- " he stopped as he bounded down the steps, suddenly feeling something for Carole. He turned back to her. "Cheer up, lady. It's not one of them telegrams, if you get my meaning. I don't do them, so it can't be news that's too bad." That said, he turned back around, hopped onto his bike, pedaled away.

Carole turned, his words making no sense to her. She heard the sound of snow crunching as the boy strained to get the bike moving. Behind her retreating figure, John secured the front door, followed Carole, walking behind her a discrete distance. He wanted to make sure he would not be needed again, should the news be bad. She stood there on the foyer landing, ripped away a small strip of the envelope's end and pulled out the telegram inside. Her eyes flew to the return address, breathed a sigh of relief that it wasn't from the government. A gasp escaped her mouth when she looked at the signoff. It read "P. Craig," in bold type.

John, alarmed, moved closer. Seeing the smile which played across her face he new it was a gasp of excitement, not of pain. He returned to his duties in other parts of the house.

Reading, Carole made her way down the foyer steps, toward the sofa. She sat. Indeed, it was a telegram from Philip. Indeed, it was good news.

Tuesday Afternoon

Mrs. Kennison cleared the dishes of the first course,

brought out the freshly baked entree. The smell of baked ham steaks filled the dining room, tickling Irene's nose. She felt her stomach ripple as the steaming hot food was brought out proudly by the cook. She looked over to Carole who stopped telling a story only long enough to allow the steaks to be served. Potatoes and peas were also served, after which Mrs. Kennison left the room. Carole continued. "Philip says that the Nazis are going to surrender within a week! He might be coming home right after and we could get married as soon as June. Oh, wouldn't that be wonderful? A June bride! Wouldn't it be wonderful?" She thrust a piece of ham into her mouth.

Irene, eating much slower, listened to every word. "But, why does he think it will be over so soon? I've heard tell, from some of the guys at the plant, that it won't be for another year or so. Autumn 1947, they say."

Carole scoffed. "Not at all. We have, Philip says, the Geris right where we want them. They're hurting." She closed her mouth around a forkful of potatoes. "They're hurting. He says that I should begin planning for the wedding. Isn't that funny? He doesn't know that I'm one step ahead of him. Several steps for that matter."

Irene was concerned about Carole's frivolity. "Maybe they can still be married," she thought. "Just in time for her to...."

"Well, dear," Irene said. "I don't think you should get your hopes up too high. Remember just last year when everyone was so sure the war would be over in time for all our boys to be home for Christmas dinner." She said it as a statement not as a question. "There have been lots of rumors, Carole. It would be nice if Philip was right; but for now, it's only a rumor, dear." Calmly, she nibbled on a piece of steak. "It's only a rumor."

They ate in silence for a moment.

"You're so mean to me, Irene," Carole protested, as she mixed her peas with her potatoes, to make them easier to eat.

"Why do you say that?"

"You don't want Philip and I to marry, to be happy. Just

because you and Joe are having a row."

"Carole! That's not it at all. Of course I want the two of you to marry and be happy, no matter what Joe and I do now or ever. What would make you say a thing like that?"

They ate in silence.

"I'm sorry. I guess in the excitement over finally hearing from him, that your words -- your wise words -- just cut me to the quick. Of course, you're right, Irene, dear. It is only a rumor. I'm just so happy he's safe, that's all. The war will be over soon."

"Yes, Carole. And maybe we can have a double wedding...."

The next two weeks were filled with a light excitement as Carole thought only of Philip, Irene thought only of Carole, and the two women worked hard at planning for the big day.

Irene had received some good news as well. Although it had been weeks since she and a large group of women had been let go from the Glenn L. Martin Company, she was still pleased when she heard the plant had been awarded its "E" pennant for excellence. Irene heard about the ceremony, the party, and the big raise everyone got (mostly only the men remained) a week after the fact. It burned her up that she was not invited to attend. It was, after all, her hard work and the hard work of all the now-unemployed women who got that pennant for the plant.

March ended and April began. There were more rumors about the end of the war. Anticipation was at a fever pitch; word around town was a big celebration being planned for the end of the war. People began to spend more money, to buy what fresh meats and foods they could, eat better, entertain more. A war-weary people were beginning to loosen up after almost six years of worry, six years of rations, six years of doubt.

As quickly as the rumors began, they ended; but not until several newspapers erroneously printed banner headlines, like

"Nazis Quit!" Indeed, it had been only a rumor, as Irene said. But the fact that it was only a rumor did little to dampen the spirits of the people of America. It seemed as though nothing could make the nation worry, now. The war was nearing its end. Things were looking good. Very good.

Thursday, 12 April 1945

In Warm Springs, Georgia, a man died of a cerebral hemorrhage. It was President Franklin Delano Roosevelt.

Carole and Irene had taken the opportunity to venture into Baltimore again to get more ideas for the wedding. After a full afternoon shopping, planning and buying, the two women had chosen the Blue Panther for a late lunch. It was after dessert that Irene noticed someone running into the club's lobby. He yelled: "Roosevelt's dead! The President's dead!" The young man ran back out of the club, down the street, into other businesses yelling the same news.

Carole turned to Irene a smile across her face. "Kids," she said. "They just don't understand how tasteless a joke like that is." She opened her purse, searched for her handkerchief. "Just tasteless."

Irene, disbelieving, excused herself from the table, walked to the telephone booth. She felt uneasy, that maybe it was not a joke. Something didn't feel right and she wanted to be sure. She called the house and spoke with Mrs. Kennison.

After a few moments Irene returned. "Carole," she said, calmly. "Mrs. Kennison said it just came across the radio. It's true. Roosevelt's dead."

They walked down the sidewalk toward their waiting car. Irene and Carole saw clusters of people standing around storefronts, straining to hear the radios that had been set up in the doorways. Irene saw tear-streaked faces everywhere she looked.

Women wiping their eyes with handkerchiefs. Men in suits and servicemen crying, openly, without effort to hide the fact.

For the remainder of the afternoon radio stations carried word of Roosevelt's untimely, though not completely unexpected, death at 4:35 Eastern War Time. Regular programming on each station had been dropped in favor of news reports giving updates on his death and the transfer of power to Vice President Truman, now President Truman. Roosevelt had had health problems for many years. He had been sitting for a portrait painter when he was stricken with a cerebral hemorrhage. He died half an hour later.

Elected in the midst of the worst depression the United States had seen, much of what was good in the country was a direct result of his New Deal policies which, as legislation, provided relief to banks, manufacturers, farmers, labor and the unemployed. Loved and admired as much as he was hated and despised, he had been a good president. His four terms in office were unprecedented. Most of what Carole and Irene knew about politics, government and the world came directly or indirectly from the Roosevelt presidency, his being in office since 1932. They both felt cheated, hurt.

Irene experienced despair the likes of which she had never felt. Not even the deaths of her brother and father had left her feeling so helpless. She felt hurt, upset, pain; but this was something bigger, more encompassing. It was as if the one leader she had known all her life had departed leaving her without anyone to look up to, without anyone to guide her or the rest of the country. It was, she knew, a time of great change.

Saturday, 14 April 1945, Early Evening

"Did you ever stop to think, I mean really take a good gander at why Lucky Strikes are in a white package now instead of that awful dark green they used to be? I mean, why would they, the Lucky Strike people, have picked World War Two to redesign their package? I don't know," he said, twisting the crinkly package in his hand, blowing smoke over her head. "I think it's strange." He punctuated his comment with one last long drag on the cigarette which he then flicked out of the open car. He turned his attention to Irene quickly forgetting the still-glowing butt which lay quietly on the ground. He lifted his right arm from beside him, moved it around Irene's shoulders without touching them. This was their first real date since the scene at the Waite's dinner party six weeks ago. It was not the first time they had seen each other or done anything together; but it was the first time Irene had let Joe spend an entire afternoon and evening with her. Before tonight, there had been the occasional lunch, a movie with Carole, dinner at the Trent home. Irene insisted, in her mind, without ever once having said it in words, that these dates should be simple, slow, innocent.

Joe had been lucky. He had his practice to occupy him, to keep his mind off things in general and Irene specifically. Since their meeting at Carole's Valentine's Day party Joe had begun the process of moving his still-new veterinary practice to Baltimore to be closer to Irene. He had told friends he wanted to escape the parental nest; but truthfully, he was so sure that he and Irene would be married that he wanted to get settled as quickly as possible. The process was simple. With his practice little more than one year old he had few regular customers to leave. These he gladly referred to other doctors in the area. The physical move was easy as well. So by the end of March all was set and Doctor Joseph Elliott was a new resident of Baltimore, Maryland. He moved to the suburb of West Lake where Carole and Irene lived -- in fact, renting Irene's house which had been closed since Carole's accident. He now lived on the other side of the reservoir from Carole.

At the time, it seemed like a good idea for Irene to allow Joe to rent her house. He would be close to her, allowing them to see each other often and long. At the time, things between them were wonderful, so why should he have to find a dreary, rundown apartment in Baltimore when her perfectly fine house sat empty? As she sat here in his brown Ford convertible, she considered her decision ill advised. Now, she was forced to see him whenever he wished. Although their dating had been limited, she felt put upon to come up with excuses to not see him. She needed to slow him down, to make him understand what she wanted.

Yesterday, he asked her to the theater. She felt she could not deny him, what with his sad blue eyes. She could have said, "Sorry, Joe, but for some reason I can't go to the show with you." But, morally, she felt like a heel. When he asked, she acquiesced. Here she was, then, now in his car with his arm placed discretely around her shoulders, trying to be a gentleman allowing her to make whatever first move she was going to make.

What did he expect of her? To turn around, wildly, thrust her arms around his neck and kiss him madly, passionately? No. He didn't think she could be so wanton. She could not understand why he would not leave her alone for a while. Just to allow her to go about her life until she could figure things out. It wasn't like she hadn't tried to understand him. How does one explain that funny feeling she felt whenever she was with him? She remembered that moment when they first met. It was a feeling she felt even now. But she could not help but feel the same tingle when she was in the same room with Bretaigne.

The more she thought of it, the more she kicked herself. If she hadn't kept on pressing Carole to see a doctor about her spells, if only she would have worried less, then they would never had met Bretaigne. She would be sitting here, in Joe's car, doing something fun. Then, it struck her: If they hadn't met Bretaigne, Carole would never had mistaken Joe for him. She would not have run up the street to catch him. They would never had gotten back together again. She felt his arm slide down the seat, around her shoulders.

"Yes, Joe. I think it's strange, too."
"What?"

"About the cigarettes. I almost liked the green package." She turned, faced him. She saw him turn, face away from her.

"Joe?" she whispered.

He turned. "Yes?"

She regretted saying anything. She felt compelled to tell him -- what? Tell him something about why she was being so distant of late; but, what could she say? "Joe, dear heart, I really like you, maybe even love you, but there was this incident in the doctor's office with this guy who looks an awful lot like you, and I just don't know what's going on inside of me..." No, she couldn't say that.

"Yes?" he asked again.

She opened her mouth, inhaled as if to begin her explanation, using whatever words tumbled out. She closed her mouth, turned her head, and mumbled, "Nothing. Can we go now?"

Disappointed, almost angry, Joe swung his arm from around her shoulders, hastily starting the car. He knew when she said his name that she was finally about to explain her feelings to him. He felt a stab of adrenaline in his chest. He didn't know why she had a problem, why she had been so cold to him of late. The only thing he knew was that she would tell him in her own time, in her own way. This was not, it seemed, that time.

The dark brown car wended its way around the reservoir and to the Trent house where it stopped long enough for Irene to get out of the car. It then sped back around the lake, to the Davis house.

It was not until the clock chimed ten times that he knew it was now very late. His rounds over hours ago, Bretaigne spent the rest of his Saturday evening hunched over his desk, her file laying open in front of him. He didn't know why these few pages and charts should hold such an interest for him; he could not stop looking at them again and again. As the last of the chimes hit he looked up, the lamp over his desk providing the only light. He sat there, in a tiny island of light, all else around him black. That was how he felt: black. Without knowing it, he and Irene were kindred spirits; for Irene and he were both feeling the same feelings of doubt, confusion, uncertainty.

Rising from his cluttered desk, he folded the cover to the file, snapped off the light over the desk and let himself out of the office. He walked down the dimly lit hallway past the nurse's station, past the rooms with people inside, past the things which, when placed around him, told him he was in a hospital. His hospital. He walked through the lobby, down the steps to the world outside, pausing only long enough to take a brief look back at his other world, the world he now left behind, and to run a weary hand through his black hair.

Sunday Morning

"Did you see 'National Velvet'?"
"Yes, I did."
"What did you think?"
"Mum.... I didn't think it was particularly true to life." She paused. "Did you?"
"No. Actually. I didn't either."
"Not many are, you know."
"True. Not many. Except for Joan Crawford's pictures."
"Oh, yes. Maybe hers."
"I think she's making 'Mildred Pierce' next."
"Elizabeth Taylor? A bit too young, I would say."
"No, silly. Joan. I heard she's all set. Even heard she's going to walk away with Oscar."
"Oscar? Which character is he?"
There was no reply.
"Curtis somebody is directing. It's opening this August, I think."
"In?"

"No," she interrupted. "Not August. October."

They walked in silence for several more feet, turned around the corner and walked farther.

"Carole," Irene said, pausing on the sidewalk for a moment.

"Yes?"

"Will you go with me?"

"Where, dear?" Carole asked, backtracking the couple feet to where Irene had stopped.

"To see 'Mildred Pierce.'" Irene felt the stab of a small pebble in her loafer and twitched her foot around trying not to move her foot too much.

Carole smiled. "Of course, Irene," she said. "Why wouldn't I?"

"Why indeed," Irene thought to herself. She was beginning to slip too often, make too many mistakes. This was the second or third time this week. Irene was not sure she would be able to keep Carole's health a secret from her any longer. And the telephone calls.... Every day for the past two weeks Doctor Fischer had phoned Irene, begging her to allow him to tell Carole the truth. "Time is drawing close," he said to her ominously. "Drawing too close. You must tell her."

Occasionally, he would threaten to tell Carole himself if Irene didn't. But Irene stolidly refused to acquiesce. "No," she told him again and again. "Not yet. I'll tell her when the time is right." And the time was coming right very quickly with the arrival of Philip's telegram. "Please let him be right," Irene prayed in silence nearly every day. She wanted the war to end as quickly as possible, then Philip would return, Carole and he would marry, everything would be fine, then she would tell her. Then, when Carole had everything she had always wanted, then would be the right time. Then it occurred to her that Carole had always wanted.... "Carole," Irene said, turning her body slightly and beginning to walk again.

"Yes?" Carole laughed. She was beginning to become accustomed to Irene's shifting moods of late. Ever since Philip's telegram. "What did you want?"

"Have you ever thought about children?"

Irene knew the answer to the question before she even thought of it. Of course she had thought about children. "Two," she had said, often. "A little boy and a little girl. Preferably, twins. I will name the little girl Marina Melinda, and the little boy -- "

"Of course I've thought of children, Irene. What's the matter?"

Irene looked at Carole. "What do you mean?"

Again, Carole laughed. "What do I mean? What is wrong with you? You keep getting into these moods. I don't know, but you had better stop playing so hard-to-get with Joe if this is the effect it has on you!"

Irene, stunned, blurted out: "This hasn't a thing to do with -- " She caught herself. Three times slipped.

"Come on, now. I've known you your entire life. Don't you think I would know when something was troubling you? I know that it's Joe, so why can't you talk to me about it, let me help?"

"This is it," Irene said to herself. This is the moment when she can tell Carole the truth.

Irene turned from Carole, resumed walking. "You're right, dear. I should have known better than to not be up front with you. It is problems with Joe."

"There now," Carole replied, her arm encircling Irene's shoulders as they walked down the path. "You can't keep a secret from me, can you? Any time you need to tell me something, don't hesitate. Just tell me."

The pair continued up the path, the sight of the Trent Estate looming over a knoll ahead of them. Trudging through the snow, they remained quiet but not because Irene had nothing to say. She began, simply, by saying "I -- "

The rest of the sentences flooded rapidly through her mind: "-- do need to tell you something, Carole. It's about your blackout over Christmas, you see. You aren't well, you're sick, very sick, and the doctor -- but what do doctors know anyway? -- says you haven't got much longer to live and, damn it all anyhow, Carole. You seem so happy, lively, young. How can anything be wrong? You'll probably outlive all of us, dear. I'm sorry, I don't know why I am so stupid about all of this, nor why I didn't tell you earlier. I'm sorry I made the fuss over everything, forgive me?"

But, she completed the sentence she began with only one other word: " -- will."

Monday Morning.

"Mrs. Kennison?"

"Yes, Miss Carole?"

"Irene is not in her bedroom; I knocked. Has she gone out already this morning?"

"I believe so," the cook replied wiping her wet hands on the bottom of her blue apron. "I saw her sweep in here a bit ago and sweep right out again with only a bit of dry toast to start her day."

Carole leaned against the doorframe, her arms crossed. "And did she say where she was going?"

Mrs. Kennison crossed the kitchen to tend to the roast she had only just placed into the huge oven. She opened the door a crack and said "No. Not a word." She closed the oven door sharply, turned to face Carole. "But, I reckon it was to see Mr. Elliott, she bolted out of here with such a fury."

"Joe?" she asked, not attempting to conceal the surprise she felt. "But, where would they be off to at this time in the morning. Why, it's only gone seven o'clock." She pushed away from the doorframe, walked slowly, confidently across the kitchen to the icebox. She opened the door, extracted a pitcher of milk, one of orange juice, and an apple. "She said nothing?"

Mrs. Kennison, who rankled at the merest hint of incompetence, placed squarely on the cutting block the carving knife which she had been holding. "Miss Carole," she started, trying to control her temper. "If Miss Irene had said anything to me, you can be sure that I would have told you straight away without having to wait for you to ask me. And," she continued, "You will not leave this kitchen with only that to sustain you for the morning! If you like, I will be more than happy to fix you a right proper breakfast. I am the cook, Miss Carole, you can ask your father about that if there be any doubt. Your health and proper nutrition is my major, first, primary, only concern. Now, scoot!" She charged after the incredulous Carole, grabbing both pitchers from her hands, sending her out of the room, laughing, still clutching the stolen apple in her hand.

Into the living room she ran, afraid that Mrs. Kennison would be in pursuit, possibly with knife in hand. As she rounded the blue sofa she felt a sudden pang of fear in her chest and that familiar fogginess in her head. Breathing heavily, grasping the sofa for support, she turned. "Mrs. Kennison!" she yelled. She was not frightened at all. In fact, irritated more than frightened. "Mrs. Kennison!" she called again, louder.

"Goodness, Miss Carole! What's all the -- " She stopped as she saw the suddenly pale woman clutching the sofa. "Miss Carole! Are you all right?"

Carole could not focus the cook into view but turned to the sound of her voice. "I -- " was all she got out before she allowed her knees to buckle under her weight. She dropped to the floor. Mrs. Kennison ran into the kitchen, summoned John from outside. They returned to the living room and moved the now unconscious woman up the stairs and into her bedroom. Mrs. Kennison phoned for the doctor. The family doctor arrived, examined Carole, pronounced her fine. She was weary, exhausted; he gave her a prescription for some vitamins. Smiling to Mrs. Kennison he left Carole's room with firm instructions to call again should her condition change. Mrs. Kennison walked him down the stairs. As they stepped up to the landing in the foyer, the door opened, startling them.

"Miss Irene!"

Irene recoiled when she saw the doctor's familiar face.

"What are you --" She caught herself. "What's wrong?" she asked Mrs. Kennison. "Is something the matter with Carole?"

The doctor smiled, patted her arm with his pale hand. "Irene. There is nothing to get excited about. She's had a bit of a faint. She's upstairs, resting. She'll be fine, if 'n you keep her in bed and not gallivanting all about. In her condition, she'll be needing more rest than usual."

Irene stood, stunned, wondering exactly what the doctor knew about Carole's condition. She hesitated about speaking, but had to know the extent of his knowledge. "Her condition, doctor?"

The old man -- who had brought Carole into the world, had tended to the late Mrs. Trent, as well as Mr. Trent and the Trent family for years -- looked surprised. He pulled his watch from his vest pocket, looked at it, smiled at Irene, then said simply: "Well, sure! Pregnancy is as much a condition as any other medical situation, wouldn't you agree?"

PART FOUR
Monday Afternoon

Carole's body moved in the bed. Irene awoke. She realized she had fallen asleep while sitting vigil at Carole's bedside. She looked quickly around, gathered her bearings, then remembered the shriek from Mrs. Kennison as she heard the doctor's words. No one -- apparently including Carole herself -- knew she was pregnant. It surprised them all. Irene decided to tell Carole the truth the moment she awoke. "This changes everything," she thought to herself as she tucked the comforter around Carole's shoulders. "Now, she has to know everything. If she can just hold on for another five or six months...."

"Irene?" Carole asked, her voice gravely.

"Yes, dear. I'm right here." Irene leaned over the figure on the bed. Carole seemed so small, helpless.

"What happened?"

"You had a bit of a spell, dear. The doctor's already been here."

"Doctor? Why? Did I cut myself or something?"

Irene laughed, the innocence of Carole's words taking her back years to Paris, to days spent on their backs looking at clouds, to rainy days and baking cookies. "No, dear. You're fine." She inhaled, played for time. "Carole," she began, haltingly.

Carole turned her face, looked up to Irene's. "Yes?"

"Did you know?" She stopped, suddenly.

"What?"

She sat erect in her chair by the bed. She smiled, wiped nervously at a strand of hair. "You do know that you're pregnant, don't you?"

"Oh, god," Carole said, turning away her face. "I thought I might be," she said, her voice almost lost in the pillow. "I had been feeling off for the last two weeks, not morning sickness, mind you, just a bit drained. I thought it was from all the hospital tests, running around for the wedding. Nothing more. I guess, somehow, in the back of my mind, I knew it was more than that."

"And you said nothing to me?"

"What could I say?" she defended, turning back to face Irene. She pulled her weary body to a seated position, filling the pause between them. "What would you have thought, me being pregnant, and not -- "

"Carole," Irene interrupted, helping her sit up. "You're my friend. What would I have thought?"

"I don't know. Philip and I -- " she stopped. The blowing wind outside the window caught her attention, again filling the pause between them. She sighed, then began speaking again. "Do you remember Christmas Eve, the party, when he asked me to marry him?"

Irene nodded.

"And do you remember when we went out onto the terrace?"

"Yes."

"Well, I don't think I ever told you what we talked about. A lot of things, really. Mostly, I was angry with him about leaving me right after asking me to marry him. I thought it was mean but I understood why. I mean, not why he left, but why he told me, asked me, to marry him." She looked at Irene. "I'm not making any sense, am I?"

"Of course you are."

She continued. "After we came back into the ballroom, you remember, we disappeared again, after most of the guests had left -- "

" -- and left me alone, to perform the role of hostess."

"We took a drive to his house, his parents were away for the evening with friends. We, well, you know the rest."

"We're experiencing 'the rest' at this moment, aren't we?"

Carole laughed. "I guess so."

Irene took Carole's hand in hers, patted it, squeezed it. "Dear, I wish you had told me. I mean, I am happy for you, but, well, the accident and all."

"Oh!" Carole said, alarmed. "Do you think it hurt him?"

"Him who?"

"Or her. The baby. Do you think my fall hurt him or her?"

"Of course not," Irene said, squeezing Carole's hand. "I'm sure he will be a perfect baby. And first thing tomorrow we find you a good doctor to get a checkup about this."

"But I have a doctor. In fact, I have two."

Irene lifted her chair, placed it back against the wall. "No, Carole. Not that kind of doctor, yet. Then it's rest, rest, rest." Irene bent over the bed, kissed Carole on the forehead. "All right?"

"Do I have any choice?"

"No," Irene replied, walking toward the door. Carole stopped her.

"Irene?"

"Where were you this morning?"

Irene froze, standing, panic filling her chest. What could she say? Not the truth, surely. Her hand got cold, her knees were trembling.

"Irene?"

"Shopping. Why?" But she thought: "No. That doesn't even sound right."

"At seven in the morning? Where?"

"Good question," she thought, but said "Joe and I -- "

"Yes," Carole interrupted. "Mrs. Kennison thought Joe was involved."

" -- went into the city to this little store."

"But at seven in the morning?"

She felt trapped. Suddenly, deciding the best defense was a good offense, she spoke, brusquely: "Carole, get some rest, will you? We'll talk later," and turned, walking from the room. The door slammed behind her.

Carole heard Irene disappear down the stairs. She bent over the bed, grabbed the telephone, lifted it and carried it to the bed. She lifted the handle. "Operator? VErnon 77319 please. Thank you." She waited. The connection was made.

"Doctor Fischer's office. How may I help you?"

"Doctor Fischer please."

"May I say who is calling?"

"Miss Trent. Miss Carole Trent."

There was a pause. "I'm sorry, Miss Trent, but the doctor just stepped in with another patient. Is there a message?"

"No," Carole replied, disappointed. "There is no message. I'll call him later today."

"That will be fine," the nurse said.

As Carole pulled the receiver from her ear, she thought she heard a sound from the speaker. She put it back to her ear, "I'm sorry?"

"I just wondered," the voice said, "if Miss Davis had yet returned."

Carole sat, the deafening noise of her heart pounding in her ears. "Miss Davis?" she asked, not sure she heard correctly.

"Why, yes. Miss Irene Davis. Or, perhaps I have the wrong Miss Trent."

Quickly, Carole answered. "No. You have the correct Miss Trent," she fumbled, stalling for time, needing the opportunity to think. "Yes. Miss Davis returned some time ago."

"Oh, good," the voice replied. "Would you let her know she forgot her compact this morning."

"I will," she replied, adding: "Forgot it? Where?"

"Well...." There was a pause. "Why, here, of course. At the office. When she left this morning, she forgot her compact. I think it slipped from her purse. Shall we send it along or will she be by again to pick it up?"

Carole paused, the telephone receiver feeling like molten lead in her hand: hot, heavy.

"Miss Trent?" the voice reminded.

"Send it along, will you please?" she replied, blankly, not hearing her own words, her mind busily sorting the information she had gathered.

"A pleasure, Miss Trent," the voice said. A click on the line signaled the connection was broken.

Friday Evening, 20 April 1945

When he set out that evening for dinner at the Blue Panther, Bretaigne had not given more thought to Carole Trent and her worsening condition. Instead, his mind was on the work at the hospital and Irene. Thoughts of the hospital ran to the number of recently admitted wounded soldiers who had been overseas. Their injuries disturbed him, deeply; ten young men clinging to life. It left a scar on his mind. How could he worry about a silly rich woman? What had she done to deserve his concern? Nothing. He thought of Irene, still unable to explain her reaction to him that afternoon in her office. He had been the object of attention for many young women, yet their reactions never gave him a second thought. Irene's impulsive and not completely undesirable reaction plagued his mind.

He sat at the table in the Blue Panther. The band began to play a swing number. He caught the eye of a passing cigarette girl, bought a piece of gum with a dollar bill, telling her to keep the change. She smiled and winked as she turned to her next customer. He ordered another drink, turned, saw Carole and Irene with another man.

He turned away to avoid having to look at her. There she was, a bright radiant young woman who would be dead within the year. She looked healthy, a few pounds heavier than last time. Suddenly, he felt a tap on his shoulder. He turned. "Good evening, Miss Davis," he said, rising.

"May I join you?" she asked.

Smiling, he offered her the vacant seat opposite him. She took it, ordered a drink from the passing waiter.

"Day off?" she said, trying to engage him in meaningful conversation.

He laughed. "Doctors do not get days off, Miss Davis. I

needed a break from the hospital, so, I came here. And you?"

"No reason, really. Like the band, I guess."

They sat, silently. Irene's drink arrived. She took a sip, then another, then set the glass on the table, her body moving closer to his. "Look, doctor," Irene said, lowering her voice. "I thought you should know...." She stopped as someone walked too close to their table, then continued. "Carole is," she started, then stopped, looking into his deep, dark eyes. They seemed the color of coal in the dim light of the club. "She's pregnant. I don't know how far along, exactly, but I would guess four months."

The glass slipped from his hand and crashed on the floor drawing little attention from others in the club. Some of the amber liquid splashed up, landing against Irene's white jacket. She took her napkin, dipped a tip into the water glass and daubed at the stain.

Bretaigne rose. "Goodness, Irene. I'm terribly sorry. You caught me off guard!"

Irene smiled, the spot virtually gone. "It's all right, really."

He sat on his chair, feeling the color drain from his face. "Four months? That means it's cutting it pretty close. Is she feeling all right?"

Irene moved closer again. "She had a fainting spell a couple days ago. She's been pretty sacked out, but her family doctor says she's doing just fine."

"How did she react when you -- " Irene's intense stare told him she had not told Carole. He recoiled from her. "Don't tell me she still doesn't know!"

Irene nodded. Words did not form in her throat.

Firmly, with a resolve he could not have planned, Bretaigne rose from his seat, knocking it backward. He moved toward Carole's table. Irene, frantic, rose, sending her chair backward into a passing waiter. She ran after him, deftly negotiating the steps down from the table to the dance floor, dodging dancers and other diners. She grabbed his arm, he did not stop. She held firm. In a half whisper, half yell, she commanded. "Stop it!" He turned. "Are you crazy? You can't just march over there and tell her she's dying! What are you thinking?"

Furiously, he yanked his arm from her grasp. "Goddamnit, woman. You've played god long enough. I'm sorry to break my promise to you, Irene, but the situation has changed. This has gone on long enough!" He started again to Carole's table. "Miss Trent," he began, fumbling with his jacket.

"Doctor!" Carole said, her surprise genuine. "How nice." She was cut off by Irene's arrival behind the doctor. "Irene!" Carole said. "But, what?"

Out of breath and desperate to save the moment Irene grabbed Carole's jacket which was draped over the back of her chair. She pulled Carole to her feet. "Come on Carole, Joe. We're leaving!" Joe, not understanding, rose from his chair to defend the two women.

"Now, see here, Irene," he began. Is this creep bothering you?" He pushed his way around the table, to confront the doctor.

"No!" Irene, screamed a moment too late. Joe swung at Bretaigne, missing. Bretaigne ducked, swung blindly, landing a solid punch on Joe's jaw. Irene screamed as the fight began in earnest. The two men tumbled down the steps to the dance floor, scattering dancing couples back from the melee. Carole turned to the *maître d'hôtel* to explain the simple misunderstanding which had caused the fight, leaving Irene to break it up. Irene waited for a moment's pause then threw the contents of a water pitcher into Joe's face, momentarily blinding him. She stepped between the two men, yelled at Joe to stop. She turned to the doctor.

"Good night, Bretaigne. I think you've done enough for one night."

Irene grabbed Carole's arm, walked from the club with Joe in tow, nursing a sore jaw. Lagging behind a few feet, Bretaigne followed them through the double doors, and out onto the sidewalk.

"Irene, what's going on here?" Carole protested when they emerged from the club. He wanted to tell me something. Why were you being so rude?"

"Carole, dear. Please stay out of this. The doctor has had too much to drink. He got a little out of control. He even threw his drink at me!" She indicated the still wet spot on her jacket illustrating her charges. "He was being rather belligerent, saying something about -- "

"I beg to differ, Miss Davis. I was not drinking anything stronger than the apple juice which stains your jacket. I was not being rude, belligerent, or mean, thank you. You know full well what it was I wanted to tell Miss Trent, your friend. And if you were indeed a friend to her, you would allow me to finish what must be said."

They stood there on the snow-touched sidewalk, Irene facing Bretaigne, Joe leaning sideways, Carole listening with half an ear. Suddenly, almost as if she had been struck, Carole felt a pain as her face flushed. Slowly, she turned, her gloves in one hand, her clutch purse under her arm.

Irene, still fighting with Bretaigne, yelled: "No! You don't know what you're talking about."

"But, she must know!"

"No!"

"Stop it!" Carole yelled. Silence descended over that spot on the street. "Stop it, both of you," she said, calmly. She turned to Irene. "Irene, dear, please say nothing. Be my friend and do this for me. Agreed?"

Irene bowed her head in acquiescence. Tears streamed from her face, gathering at the edge of her chin, finally dropping onto the sidewalk. "No," she said, her strength nearly gone. "Please, no."

Carole turned to Bretaigne. "There was something you wished to say?"

Bretaigne felt like an animal caged. He turned to Irene, she had turned from the group, begun to walk down the street.

He turned to Joe who followed Irene with his eyes, massaging his chin. He turned to Carole, felt a pain stab deep in his heart. He thought of the injured soldiers in the hospital and suddenly realized why Carole was so much more important to him than as just merely a patient. He stood there, gazing into her hazel eyes, her face touched with flakes of newly fallen snow. He saw those strong, angular bones which created her face, made stronger by the light from the streetlamp. He reached out his hand, lightly touched her blonde hair. She backed away a step.

"I -- " he began.

Could it be really happening to him? He had not felt this way since long before he saw his mother and father -- No, it couldn't be true. Why had Irene kissed him? Why had it preyed on his mind for so long? He knew, now, why. There was a truth to be told, here. And he knew now was the time. "I think I'm in love with you, Carole."

She accepted the cup of hot tea from a weary Mrs. Kennison who did not appreciate being taken from her book. As she sipped from the blue porcelain cup, Irene glanced over he shoulder to the clock on the mantle. Mrs. Kennison slipped quietly from the room. "I would rather you had received the news another way, Carole," Irene finally said, placing the cup of tea on the table. She leaned back, crossed her legs, removed a strand of hair from in front of her eyes. She sighed. "I told him I wanted to tell you, but he wouldn't hear of it."

Carole turned away from the window. "*You* wanted to tell me?"

Irene, surprised at Carole's excitement, spoke slowly. "Yes. I told him that the right time had to present itself before you could be told. I felt the news should come to you calmly, quietly."

Carole crossed the library toward the fireplace, her walk strong.

"What were you afraid of, Irene? That I would fall apart

or something?" She turned her back to the roaring fire. "You know me too well to think I would let something like that get to me."

Irene could not help but look surprised. She was unsure how someone could take such bad news with so little care, so little worry. Maybe it just hasn't sunken in yet. She rose from the sofa, joined Carole. With a hand on her arm, Irene spoke. "I'm sure you're right, Carole. I must admit, though, you're taking the news a lot better than I ever could have. I'm surprised."

"Why? Haven't you had men tell you they were in love with you before?" Carole walked away from the fire, sat on the edge of the big desk. "I don't understand why you're making such a big deal about it, honestly."

Irene immediately understood: Bretaigne had *not* told her. She turned, faced Carole. Stunned for the moment, she couldn't think of the next words to say -- and she almost slipped and told her herself. "I, uh..." she started, covering her clumsiness with a fake cough. "Excuse me," she said. She stepped toward Carole. "I guess," she began. "I guess I was just surprised that he told you he loved you."

"But, why did he tell you, Irene? He hardly knows you."

"Yes, well, when we talked, he -- "

"Talked when, Irene? Monday morning?"

Irene's eyes opened in shock. How did she know about that? Did Bretaigne tell her that too? Irene needed time to think. She turned from the desk, returned to the sofa, picked up her tea cup. Carole went to the desk, opened a drawer. Irene watched over the edge of the tea cup, saw Carole remove a small, neatly wrapped package of brown paper. There was some small, neat lettering on the package. Irene quickly knew it had been delivered, not sent through the mail. Closing the desk drawer firmly, she walked back to the edge of the desk. Extending the package held loosely in her hand, she said, "Here."

"What is it?"

"Come see," Carole beckoned. She moved her hand with the package a small bit closer to pique Irene's interest. Irene reached for the package which lay several inches from her grasp. "I can't."

"Come get it, Irene." Carole's voice grew suddenly calm, soothing, yet hard edged. Irene felt a tingle up her spine as she rose from the sofa, placed the tea cup on the table, walked toward Carole, her eyes unwavering. Irene gently took the package from Carole's hand, resisted opening it. "Aren't you going to tell me what this is?" Carole smiled, but said nothing.

Irene's hands shook as she opened the package. "It isn't my birthday," she offered to Carole's blank stare.

Anger welled in Carole and she walked from the desk and the closeness of Irene, returning to the fireplace. Her back to Irene, her face warmed by the flames of the fire, Carole heard Irene's gasp after the crinkle of the paper ceased.

"Oh, my," Irene said, the truth clear to her.

Carole did not turn around.

Irene's mind worked frantically. "Where did you get this?" She knew, but there was still hope.

"It was delivered." The warmth of the fire was too hot on Carole's face, but she would not turn around.

"By whom?"

"A delivery boy."

There was a heavy pause. Irene could see Carole's back heaving. She knew she was crying.

Irene's throat tightened, dried up. She felt her voice crack as she asked, "From where? Where did you get this?"

Slowly, painfully, Carole stepped to the side, turned to face her friend. She raised her head, focusing through tear-filled eyes at the woman who was once a friend. A woman for whom, once, Carole would have given her life. She wiped her eyes, but was still unsure who she saw on the other side of the library. She had been betrayed, she was hurt. They had been friends almost their entire lives. Before her, now, stood a woman who had lied to her. The fact of the lie hurt, but the reason for the lie hurt more.

"You know Mrs. Sharp?"

Irene's eyes flared open. "Of course. She's a nurse at the hospital."

"Yes. She phoned me Monday afternoon. Actually, I called the doctor myself. Why, I don't remember. Mrs. Sharp, as an afterthought, asked if you had returned home yet because you had forgotten that!" She motioned at the compact Irene held. "Forgot it in the office. She asked if you were going to pick it up or if it should be delivered."

Irene, hurt, said, "Carole, I -- "

"I know, Irene. You lied to me. It's as simple as that."

"But, Carole, I did it -- "

Fury blazed through Carole's mind. She walked past Irene, bumping her shoulder. At the other end of the library, Carole wheeled around, faced Irene. "I don't care why you did it, Irene," she snarled, her voice deadly calm. "The fact that you did it is painful enough. The whys do not interest me in the slightest."

Irene, too, was crying. She knew what she had done was wrong, but had no idea how she could explain her actions to Carole. Carole had been her friend, and now she was all Irene had left. "But -- "

"Shut up! Shut up! Shut up!" Carole yelled, covering her ears with her hands. She walked around the library. She wanted to escape the confines of the four walls but could not leave until she threw Irene out of the house and her life forever.

"Carole," Irene pleaded, tears streaming down her face. She was sobbing strongly, trying to form sentences in her mind. Everything she thought to say sounded too flimsy. "She's right," Irene thought to herself. "I lied. That's bad enough."

"Good god, Irene!" Carole shouted, her voice echoing against the rich wood paneling of the library. "We've been friends forever. You are living in my house, sharing every intimate moment with me." Her voice grew static, hoarse. "In case you haven't known this, Miss Davis," she said, spitting out the words like a piece of bitter lemon, "I love you. I love you more than my own life. My mistake: I loved you like that once, now, I don't think I can."

"Carole, don't say that," Irene cried. She crossed the sofa, fell onto it, sobbing, drained, hurt.

Carole crossed to the sofa, almost as an animal moving in for the kill. "Why? How can I trust you ever again? You've never lied to me -- or have you?"

"Carole," it was a weak effort. "Please."

"Please what, Irene? I don't know you any more. I could never trust you again. No one I love has ever lied to me. Until now."

The room was silent. Carole could hear Irene's sobs over the quiet crackle of the fire. The wind outside howled almost silently. A long moment passed.

Irene lifted her head, searching for some compassion in Carole's eyes. "Please, Carole. Please. If only you knew why."

Carole sat on the desk. "I don't care why, Irene. I don't care."

Irene lifted her tired body from the sofa, sat back against its softness. She said nothing.

Carole rose from the desk, moved toward the fire. "Nothing you could say, no reason you can name would be enough for me to overlook -- " At first, Carole was not sure she heard Irene's words correctly. There was a heavy thumping in her ears as she turned to face her. "What?"

Irene lowered her face into her hands, the sound of crying filling the room.

Carole angrily crossed to the sofa, grabbed one of Irene's arms, yanked her to her feet. "Tell me what you said," she yelled.

Irene looked up, her eyes meeting Carole's. "What I said was that you are dying, Carole. I went to the doctor because he's been insisting on telling you. I've been trying to fight him, convince him not to tell you."

Carole released Irene from her vice like grip, heavy red

marks remained on Irene's skin. Her face went white as the blood drained all at once. A look of shock and disbelief was fixed in her eyes. Carole walked to the window, looked out. "Then it's true."

Irene, rubbing her sore arm, walked to Carole. She stood next to her, wrapped her arm around her shoulders. She said nothing.

A few minutes passed. Carole stopped crying, turned to Irene. "How long have you known?"

"Since you were in the hospital. Doctor Fischer wanted to tell you then. I guess I didn't believe it was true and didn't want to upset you if they later found out they were wrong. Then, Philip's letter arrived, you were so happy. How could I tell you then? And, of course -- "

"I'm going to have a baby," Carole whispered.

"Yes. When I found that out, how could I tell you? When I told Bretaigne tonight, well, he thought you had to be told. And I thought he had told you outside, on the sidewalk. I was walking down the sidewalk, so I couldn't hear. I didn't want you to find out, not like this. I guess I did the wrong thing. I'm sorry."

Carole looked at her friend, smiled. She ran her hand over Irene's richly dark hair. Leaning forward, she kissed Irene, lightly, on the cheek. "Irene dear. I wish you had told me but your heart was in the right place. For that, I thank you." Irene looked at her friend, the fire from the fireplace casting a faint glow onto her face. They stood there, holding one another, saying nothing. After a time, they moved silently from the library, up to their separate bedrooms where they both slept, peacefully.

Saturday Morning

Carole awoke. She merged slowly from deep sleep to a state of wakefulness. It was a peacefully smooth transition from one state of awareness to another. She felt the softness of the bed linens against her arm before she opened her eyes: she knew she was awake before she actually woke. The soft, rumpled comforter warmed her body as her awareness spread from her arm to the rest of her still unmoving body. She did not move at first, and then worked hard to keep her body motionless. It was a struggle as she fought to keep her legs still; to prevent her heart from beating too strongly. She was not sure how long she had lain there. Time passed slowly; time passed quickly.

Suddenly, an uncontrollable urge to stretch consumed her and she shot out her arms in different directions, her legs down the length of the bed, and arched her back violently, hard. She held this stretched position for several beats until she was exhausted from the action. She opened her eyes wide, stretched a half stretch, quickly yawned. She rearranged her body into alignment with the bed, sat up using the pillows for support. Her room was awash with bright sunlight. She quickly glanced out the window to see a light covering of white over the ground. For the first time, she realized it was spring outside.

She heard sounds from outside, the likes of which she usually did not notice until she was outside riding, walking. Then, she made it a point to notice these sounds; now, they were unavoidable. She looked around the room at all of those all-too-familiar things which made this room *her* room. She noticed how bright were the colors. Could it have been the sun's light making them seem more vivid? Somehow, she knew this was not the reason. The events of the last four months combined to make each sound more clear, each color more bright, the sunlight more intense. Without being conscious of the effort she found her hand resting on her stomach. "I'm pregnant," she thought. "And I'm going to die." She looked out the window again and sighed.

Things would be so different now. No more did the little things seem important to her. No more did she worry about the war in the way she did yesterday and all those yesterdays before.

No more would ration stamps plague her mind; no longer would canned salmon be less desirable than fresh. How can she feel so differently now? Is she a person different from at this time yesterday? No, she was still Carole Marie Trent. She was still twenty-four years old until July. She still had blonde hair and, although she had no proof, she was sure her hazel eyes had not changed color overnight. No, she was not anyone other than herself. Then, why did everything around her look so different?

She looked to the little round clock on the stand next to her bed. It was just after 6:00 and hours before she was accustomed to awaking. Why did she have so much energy surging through her body? She felt alive for the first time in her life. That was it. She felt alive. "How long do I have?" she wondered. Well, her list for today would have that item as top priority. How long?

Again she sighed. Item two on the list: what about her baby? She allowed her other hand to rest lightly on her stomach. She applied a small bit of pressure from both hands and felt nothing different. How soon until he or she kicks? What was it that suddenly took her attention from her thoughts? Why did she feel the prick of a tear in each eye? Why did she begin to laugh as those tears began to flow freely down her happy, smiling face? Her hands rested lightly on her stomach. She felt a hearty kick. Suddenly, she felt so happy, so immortal. More alive now than only a few moments ago. She knew, no matter how long the doctors gave her, she would indeed live long enough to see the life within her living and breathing on his or her own.

The sun's rays and the shadows it made moved across those things in the room which made this her room. Carole laid in her bed, the bed linens shoved down around her hips, her hands resting lightly on her stomach. She fixed all of her attention of the life within her, and waited there, for many hours, for another healthy kick.

Saturday, Late Morning

Irene woke, bathed, dressed, ate a small breakfast, took a quick stroll around the grounds, read the morning paper while Carole remained in her room, quietly. Irene did not want to wake Carole and, so, did all of these things as quietly as possible. She was happy, somehow, when she should have been feeling an unease over the events of last night. No. She felt happy, comfortable, and at peace with herself. She thought, standing at the French doors in the dining room, that she was wrong to have kept the news of her health from Carole. She would have done things differently if she could have, with all she knows now, but did not think she had done so badly, after all. Now, though, she had to focus her attentions on other matters, more important matters. No longer did she feel that sense of dread about the war that had permeated her thoughts for the last five years. She felt good, actually, about the war, and would almost say she felt the war's end would come very soon. "By autumn," she said aloud. "By autumn."

She turned from the windows and walked through to the living room where she sat heavily upon the blue sofa. She sat for a long while thinking of children playing in the sun along a bright, white beach, the waves playfully lapping at their heels as they ran along the water's edge. She thought of flowers blooming in the gardens, fields, meadows and glens around her. She thought of the newly born, small versions of the animals around her: baby birds, baby deer, baby people. She thought of how nice the colors pink and light blue were. Not thinking of babies but of weddings. She knew there were scarce months left until Carole would....

She rose quickly from the sofa, the motion driving that thought from her mind. She knew her top priority was Carole's baby. Timing was of essence now, if the doctor was correct. Carole might have two months left, or four. Maybe six, maybe more. Calculating quickly, Irene figured Carole would be almost four months along. She counted on her fingers: December 24th to January, February, March, to April 21st: today. Three more days and it will be four months. Five months from now would be September 21st. Carole would need to hold on until then. But, the doctor has given her maybe another four months: August 21st. There would not be enough time if he was right. Carole needed to hold on another five months, not four. "Damn this war anyhow," she said aloud, the sound of her voice startling her. She thought Philip should be here with Carole, now. He probably doesn't even know he's about to be a father. Carole doesn't know where he is and she's pregnant. Irene did not know what she should do. She could phone Mrs. Craig -- Philip's mother -- to tell her what's happening. No. It doesn't seem like so good an idea. She could use her contacts and try to locate Philip herself, but that doesn't seem ideal, either. There was nothing for her to do but wait. Wait. Wait. She would do whatever Carole wished. Plan the wedding, if that's what she wanted. Travel, if that's what Carole wanted. Irene would do whatever Carole wished. Until Carole could wish no more.

Saturday Afternoon

She sat on the hard, cold, wooden chair with her legs crossed correctly one over the other. She folded her gloves over her purse, then under. Over then under: unable to make up her mind just how they should be held. Over was best, she decided, grasping her purse and gloves with her left hand while lifting her right hand to the strand of pearls around her bare neck.

She was acutely aware of her posture. She sat snuggly against the corner of the chair, her back straight as a line. Her wide-brimmed hat, in a grey velvet material which matched her suit, slightly askew on her head. She titled her head as she gazed down the seam on the back of her top leg: it too was straight. Her black patent-leather shoes glowed in the reflected light of the office -- an office where light was at a premium: only one lamp was on in the room; it cast a broad pool of light onto the desk where he sat, uncomfortably leafing through the file, trying to summarize his findings, trying to find a nice way to say he was sorry but there was nothing more that could be done. Trying to find a way to look at her.

"What is it that I could say," he began, still looking through the file and not at her, "that you don't already know?"

She changed her mind; she folded her gloves under her purse. "You're the doctor," she said, stiffly. "Not I. There must be more than what you've already said."

He rose from his desk, slowly, haltingly, and walked around it. He sat on the edge of the desk directly in front of her. He sighed. "Miss Trent, you must understand that anything and everything that could have been done for you has already been done. There is nothing more to do, say, or try. I'm sorry."

Carole's neck began to ache from looking up to the doctor. She looked away, fumbled again with her gloves, then looked at him again, directly, eye to eye. "So you are saying within three months I will be dead."

"I am saying nothing of the kind, Miss Trent. I wish you would try to understand just how difficult something like this is for us."

"No more difficult for you than me, I assure you, doctor."

"Of course, Miss Trent; that's not what I meant. I've been trying to explain to you how difficult it is for medicine to determine exactly how soon a condition like yours will prove fatal. There are so many unknowns; but what we know is this: there is an abnormal growth in your brain. We know that the area sometimes bleeds -- causing your blackouts. That bleeding will continue. Due to the location of the growth, we are unable to get in there and operate without a tremendous risk to your life. We have tried to find some way to stop the flow of blood. It has never been a question of whether this growth will prove fatal, Miss Trent, only when. The best estimates, by the best experts in the field, give you from two months to six. Eight months at the most. But not even this is certain. The bleeding is minute and it has not stopped. The small flow of blood is, to the best of our ability to tell, building up within the cranial cavity. Somehow, someway, there is a very small chance, Miss Trent -- a very small one -- you may go on to live a normal, healthy, happy life. You may indeed outlive us all but I would not think that is a probable outcome. To the best of our ability to tell, you have six months from the date of your first blackout. Medical records and other case histories are the basis for our conclusions."

He continued to look at her; she turned away. What could she say? It was hopeless.

The doctor tried to reassure her. "Diseases of the brain are very complex, Miss Trent. There is anecdotal evidence that a person with a growth such as yours could live a long while. We could be wrong."

Carole's eyes darted to his face, her eyes searching out his.

"Could be, Miss Trent, but are not."

She lowered her eyes again.

There was a long pause between them. Neither knew what to say or ask next.

"How will it happen, doctor?"

He stood away from the desk. "The end? It's hard to say for sure. Best evidence indicates you should do well until shortly before the pressure build up that finally interferes with the functioning of your brain. Hours, possibly days before that, you could find yourself having difficulty walking, seeing clearly, thinking. You might start forgetting things. There may be more symptoms and again there may be nothing. It's difficult to know."

"What's happening inside my head? Why would I feel these things?"

"Oh, that's very simple to explain. Blood is flowing into the fluid-filled areas of your brain where blood should not be. There is only so much room in these areas and the bleeding is putting more fluid in them than can fit naturally. This causes pressure to build up, which, in turn, puts an unnatural pressure on the areas of your brain near the bleeding. In your case, near the brain stem. Through this area all nerves flow sort of like a railroad station through which all trains must come at one point in their schedule. These nerves continue down your spine and branch out to areas all over your body. Every sensation you experience is related to these nerves. A disturbance to the area where the nerves gather could cause problems to any one of a hundred areas of your body. There's no way for us to know for certain."

"What about -- "

"Your baby?" He walked around the desk, moved her file, sat on the edge. "Again, it's impossible for us to say for sure. You're apparently doing just fine in your pregnancy. You are how far along?"

"About four months."

"Yes. Well, as things are now, the pregnancy is going along just fine. There is no indication that your baby has been affected at all."

"But, it has."

"I'm afraid I don't understand."

She uncrossed her legs, crossed them again, opposite to the original way. "If, as you say, I have only six months -- "

"Possibly eight."

"Six or eight months from the date of my first blackout, which was Christmas, then I will not live long enough to deliver my baby full term."

"I have contemplated that."

"And?"

"There are three options available to us. They are three difficult options to be sure, but only three."

"Please tell me," she said, leaning back against the chair.

"All right." He returned to his chair behind the desk and sat. "First, we do nothing, hope for the best, that you will survive long enough for the baby to be born on his or her own and that all will be fine. Next, we can leave the baby until its seventh or eighth month and force delivery."

"Lastly?"

He paused, thinking. He looked up, his eyes meeting hers. "You end the pregnancy -- now."

Carole knew her options long before she called the doctor to arrange this meeting. She knew the chances were slim at best of her being able to carry the pregnancy full term. She knew that the baby could be delivered early, with a slight chance of survival. She had even thought about -- "Aren't we, I mean, aren't I too far along to end the pregnancy?"

"Technically speaking, yes, you are. But in a case like this, where the life of the mother is in jeopardy -- "

"In jeopardy? This pregnancy is a risk to me?"

"Possibly. The added strain of a pregnancy in your condition could increase the bleeding, thereby increasing the pressure on the nerves, and...." He stopped. Too fine a point had already been put on the issue. "So, yes, the pregnancy could be considered a risk to your health."

"But, you don't know that for sure. Anyhow, I'm dying. What difference could it make?"

"Quite a lot, Miss Trent," he said, leaning forward, his elbows resting on the desk. "There is a chance you can survive this condition, as I have said before."

"How much chance?"

"Maybe five percent."

"Ninety-five percent chance I'm going to die."

"Yes."

"And if I decide to continue this pregnancy?"

"Your life will end within the next four months. Maybe two. Maybe sooner."

"If I," she paused, "end the pregnancy?"

"Miss Trent, there are no guarantees. We could terminate the pregnancy -- "

" -- and I could still die next week."

He leaned back in his chair. "The possibility does exist."

"Is there any way for me to," she paused, her throat dry, constricted. "Is there any way for me to, for you to..." She stopped again. "What chances do I have to carry this pregnancy to full term?"

Doctor Fischer rose from his chair, walked around the desk, stood facing Carole. "Now look, Miss Trent. I don't want you to get your hopes up. I can't say anything for sure as far as this is concerned. Generally, if you take it easy, don't excite yourself, don't do anything strenuous like horse riding, eat a good, healthy diet, get plenty of rest, maybe -- and I stress the word maybe -- you can take the pregnancy full term. But, it's going to be a big strain on you, Miss Trent. It could kill you. There are no -- "

Carole bolted from her chair, her gloves in one hand, her purse in the other. " --guarantees. Yes, doctor, I know. How often do you have to say it? I know there are no guarantees. I know it." She walked around the desk, stood looking out the window in the office. She turned to face him.

"What would you think best?"

"I can't make that decision for you."

"I am not asking you to make any decision for me, Doctor Fischer. I am simply asking your medical opinion."

He looked away from her, thinking. He turned toward her, took a step in her direction. "As your doctor, I would suggest we check you into the hospital today, do a clinical abortion on the grounds of endangerment to your life."

She stood there, at the window. "Abort my child?" she thought. "No, I could never do that. This," she touched her stomach gently, "is the product of one night's love. Our love. Even after I'm gone, Philip will have our child."

Carole walked from the window, stood facing him. "Thank you doctor, for your candor. I'll let you know when I've made my decision." She turned, strode from the office. Doctor Fischer sat at his desk, looking at the door long after it had closed and knew that his love for her was stronger now than ever.

Sunday Afternoon

Irene had not left her room all day. She called down to the kitchen and asked Mrs. Kennison to bring a tray of fresh fruit. Carole had been strangely quiet since her return from town yesterday afternoon -- and for Irene, that was all the better for she had something else on her mind, something of more immediate importance. She could count on one hand how many more months her best friend had left. Four months. So much could happen in four months, but never as much as should happen. It was almost as if someone had taken a rough knife to her bosom and carved out her heart. She felt such a heavy, empty feeling in her chest that it almost made her cry. As it was Irene had cried herself to sleep yesterday evening and awoke with a solidly heavy, depressing feeling gnawing at her innermost self.

For now, her life was Carole's. In order to facilitate the decision Irene had made, she knew she would have to end things with Joe: not because she had no desire to see him. She had -- in fact, she now felt more strongly about Joe than ever before. She knew that, were he to dare to tread that fine line again and ask her to marry him, she would not be able to refuse him his wish. Now, it was her wish, as well. She could remember, at this very moment, the exact feeling when she saw Joe for the first time. The first kiss, his touch, the sound of his breath against her hair.

She sighed heavily, pulled the covering off her lap and allowed it to fall onto the ground at her feet. She put her hands, palms down, on her legs, sighing again. She looked out the window at the spring outside, mocking her in all her despair. Outside, the freshness, the newness of a re-emergence of life were calling to her and telling her of her loss, drawing attention to each newly bloomed flower, each newly born animal as if saying "for us, but not for you." She turned from the window, fighting against the bitter pain which stung her eyes. Tears rolled down her cheeks, anew. "Damn it all," she shouted to the empty room, the echoes ringing in her ears, calling her fate to her again. "Damn it all!" She pounded her clenched fists on her legs, her body bending forward, sobbing. "Damn it all." She allowed her body to be wracked by the heavy sobs for a long while, breathing sporadically and with great effort, knowing this would be the only time she could allow herself this luxury. After this, never again.

She remained bent over for many minutes, finally, she straightened up at the sound of a knock at her door. "Yes?" her voice asked, tired. She remained seated, but wiped her eyes with her hands, quickly. "Yes?"

From the other side of the locked door, a muffled voice came through. "It's Mrs. Kennison. May I take your tray away?"

Irene quickly glanced across the room to the empty tray at the window. "Yes, Mrs. Kennison. All right." She rose from the other side of the bed and slowly, cautiously, walked to the door, unlocking it with a simple, quick flick of her wrist. She turned her back to the door, walked to the window.

The old woman walked through the door, attempting to be bright and cheerful. "It's going to be time for dinner, Miss Irene. Should I expect you downstairs or would you rather I brought up another tray?" Irene stood silently at the window looking out, her eyes red. "I've got a great big roast that's been cooking all day. There will be mashed potatoes and a great big gooseberry pie -- your favorite."

Irene did not turn from the window. "That will be fine." Her voice, soft, sounded worn out.

Mrs. Kennison walked across the room, quickly checking to insure that the fire was well stoked with extra logs and to the window table where she began to collect the breakfast tray. "Shall I bring you something?"

Irene turned from the window, walked past Mrs. Kennison without a word. As she sat on the edge of her large, rumpled bed, she spoke. "Mrs. Kennison?"

Welcoming the opportunity to break through Irene's depression, Mrs. Kennison wheeled around to face her. In her haste, tipping the bud vase off the tray. It shattered as it hit the wood flooring.

"Leave that for now, Mrs. Kennison. I need to speak with you."

"Of course." Mrs. Kennison straightened her weary, old body, remaining by the window. Across the front of her apron she folded her hands, her chin lifted, her legs straight. She assumed the pose one assumes when willingly accepting the responsibility for the completion of a task, or when one honestly accepts blame for its failure. For many years this proud woman had accepted responsibility for running the Trent household -- from raising the owner's daughter, Carole, to tending to Mrs. Trent when she fell ill shortly before she died. She tended broken bones, injured souls, and torn drapes always with a pride of workmanship and duty that could never be questioned. Now, as she stood in the half light of a dying afternoon, not knowing which responsibility she would be asked to assume, whether command or blame, she possessed a dignity which almost belied her station in life.

"Mrs. Kennison," Irene said "I'm going to request your utmost cooperation over the remainder of the year."

"Yes, Miss."

"I'm going to ask you to enlist the help, loyalty and cooperation of the entire staff as well. I'm charging you with this responsibility."

"Yes, Miss."

"Carole is dying and it is up to us to make her last days as comfortable as possible."

Irene looked to Mrs. Kennison, their eyes communicating what decorum insisted could not be said aloud. Mrs. Kennison, forcing her knees to remain rigid, twitched, trying to restrain herself from running to Carole, to comfort, to question -- fighting, every inch of the way, the maternal instinct which now told her to protect the child at all costs. She said only, "Yes, Miss."

Irene reclined against the pillows propped against the

headboard, looking away from Mrs. Kennison. "You may remove the trays now. I will be down for dinner."

Silently, tears rolling down her cheeks, Mrs. Kennison walked across the room, toward the bedroom door. Before she exited, Irene called to her. "Yes, Miss Irene?"

Slowly, Irene turned to face the old woman who had come to be the mother Irene knew so little of. She smiled and winked. "As for dinner tonight, Mrs. Kennison, go all out."

Grasping the opportunity to return the kindness just offered her, the old woman forced a smile to her face, sniffled back a tear. "Of course, Miss. Of course." She walked through the heavy, old, oak door, closing it behind her. Irene knew, behind the barrier, she was crying.

Irene sat up. Now, the easy part was over. She still had to find some way to deal with Joe, to tell him they would not see each other again. She looked down at the fragments of the crystal vase lying so peacefully on the clean, shining floor, then reached across the bed, lifted the receiver from the telephone, and said: "Operator? Please connect me with VErnon 70727."

Thursday, 10 May 1945

She was surprised, astonished, really, at how simple the whole affair had been. One little phone call and Joe was out. It almost angered her that he did not protest. He fell silent for a moment then said only, "If that's what you want, Irene, then all right." He didn't sound hurt, angry or upset. He stated the fact. "If that's what you want." She could have screamed at him: "Why don't you argue with me? Fight me, Joe. Show me that you love me by fighting my decision!" But she said nothing more. She waited to hear him raise his voice. He did not. She would have been happiest for him to yell at her. He would not. She wanted him to slam the receiver onto the telephone, drive to her house, grab her, shake her. He did not. "If that's what you want," was all he said. For that, she hated him.

This was all two weeks ago. She saw nothing of him or heard anything. He had been too easy: too easy to meet, too easy to love, too easy to leave. Too easy. Her life had always been filled with ups and downs. She felt she needed something to stabilize her life, to prevent the ups and downs. Why then was she so filled with a burning hatred of Joe? He was a doctor with a good veterinary practice. He loved her. He was devoted to her. No better a stabilizing force she could find. But, it was when she faced her responsibility of living in a stabilized world that she realized just how much the thought made her ill. Not just mentally ill, but physically nauseous. When the operator connected her to Joe, as she began to explain her feelings to him, a horrible wave of nausea came over her. She had to rise from her bed, pace the room, breathe deeply in an attempt to fight off the sickness she felt in the very pit of her stomach.

The moment she hung up with Joe she realized her futile attempts had little effect. She ran down the hall to her private bathroom, threw up into the small toilet. She heaved and heaved until her coughs were dry and painful. She fell limp onto the floor and cried until her eyes, too, were dry. For a long moment she stayed there, limply, on the floor, breathing and sighing. After a time, she lifted herself from the cold tile flooring, slowly walked back to her room. The whole distance back she repeated in her mind. "It's over. It's over."

How does one argue with someone who knows everything? Not someone who only thinks she knows everything, but actually does. She had often joked to Irene, "It's one thing to be arrogant. It's quite another to be arrogant AND right." This was the bind in which Carole now found herself as she stood, carefully, in the kitchen, her eyes boring through Mrs. Kennison's who stood on the other side of the cutting board.

"Goodness, Mrs. K." she said, exasperation filling her words. "The doctor was very specific about the foods I could and could not eat. He gave me the list which you so conveniently lost. What do you wish to do, kill me?"

"Miss Carole! How could you think something so terrible of me? Why, I have always loved you like my own daughter, and this! You treat me like this!" The old woman began to cry. It was the only argument that Carole could not defend herself against. She hated when anyone cried, for any reason, but to see this special woman crying was unfair.

"Oh, would you stop that! You know how I hate it when anyone cries. And you have tried this already, once before."

"You are a wicked, wicked woman, you are. That poison the doctor suggested could kill you. That tripe! Goodness! After all this time, after all the young ones I have cared for, you think I don't know what is best for you now that you are...ah...." She hesitated. "Now that you are in a family way."

Carole rolled her eyes at the old woman, turned from the table, ventured to look through the icebox. "Goodness."

From that point forward, Carole and Mrs. Kennison never again would discuss the topic of her diet. Instead, Carole obediently ate whatever Mrs. Kennison provided. And she made the point of eating everything: no questions asked.

Carole and Irene seemed to grow more distant than at any time in their past. Irene was, it seemed to Carole, preoccupied with her social life. Irene seemed to be on the phone an awful lot, going out without explaining where, generally being more secretive, distant, solitary.

To Irene, it was Carole who seemed to be pulling away from her. Carole was now thinking only of a proper diet, baby clothing and how soon she would die. To Irene, Carole was beginning to draw life in around her at the expense of all else. Only when one on the outside looked in could the truth be seen. But, there was no one on the outside who could look in.

For a reason Carole did not know, and would not dare to ask, Joe was nowhere to be seen. He suddenly stopped coming around to the house. Irene never mentioned his name to her.

Was there someone else? Carole did not want to know for she did not care. Now, her priorities lay elsewhere. Baby, first, then Philip, then everything else. She came last. She had her whole life, what little was left, planned perfectly. Almost to the minute. The blueprint had been drawn; construction underway. Deadline: the day when the bleeding in her brain finally killed her. It was a deadline she thought of often, but always with distaste.

Later that afternoon, as the sun's warmth heated her body while she rested on the terrace outside the dining room, the lone fault in her plan struck her as if a swiftly moving hand on the end of a strong man's arm: she would do everything within her power to see the baby was born healthy, strong and happy; but she had, to this point, never taken her thoughts beyond that moment, the very moment of birth. Now she knew she would have to.

Friday Morning

The sun rose, filling the day with a powerful, unseasonable warmth for which Carole had not planned. She had dressed warmly, unaware that the day's temperature would rise rapidly, unfalteringly. As she sat in his office again, in the same old, wooden chair as before, she felt the heavy beads of perspiration run in tiny rivulets down her back as she fanned her face with her new issue of *Vogue*.

She sat in the tiny, hot, oppressive room, awaiting the doctor's arrival from a sudden emergency with another of his patients. She angrily set the magazine onto her lap and stared at the almost-abstract cover and read the small blurb in the bottom right-hand corner: *"Vogue is regularly published twice a month. Because of wartime emergencies, it will be published once a month during June, July."* She sighed again. Once, at a time not too long ago, this little inconvenience would have bothered her, angered her. Today, she understood. She allowed her eyes to pass swiftly over the cover and settle on the words on the cover:

"To The American People:

"Your sons, husbands and brothers who are standing today upon the battlefront are fighting for more than victory in war. They are fighting for a new world of freedom and peace. We, upon whom has been placed the responsibility of leading the American forces, appeal to you with all possible earnestness to invest in War Bonds to the fullest extent of your capacity."

She looked at the names scrawled at the bottom of the text. They were the names of the leaders of the various military forces. She wondered who these men were. She wondered if any of them knew Philip or where he was. She made a mental note to stop at her bank on the way home and purchase a few more War Bonds.

Carole thumbed through the magazine again, for the third time. Not reading it; merely passing time through the mechanical act of turning pages, one page at a time.

The doctor finally arrived. "Thank you, Miss Trent. I'm sorry, but you know how these things are."

She placed the closed magazine onto her lap, smiled, said: "No apology is necessary, I assure you I have nothing but time, as you well know."

He looked sharply at her and sat onto the creaking chair behind his desk. He said nothing.

"I'm sure you are wondering, doctor, why I requested to see you."

"No."

Genuinely, she was surprised. "Really?"

"I expect you and I will see each other a lot in the next few months." He said it simply, implying nothing.

Carole laughed, suddenly, brightly. "Of course. Surprisingly, the thought hadn't entered my mind. Suppose I am a bit too preoccupied."

He smiled. "That's to be expected."

"Well," she tossed the magazine and her purse onto the small table to her right. "I have decided to do everything I can to see this baby born healthy, happy and taken care of."

He leaned back on his chair, folding his hands in his lap.

"I've already seen to it that a trust fund will be started for my son or daughter, and will soon choose someone to execute my wishes and desires with regard my child." She stood quickly, efficiently from the chair, lightly brushing her hand across the front of her skirt, straightening the folds. "My fiancé, Philip has been away for months and I don't know when he is due to return. To be frank, doctor, I do understand there is a chance he will not be returning at all." She looked down at the doctor, saw only a blank, although interested, face looking back at her. "That doesn't surprise you, doctor?"

"Not at all. You've always struck me as a bright, intelligent, above all pragmatic woman, Miss Trent. I assure you that little you could say would be unexpected."

She thought: "Extra points for you doctor," but said nothing. She tilted her head in affirmation of his compliment, quickly smiled. She walked toward the window overlooking the hospital grounds and continued. "That's why I've come here."

She heard the chair squeak, the doctor turned to follow her regressing figure.

"What can I do to assist you?" he asked.

"The baby needs a mother."

"Yes."

"That's me, for the time being, that is."

"Yes."

"The baby also needs a father. This is where you come in."

Carole wasn't sure, as she was not looking in his direction, if the chair slipped from under Bretaigne or if he fell trying to rise from the rolling chair. Either way, she heard a thump as his body hit the hard floor. She ran the couple steps to the desk, helped him up. "Goodness! What happened?"

"I'm not sure," he said, slightly dazed. "The part about the father," he gasped for air. He was either laughing or choking, she could not tell for sure. "I think you actually did it."

"What?" she asked, straightening his jacket.

"Said something that surprised me."

Carole walked around the desk, sat again on the old chair. "I knew it was only a matter of time, but I'm sure you misunderstood my intention."

He seated himself firmly on his chair, cleared his throat. He smiled. "I don't think I even gave a moment's notice to your intention, Miss Trent. It was just the concept of a pregnant, dying woman looking for a father to her child. It is not one I encounter often."

She laughed, the interpretation clear. It was a bright, sincere laugh. Carole enjoyed those moments when she laughed, now. It seemed as if she had never laughed before. Now, there was so little time to laugh. She wanted to do it as much and as often as she could. "Yes, I quite understand. You see, I do not put my faith in providence to see Philip home safely. I know that he is safe and I know that one day he will return; but I do not feel I shall ever see him again. I have hopes to marry him, one day, but -- " She stopped, looked at him. "Doctor, have you ever known something, but -- how should I put this? -- but felt that it was not true, or not going to happen?" He nodded. "This is like that. I am probably wrong but I do not feel Philip will return before I die." She smiled. "And, until he does return, I need to see to my child's future."

"In what way?"

"He needs a father and a mother, until such time that Philip can find someone to marry who will raise my child as her own."

"Well, Miss Trent, if I can think of any suitable candidates to fill your opening, I will be sure to call you. But, as it is now, I don't know of any young men or women who could possibly fit your bill."

Carole rose again. "You misunderstand me, doctor. I already have the right woman in mind."

He allowed a puzzled look to cross his face. "But, then, what reason do you have for telling me all this?"

"I also have the perfect man in mind."

"Then, I have even less understanding of why -- "

"Bretaigne," she said cutting him short. "That man is *you*."

Friday Morning, 10:37

"It's all quite simple, really. All I want you to do is to get to know Miss Davis, you know, Irene. She's a very nice person, really. You get to know her, like her, you don't have to love her if you don't wish, then marry her. I'll draw up the necessary papers so that you and Irene will get temporary custody of my child until such time that his or her father can take proper custody. I realize this favor will interrupt your routine for at least several months and for that inconvenience, I am ready to pay you handsomely."

She walked away from the window in his office toward the table where her purse still sat. Flipping open the snap, she extracted a large, thin, envelope which she opened. She walked toward his desk, setting the purse on one edge. "Here is a check for you in the amount of twenty-thousand dollars. Much of it is for you, Bretaigne, but the rest is for start-up costs for your own private practice. Also, I expect you to close up your practice here, in the hospital, engage a staff to help you in your new office, and hire the best nurse for my child that you can find. I'm sure with all your professional contacts, you can find someone suitable." She laid the envelope on the desk in front of him. She picked up her purse, walked back to the wooden chair, sat. "There will be more money. After I have died, and after you have fulfilled your part of our deal, you will be a very rich man, indeed. I realize immediately that I am asking a lot, but I do not make such requests lightly." She smiled at him, her eyes not wavering from his.

Bretaigne sat in his chair, stunned, motionless, silent. "I," he said, then swallowed heavily. His throat was parched, his eyes painful. He rose to the table behind him, poured a glass of water from the porcelain pitcher, drank it quickly without breathing. He walked a few steps, turned to Carole, leaned against his desk. "You are surely jesting, Miss Trent. What you are asking is... is... Good god woman, do you know what you are doing?"

"Please sit down, doctor. You don't look well. May I get you something else? Some tea, perhaps?"

He moved toward the chair behind the desk, dropped into it. "No. Thank you."

"I assure you I have given this matter a lot of thought. After, if you so desire, you may move to have the wedding annulled. I see that there will be little problem if any."

"Little problem? You can't just come in here, no matter how rich you are, and ask a man to do something like this! What are you thinking?"

Carole rose, firmly. She was as a mother lion defending her cub. It was all or nothing. "I am thinking of the safety and life of the child within me, doctor. There is no higher priority at this time. I'm sure that you, an intelligent man, can understand a mother's love for her child. How difficult can something like this be? And think of the money you will make for only a few month's work! You will make more from this little venture than you could hope to make if you stayed here, in the hospital, for the rest of your life. What do you make now, doctor? I happen to know even the best-paid doctors make little more than three thousand dollars each year. And, I also happen to know you are not one of the highest paid. I assure you, I've checked you out. Think of it. You will be set for life, in your own private practice. Anywhere in the country you want. I'm a rich woman, doctor. I know you know that. I'm going to die and I cannot spend half of what I have before then. After my father dies, I will have much more, so what is there for me to lose? And, if giving say, one-hundred-thousand dollars to you will help insure my child's welfare, then it's a small price to pay. Wouldn't you agree?"

He said nothing.

"I'm sure you will like Irene. I saw in her eyes that she likes you. I also think that she has broken off all ties with the man she had been previously seeing, so the time is right for your move. It's simple."

She picked up her purse, returned to the wooden chair. Calmly, she pulled a small, silver and black, geometrically designed compact from her purse, opened it, then pulled a small, plastic-cased lipstick from her purse and redid her lips. A quick bite on the linen handkerchief in her purse and she re-checked the mirror. Satisfied, she replaced the compact and mirror. She sat there, looking at him. "Cat got you tongue, doctor?" She smiled. It was becoming a game for her. A game with serious consequences.

Bretaigne looked at her, closely. He was stunned that his woman could be acting so callously. Then he thought about the money. One-hundred-thousand dollars. He looked at the check, which stuck partway out of the envelope. Twenty thousand already his for the taking. The chance was certainly too good to pass up. He looked at Carole again, then at the check. He sighed in defeat, leaned back against the creaky chair. "All right, Miss Trent. I'll do whatever you wish."

She smiled at him. The battle won.

"But," he said, as she began rising from the chair. "I have one question to ask you."

"Of course."

"Why me? I mean, I understand why, but how could you have ever hoped that I would say yes? There's no way you could have known positively."

She rose from the chair, ran her hands over the folds in the front of her dress, walked to the office door, stopped, her hand on the glass knob. She turned. "That's where you're mistaken, doctor. I did know, positively."

"How?"

"Remember that night outside the Blue Panther? The night you made such a fuss?"

He nodded, understanding.

"You told me then that you loved me."

His face flushed, red. He smiled, looked away. "Yes."

She opened the door, placing her purse under one arm. "I knew then that you would do anything I requested of you. For that, I return your love and the deepest respect I can offer another person." She turned back, quickly, walked through the door without closing it. He heard the clicking of her pumps as she walked down the tiled hallway.

He picked up the check, rose, walked to a file cabinet where he locked the check inside.

Sunday, 27 May 1945

Carole was amazed at how simply her plan took effect. One phone call to Irene, and Bretaigne and she were on their way. First, he took her to the Blue Panther for a nice dinner and show. A couple days later a movie and ice cream. Carole so easily acted the part of innocent bystander; she had her baby and her own life to worry about. She listened as Irene came to her questioning the doctor's intentions. "I don't know, Irene," she would say, her hands busy with the knitting she took up as a pastime. "He seems awfully nice. What's the harm in going to dinner or a show? Go ahead. If it doesn't work out, what harm was there?" The needles would click in the silence that followed. Irene could not find the words to argue although she felt in her stomach that something was not right. Next, it was a day trip into the mountains fishing and a picnic. "Go ahead, Irene," Carole said, looking up from her new issue of *Vogue*. "It's only a picnic. Not a honeymoon." So, off they went. And, only yesterday the two of them returned from a few days in New York where they saw shows, had dinner, walked, talked and had, to Irene's surprise, a very good time. Carole was pleased.

There had been no word from Philip, his parents, or her father. The last telegram from Philip arrived, it seemed, years ago but was only months. Mr. and Mrs. Craig said they heard nothing; Carole had no reason to believe otherwise. Her father, again in Europe on business for the government, was incommunicado. As far as this was concerned, Carole was far from pleased. But she had other thoughts, other concerns. The baby was five months along now. She had visited her family doctor nearly every day to the point of irritating the old man. She wanted nothing to go wrong; would leave nothing to chance. She had visited Doctor Fischer only once more during the past two weeks; surprisingly, she spoke only of his relation with Irene, never once mentioning her health, the possibility he was wrong or that something could be done. She had finally reconciled herself to the fact that her days were truly numbered. She ate well. Mrs. Kennison, who had only once slipped in her control of her emotions, had practically devoted herself to Carole's care. Like a saint, the old woman looked after Carole's every need. Once, not long ago, Carole would have resented this intrusion into her privacy but no more. She was no longer living life for one, but two.

The entire Trent house seemed to be living under a pall of destiny. It was like all those within the house felt the coming fate. All except Carole. It amazed everyone -- servant, friends, people who stopped by the house to deliver packages -- how happy Carole was. Not once did she seem depressed, unhappy, upset. As a matter of fact, it was easy to confuse her with a woman who had just given birth, or just inherited a fortune. It seemed to all around her that Carole was living a charmed life.

She was here, now, in the library, knitting away calmly on a small jacket for her baby. Her mind was wandering through many thoughts. She could not remember when last she took a drink. She thought about her last night with Philip, stopped knitting, twirled the ring around her finger. She felt sadness no more, neither did she feel emptiness, pain, sorrow. In fact, she had realized long ago that she would never see him again. She still could not explain to Irene why she felt this way, or how she knew that her eyes would never again caress Philip's; that her hands would never again hold Philip's; that their lips would never again meet. She paused. She sighed. After a moment, the clicking of the needles resumed, the thoughts in her mind flowed again.

After a time, she heard a knock on the library doors. They squeaked when Irene pushed them open.

"Hi. Stand some company?"

Carole placed the knitting on her lap, yawned, smiled. "Always, Irene dear. Always. Come in."

"I'm sorry to disturb you Carole, I -- "

"Goodness, Irene. I'm fine. Would you please, please try to understand? I can't have you continuously acting like you're walking on egg shells. Just be you. Just be the Irene Davis that I've known and loved all this time." She paused. "Okay?"

Irene laughed. "Okay."

"Come sit here on the sofa with me."

Irene walked across the library, forgetting to close the door, and sat cross legged next to her friend. She smiled. "How's it going?"

"Hmm?" Carole questioned, following Irene's glance to the knitting resting in her lap. "Oh this," she laughed. "Goodness. If I had known knitting little baby garments was a requirement for being able to have a baby, I would have thought twice about the whole affair." They laughed. Together, for the first time in many days, the two women laughed, sincerely, together, echoing through the library. So like before, when they were children, school girls, high school students, college girls. "It's fine. I think." Carole held up, with a finger and thumb at each corner, a small blue and pink creation which she turned sideways, then upside down. "What do you think?"

"It's a beautiful little blanket. Your baby will be very comfortable in it."

Carole laughed. "It's a jacket!" Again, they were laughing. Soon, however, Irene stopped. "Irene? What is it? What's wrong?"

Tears began to stream down Irene's face, her eyes red. She began to sob, heavily. She spoke in broken phrases through the spasm of crying. "I don't... want..." she coughed. "I don't want to lose you, Carole. I couldn't handle it if you were... to...

die." She cried harder. "You're being so damn brave about the whole thing. Don't you know it makes it harder for the rest of us? I can't stand it, Carole. You're driving me mad." She flew from the couch to the window. Her words had gone from sad frustration to angry bitterness. "Can't you see what this is doing to me? to us? Can't you? I can't stand to see you so... so damn happy about the whole thing. It's not fair, Carole." She looked through the window, silently beating her fist against the sill. "Damn it all. It just isn't fair." Her body crumpled to the floor. Exhausted, she could only cry. So many hours of silent acceptance of the situation had broken through like a weak dam straining to hold back a reservoir's total capacity.

Carole rose quickly, rushed to Irene's side. "Irene... Shh," she comforted, running her hand over Irene's hair, pulling a few strands from her face. Irene opened her eyes, looked at Carole. Carole smiled. "It's all right, Irene. Really. I know how hard this must be for you. But, I can be nothing now but happy. Can't you understand? Think how hard this is going to be for me. I love Philip and I know I will never see him again."

"So you've said."

"And, so it will be, Irene. I know it. I will not live to see my baby grow. I'll miss his first, halting steps. I'll never hear his first words. I'll miss his little hand grasping my finger. Think of how hard this is for me, Irene. Maybe then you'll understand why it is that I'm so happy. Maybe then it will be less difficult for you."

Irene looked up through tear filled eyes. "But how? How can you still be happy. You've mentioned all the most important things in life that you're going to miss. How can you still be happy?"

Carole lowered her body to the floor next to Irene's. Her face a calm bay in an angry sea, her eyes filled with a light which did not come from the sun's reflection outside the window. Irene could only describe it in her mind as the look of total serenity, peace.

"But, that's just the point, Irene," she said, smiling.

"Those very things that I am going to miss are why I am happy, because I know that here, in me, right now, is the product of a very special night of love. My child is part of me, part of Philip. Just because I won't be there doesn't mean I won't enjoy those things. Do you see? That I am making it possible for him to do these things, even without me, is my reason for happiness. I can imagine in my heart and see in my mind, what my son will look like. I know Taylor Christopher will be happy, healthy. He will grow to be a strong boy."

She stretched her legs beyond her body, leaned on one arm and sighed. "I'll miss all those things, but I'll still enjoy them. Because I know that what I am doing now will make all those later, other, wonderful things, possible. In a way, I have to... to die in order to allow my son these things. Do you understand?"

"But you don't have to die."

"I do, Irene. I do. There's apparently only marginal hope that I'll survive this. Doctor Fischer says that in choosing to continue this pregnancy, I am lowering my chances of survival even more. But I have, I had, no choice. It was either a few extra months for me, or a lifetime for my child. There really was no choice."

Irene turned her eyes from Carole. Slowly, she lifted her body from the floor, straightening her outfit and seating herself on the sofa. Her eyes red, her face moist. "Of course, Carole. I should have known you had figured this from every angle. You're too smart to let even something like this get to you. I'm sorry."

Carole followed Irene to the sofa, sat next to her. "No, no, Irene. There's no reason for you to be sorry. You are my very best friend, my only best friend. You are showing for me the same concern I would were you in this situation."

"Thank you for understanding."

"It is you who deserve my thanks, for staying by me this whole time. I know it's not been easy. You have proven your loyalty again and again. I couldn't be luckier. Now!" she said, slapping Irene's leg lightly. "Let's drop this talk, agreed? How about lunch?"

"Great," Irene replied, forcing a smile.

The two women exited the library hand in hand, smiling, telling funny stories from their childhood. They entered the dining room as the clock began to strike twelve times. Mrs. Kennison emerged, her hands holding trays laden with food. "It's suren good to see you two arriving for lunch at the proper time, for once."

Carole shot a sideways glance to Irene. They laughed more. Mrs. Kennison stopped in her tracks. Her feet planted firmly apart. "Now, then. What's so funny?"

"Nothing," Carole replied, smirking. "What's for lunch?"

Mrs. Kennison set the dishes on the table and returned to the kitchen for more. She replied to Carole as she walked out of the room: "Some great big turkey sandwiches, mashed potatoes, gravy, and a big fruit salad for each of you."

Lunch began. The two friends talked about unrelated events. Carole talked about her wedding which she continued planning even though she was sure it would never happen. Irene talked about every event under the sun but never mentioned her dates with Bretaigne. Finally, Carole could no longer stand the suspense. "If you don't tell me about him," Carole said, between bites of a turkey sandwich, "I'm going to throw the rest of this lunch at you. Tell me!"

Irene laughed. "All right. I knew you couldn't hold out too long."

None of what Irene said was new or unexpected. Carole felt she had written the story which her friend was now telling. She calmly ate the rest of her lunch listening to the words flow from Irene. Here and there she would ask a question of interest or make an appropriate comment. She kept her comments short, the brevity not holding back Irene's torrent of words. Irene seemed pleased about the turn of events in her life, as she spoke happily, giddily about the first date, the next, the trip to New York. Carole, too, was in her own way, pleased. It had been a long time since Irene had seemed so happy.

For the first time, here at lunch, listening to her friend's happy words, Carole thought of Joe. Carole wondered what made Irene decide against seeing Joe. Was it just that they were not compatible? Could it have been Carole's illness? She scooped up the last of the potatoes, pushed her plate to the side of the table, leaned back onto the wooden chair.

Irene finished her story, bringing them up to the events of last night. "...and he leaned forward, kissed me, then smiled. I don't know what it is about him, Carole," she said with a devious smile on her face. "I really think I love him. What do you think?" Irene leaned almost imperceptibly forward, awaiting Carole's verdict. A study in contrasts, Irene's plate still filled with food, Carole's empty. Mrs. Kennison walked into the dining room, removed Carole's plate, frowned at Irene.

"Finish your food and stop all that gabbing!" she said, then left the room.

Carole taunted Irene by sticking out her tongue. She laughed an affirmation of how perfectly well her plan was going. Somehow, she knew that at that exact moment, the cook would enter the room, say those exact words, turn and leave.

Irene looked hurt but tilted her head, awaiting Carole's reply.

"If you're happy, Irene," she said, folding her serviette. She placed it on the table as she pushed back her chair and rose. "Then, I'm happy also. You know that."

Irene ate her lunch; there was no more to be said. Irene was contented at Carole's words. She ate steadily, her mind thinking of how right her friend had always been, how perfectly correct about everything. Lunch finished, she rose from the table, went to her room, happiness filling her.

Wednesday, 06 June 1945

It had been one year since the Allied forces under the

command of General Dwight D. Eisenhower landed in France and liberated the French. Since then, fascist leader Benito Mussolini, who had ruled Italy since 1923, was executed by Italian partisans in April 1945 -- his head stuck on a pike and paraded around the squares. On the twenty-fourth day of the same month, American and Allied camera crews entered the first Nazi concentration camp and began to make a film record of the liberation of all those who had been consigned there to die; word was not slow in reaching across the Atlantic to America. Eisenhower's armies liberated Western Europe and rolled into Germany.

Last month, on the seventh day, German military leaders signed an unconditional surrender; Victory in Europe Day, VE day, was on the eighth. Shortly thereafter, the death of Nazi leader Adolf Hitler was announced. There was an unbridled anticipation about when the war would end. There had been rumors abounding about a secret weapon which would make America invincible; rumors about Japan surrendering within a month; rumors that the war could not end until at least the spring of 1946. There was hope in the air; but there was also fear.

No word had come from Philip. His parents told Carole they had no idea at all as to his location. Was he in Europe? Was he in the states? Was he even alive? No one knew. Carole had not expressed any surprise that she had not heard from or about him.   Irene and Bretaigne had seen each other again. It was unusual for a day to go by without them spending time together. Carole was not surprised that Irene and Bretaigne could find so much comfort in each other's presence. She knew in her heart this match was right, her plan justified in her mind. She rationalized the presumptive nature of her actions, found she had a fine father and mother for her child and a perfect mate for her best friend: something she had always wanted to do for Irene. With all the events of the world going on around her, she felt contented, still. She rarely picked up a newspaper anymore, or a magazine. Instead, she filled her time with knitting or writing in a journal which she had recently begun. She wanted to write down all the advice she would give her son, if she could. All those things a mother would have the opportunity to say to a child during his long life she wanted to write down in her journal. Someday, she knew, he would read these words and know how much his mother had loved him.

Life in the house adopted a calm, serene manner. Carole frequently thought of how magnificent their house was and how, one day, Taylor would be sitting, just as she often did, in the library, reading her journal. She wrote about the house in which she grew up, how she first met Irene. And explained why that house was no longer standing.

"The old Trent House was very large," she wrote. "At the end of 1939, your grandfather was called to Racine, Wisconsin, to visit with some officials from the Johnson Wax Company, a company with whom he had done years of business. The meeting was held in the newly completed headquarters building designed by Frank Lloyd Wright. Your grandfather was immediately taken with the beauty of the building, the mastery of the open spaces, the innovative columns, the humanness of the great expanses of glass. The moment his business was completed there, he contacted Mr. Wright and commissioned him to build a new Trent House. In 1942, the new house, the one you live in now, had been completed on the shore of West Lake, next to the old house, which was subsequently razed and removed. No sign of the old house remains and none of us miss it. The new house looked as if it had been here since the days when the first trees grew along the banks of the lake when the mountains themselves were formed. Everyone was pleased at the fine job Mr. Wright did. Last year's fire meant another commission for Mr. Wright who rebuilt the damaged portions of the house while your Aunt Irene and I were in New York, seeing 'Oklahoma!' That was where we celebrated our last New Year's Eve together before I died."

Thursday, 07 June 1945

The decision had been easy: since Joe Elliott vacated the Davis house across the lake from Carole's and it was still staffed, although empty, Irene could find no fault in Carole's suggestion that Bretaigne become a temporary resident. His study at the hospital now ended, the doctor busied himself setting up in private practice, finding an office, hiring staff, ordering furniture and consulting. The time he spent with Irene and sometimes Carole increased as each day went by. Irene, for her part, enjoyed the idea of Bretaigne living just across the way. She felt a security knowing she could stay with Carole and still see Bretaigne. When the couple spent time at her house, Irene was just a five minute drive from Carole should there be an emergency. For all concerned, the situation was ideal.

Carole contented herself, supervising a plan that was proceeding smoothly, flawlessly. As each day went by, as Irene and Bretaigne saw more of each other and seemed more comfortable with each other, Carole relaxed. Her child would be cared for until Philip's return and, should things keep going, her best friend might actually find herself married to the ideal man. Sometimes marriages of convenience do end happily.

Monday Morning, 16 July 1945

Almost before the sun rose, Carole was awakened by a telephone call from Western Union. It was from Philip. She fumbled for the telephone, shot a quick glance to the small, round clock on her vanity. It was 7:38. "Yes?" she asked groggily.

"Telegram for Miss Carole Trent." The voice on the other end of the line was very high pitched and irritated Carole.

"This is Carole Trent," she spoke.

"The telegram reads: 'Dearest stop," Carole could almost

imagine the youngish woman chomping on gum while she read the telegram. " 'All went well with test five thirty this morning my time stop. End to war soon stop. Be home soon stop. Expect a big wedding stop. Love Philip stop.' " The woman read it flatly, without passion. "It's signed Philip Craig. Do you wish the address?"

"No," Carole replied, the heart in her chest beating.

"Will a paper copy be needed?"

"No," she said. Quickly, she changed her mind. "Wait. Um, yes. A paper copy will be needed."

"Thank you," the voice said, punctuated by the crack of gum. "Expect delivery this afternoon." There was a pause. Carole could not decide if the crackly noise she heard was static on the phone line or gum in the woman's mouth. "Is there a reply?"

"Yes," Carole thought to herself, but only said: "What is the return address? Is it Maryland?"

"Yes," the bored voice answered quickly.

"Then no reply will be necessary. Thank you." Carole hung up the phone. Just as she thought: he used his home address for the return address. She knew he would not have been able to tell her where he was. She ran her hand through her tousled hair as she propped her body into a roughly sitting position. The words of the telegram filled her mind. She wondered what test he meant. A promotion? She wondered if he needed to take a test to get out of the service or to come home. She couldn't understand. She looked at the clock again: 7:44. She wondered what time it was Philip's time. Where is he? She slowly slid back into a supine position. Shortly she fell into a very sound sleep.

Monday Afternoon, 16 July 1945

She sat at the small wooden table in her kitchen where she usually ate breakfast, and re-read the letter from Bretaigne she had received in the morning's mail. Finishing the last of the letter's nine handwritten pages she set it down, clasped her hands under her chin, gazed out at the trees in the forest, watching them sway lightly in the wind. She thought of the words she had read:

"Dearest Irene," it had begun. "You cannot know how much this task hurts my heart, but I felt it only fair to tell you that it would be unwise for us to continue seeing each other."

Page three contained the words: "Believe me, please, when I tell you it is not your fault. In fact, were any fault to be affixed, I assure you it would fall on my shoulders."

Page seven: "The reason why would not make sense to you, so I will not explain it here. Someday, as I gaze, once again, into your beautiful eyes, I know I will find the courage to tell you everything; but for now, my word must be enough."

The letter closed on page nine: "As much as I would have things be different, they cannot be. Please honor my request; it will be easier for both of us this way."

It closed: "There shall always be a piece of my heart yearning for you, my love. B."

She felt her eyes grow moist as the words coursed through her mind. She watched the leaves dancing in the breeze and followed an occasional one tumbling to its death on the green grass below. She sighed. "How could this have happened?" she wondered aloud. Each person she loved left her life in one manner or another. She had been so sure things were working out with the young doctor. She searched her mind for possible explanations. She wondered what she had done that sent him away. She wondered what words could be said to make him change his mind.

She watched the path followed by a squirrel as it darted up one tree then down again; scurried across the bright lawn; stopped, frozen, its nose twitching as it smelled the air for danger signs; dropped forward onto its forepaws, froze again; then scampered up a neighboring tree. "How simple life must be for them," she thought.

She rose from the small table, pushing the chair back deftly, and walked into the sunroom where she sat at her writing desk. From the small powder-blue box she removed a handful of stationery and a long envelope. Affixing the three cent George Washington stamp, she was reminded once again of the war which raged around her. Once, she would have been thankful that her wealth and position served as ample insulation from the war and its effects; now, however, she realized just how permeable that insulation was. She set the envelope aside, pulled one sheet of the blue stationery from the pile, positioned it in front of her and began to write. "My Bretaigne," it began.

Carole awoke. It was nearly dusk. She pushed aside the bed linens and sat up. She looked down at her swollen stomach and gently placed her left hand on it. "Soon," she thought, patting the swollen haven with tenderness and kindness. With great care she rose from the bed. She had been warned that sudden movements could aggravate the bleeding in her brain. And now, with the delivery date of the baby so near, she would take no chance. She plodded to the window, pushed aside the yellow lace curtain, looked at the lake stretching to the mountains on the other side. She felt a strange calm and serenity come from the lake and its flatness. "Like that lake, I am," she thought. "Calm and undisturbed."

For the first time since learning of her condition, Carole allowed herself the opportunity to reflect upon her life. She had avoided doing so earlier; she had more important matters to concern her mind. But now, with the future of the baby insured, she could allow herself the luxury of review. She did not, right now, worry about the doctor. She knew, in her heart, he would fulfill his part of the agreement. She had given him the second check only last week. So, with that temporary problem well in hand, she turned her mind inward, to her life. She was struck with an unfamiliar but not unwelcomed thought. "I am ready to die." It was not, "I want to die," but, "I am ready." In making that fine distinction, she was able to understand it.

She had lived a full life, a good life. She was happy. She had met and loved a man who existed only as a fantasy to her before she met him. Philip. She thought of how she met Philip. The first thought that came to her was not how she met him as much as how she felt her heart stop when she saw him for the first time. It was the year before her trip to Europe. She had finished her first year of college. Her friend Irene was excited about her last year of prep school and Philip, whom she had not yet met, was about to begin his first year in college.

The three of them crossed paths at a party on campus. Carole was there as a student, Irene as her guest. Philip had been invited by an older friend who was one year ahead of Carole. By coincidence, Irene knew Philip's older friend, Jonathan. When Irene saw Jonathan, she walked briskly toward him, champagne glass in hand, Carole in tow. Jonathan stood alone and brightened when he saw her approach. Carole remembered watching as he turned to his right, whacked someone on the back and said, "Turn around, Phil. Here comes another one of my swell pals -- and boy, look who she's with!"

Carole would learn later that Jonathan had been trying futilely to fix up Philip with someone, anyone. Philip had been leery of the women he met at school. He had not found anyone with whom he felt comfortable. Jonathan knew Irene would be perfect for him. But when Philip Craig turned his eyes saw Carole and nothing else.

On the other hand, Irene had been trying, equally futilely, to find someone with whom Carole could spend time. Carole resisted going to social events alone because she feared she would leave alone, not having danced with a soul. Irene's intentions, therefore, were to fix Carole up with Jonathan whom Irene saw as dashing. She knew they would be a perfect match and was surprised she hadn't thought of it earlier. But when Carole saw Philip turn around, she only had eyes for him.

Carole remembered little of the social chitchat during and following the introductions. She could only remember how beautiful she found him, how inviting were his sky-blue eyes, how handsome he was with his jet-black hair falling onto his forehead, scattered, unkempt. She wanted to reach across the short distance and replace the stray strands, but willed her hand not to move from her side. Philip noticed the effort with which Carole remained restrained, proper, polite. As if saying, "I feel the same way, too," he smiled a furtive smile at her and winked. Carole, in reply, almost allowed her glass to slip from her hand. It was a problem she encountered with him often but never once did the glass actually fall.

She felt a warm feeling in her heart for that first moment when they met, accompanied with the warm glow for each and every thing they did together from that day onward.

Philip and Carole saw each other every day. There was, however, one day when she refused to see him. It was Christmas Eve, 1941: the day Philip enlisted. He had told her the night before of his plans and she felt then the sense of dread which had plagued her since. She could never explain her fears to herself or anyone. That was not the case now.

Every other day, however, was bliss. They strolled together along the long winding paths around the Trent house or by his parent's home. They sat intently in front of the roaring fire reading to each other from books of poetry or works of fiction. It was an idyllic existence. She could not remember an incidence where they argued or even disagreed. No, their relationship was perfect. And it was topped off by his sudden and completely unexpected proposal at dinner last Christmas Eve. She had been so happy, then.

She allowed the curtains to fall back into place, and walked across the room, peace filling her mind. Carole walked the long stretch of hall, past the open door to the sun room.

"Carole?" she heard from inside, and stopped to look into the brightly lit room. Although it was late in the afternoon, near dusk, the sunroom was at its brightest this late in the day; the sun shone through, partially reflected off the lake outside.

"Irene? I didn't realize you were in here." She walked

into the warm room and chose a brown, overstuffed chair in which to repose. "What's that?" she asked, referring to the stuffed envelope on which Irene was writing Bretaigne's name.

"A letter."

"To whom?"

Irene rose from the desk, smiled, joined Carole on the mate to the already occupied chair. "Bretaigne."

"A letter? Why?"

Irene sighed, turned from Carole. "I don't know," she said, evasively.

Carole reached across the short distance, touched Irene's arm. "What is it? Is something wrong between you two?"

Irene laughed.

"What is it?"

"That's the problem, Carole. I don't know. He wrote me this long letter, telling me he didn't want to see me anymore."

Carole was prepared for this possibility. She showed no surprise. "Did he say why?"

"No," she sighed. "He said it wouldn't matter why and that I probably wouldn't understand."

"What do you think?"

"I don't think about it. I don't want to get hurt again."

"Do you have any idea why?"

"I think he's afraid. He seemed to be moving into this awfully fast in the first place. And then, moving him into my house. Maybe that's all part of it. Maybe he's just afraid."

Carole did not reply. After a long moment's silence, Carole asked, "What are you going to do about it?"

Irene turned slowly, looked at Carole. "Why should I do anything about it? There are other things of greater importance to me right now -- you."

"Don't say that, Irene. You can't continue to use me as an excuse to stop living your life! I know how hard this is on you. What are you going to do once I'm dead? Find someone else who's dying?"

"Stop it, Carole! Stop it!" Irene rose quickly from the

chair.

But, Carole would not stop. Irene must break through this obstacle and now was as good a time as any. "You have your own life to lead, Irene! Lead it! If you love him, go to him."

Irene said nothing.

"Do you love him, Irene?"

Irene still said nothing.

Carole knew the silence was an affirmation. She rose from her chair, placed her hands on Irene's shoulders. "Go to him, Irene. Fight for him. You've done everything for me that you could possibly do. More, in fact, than anyone ever expected from you. You deserve better than this. You deserve a life of your own. A happy life. You've helped me to have the best possible life. Now, it's your turn."

Irene's eyes met hers.

"Go to him," Carole said, almost in a whisper. "Tell him you love him."

"Why are you so concerned about him, Carole?"

"Why?" she began, caught off guard. "Because I care for you and I want to see you happy."

"Then, why not this talk when I stopped seeing Joe? Didn't you care about my happiness then?"

Carole gave a moment's thought. She was not sure why she didn't express an opinion then. "My mind was preoccupied then, Irene. But, you're right. I should have said something. Somehow, though, I didn't feel that you needed me, that you had any doubts about you and Joe."

"I didn't," she smiled. "There was a time when I did, though. It was so remarkable meeting him again after all that time. He was my first love, my first kiss, my first crush. I was so young, Carole. He was just everything I ever imagined my knight would be: dashing, handsome, smart, kind, considerate. But time has a funny way of playing tricks on you. When he stood there at your party in February my heart just fell. The sight of him brought back all those emotions, all the happiness -

- no, giddiness, really -- I felt when on the ship with him. Perhaps... maybe because I thought him dead, the memories were so much stronger, more alive, more vital."

"So, what happened?" Carole probed.

"I don't know, really. After I spent time with him I was so, well, you might think this cruel, but I was bored with him. Everything I remembered about him paled when placed next to the real thing. I guess the momentous nature of those first emotions had been so magnified through the last few years that when I was face to face with him again I saw the real him, not the fantasy I had built up in my mind over the years."

"I see."

"No, Carole. You don't. There's more."

Carole's eyebrows lifted in curiosity, encouraging Irene to continue.

"Remember when we went to the hospital for those first tests?" Carole nodded. "When we met Bretaigne in your room? and what you said?"

Carole chuckled. "I told you you were in love with him, that it was obvious."

"Yes. It was. When I spent more time with Joe and saw Bretaigne more often, I started to sort my feelings out. I was so confused probably because they looked so alike, although that could just be the easy way out, that I didn't know which way was up. It took me time but I finally realized the source of my feelings." Pointedly, Irene did not tell Carole the real event which made her feelings clear: that day, in his office, when she kissed him.

"Bretaigne?"

"Yes. The letter on my desk," Irene said. "It's a letter to him in reply to his."

Carole grasped Irene's shoulders tightly, shook her. "Then deliver it to him, if that's what you want to do. Wait until he gets it, then go to him. You've discovered the source of your feelings, now don't lose it."

Irene smiled. "How do you know what's in the letter? I

could have told him I never wanted to see him again in agreement with his own wishes. What then?"

Carole smiled, her arms dropped to her side. She leaned forward, kissed Irene lightly, her lips brushing her cheeks. "But, you didn't, did you." It was a statement, not a question. "I know you better than you know yourself, Irene." Carole hugged Irene, and thought to herself, "Maybe I was more right about you and the doctor, Irene, than I may have first thought. He may have been Mr. Right from the start." Suddenly, Carole laughed a small bright laugh.

Startled, Irene looked to Carole. "What is it? What's so funny?"

Carole shook her head, said nothing.

Wednesday Evening, 18 July 1945

Dinner cleared, they sat on opposite ends of the rectangular table in the darkened dining room. The candle's light cast a glow over the wooden table, the floral centerpiece and the two diners. She smiled across the distance at him. He did not return her smile.

Earlier that morning the chauffer drove to the other side of West Lake and delivered the small blue note card to the resident of the Davis house. It was an invitation requesting his presence at a small dinner party that evening. The bottom right-hand corner of the card bore the legend "Black Tie." The left corner, where he would have expected to see the letters "R.S.V.P." was conspicuously blank. At first, he refused to even think about going. He tossed the invitation carelessly into the black lacquer waste basket as he left the house on his way to work. During his lunch break, he gave in to the nagging presence the invitation occupied in his mind. He drove back to the house; thoughts of seeing her again, after having sent that letter earlier in the week, plagued his mind.

He retrieved the blue card off the top of the trash in the

basket, read it again. He sat on the steps leading into the living room, rereading the invitation, trying to infer whatever intentions were implied.

He walked around the living room in a daze, his mind trying each combination of events, trying to work out what actions he should take. He placed the card on the writing desk, went into his bedroom. He lay on his bed for a long time, thinking of her, seeing her, touching her, being with her, rehearsing what he would say to her, what words she would say in reply. Here, he lost all track of time. Glancing at his watch, he realized the lateness if the hour, the day gone behind him. He walked from the bedroom, removing his clothes item by item, preparing for the evening which lay ahead. At eight o'clock, his car arrived at the Trent house.

Across from him, he watched her face as she smiled. He hurt so much inside that he could not return the smile. He wanted to, but the pain in his heart fought against the effort of his mind over his facial muscles. Her smiled stabbed like a knife into his heart.

"Shall we have coffee?" she asked. He nodded, rose from the table, followed her into the living room. He sat on the blue sofa, looked around the room. He admired the crisp, black streamlined vases, picture frames, decorations. Everything, together, looked perfectly urbane. Touches of wood here and there broke the rhythm of the room. Rose-and-white marble framed the fireplace. He looked at Irene, so cool, comfortable in this room. Almost her room. He watched her move in her soft silk blouse and skirt. He followed the line of her leg through the silky skirt, down the silk nylons, ending with the crisp, black, patent leather pumps which softly caressed her feet like hands. He loved to look at her, all of her, from her feet to her ravenous, soft, silky, brunette hair. He thought of her and wondered how he could ever have written the letter.

"Black?" she asked, sitting in front of the coffee set. Again, he nodded. He watched her rise, walk around the table separating them, hand him his cup of coffee. She turned, walked back to her chair. "I thought ahead, gave the staff the night off. So, it looks as if we are going to have to wing it on our own." She sat into the rounded chair, smiled at him.

"And Carole?" he asked, sipping from the cup.

"She's spending the night with Bette Davis," Irene replied, calmly. She looked at Bretaigne, awaited his reaction.

"What?" he asked, astonished.

Irene laughed lightly: she had not been disappointed. "She's at the picture show. One of her friends got her an invite to a sneak showing of "The Corn is Green," her newest film. It doesn't come out until next month; Carole was thrilled at the invite."

"I'm glad." He smiled back at her. "How is she?"

"As well as can be expected, Doctor," Irene said in jest, leaning back into the plush chair, coffee in hand. "The baby's doing well and her new doctor is quite pleased with her attitude about -- " she paused, "things...."

They sat there, Irene sipping her coffee. "Unfortunately, he agrees with your prognosis." Silence fell between them. After she finished her coffee Irene joined Bretaigne on the sofa. She looked deeply into his eyes, trying to divine the secret, the foundation of what he was. Another silence filled the room. She watched as he reached across the table, lifted his cup, drank the last of his coffee. She watched his well-formed hand grasp the cup, his strong mouth joining with the cup's rim, the glints of light bouncing off his eyes. She inhaled deeply, breathed in his smell. What was it, this fragrance of his? "The fragrance of love," she thought to herself. "More?" she asked, eager to do for him, to cater to his desires.

"Thanks," he said, not looking at her. "Maybe later." She nodded. He leaned back into the soft, cushioned warmth of the sofa, his eyes meeting hers. There was another, longer pause between them. "I got your letter yesterday," he said.

"Which letter?" she asked, not thinking.

He smiled in reply.

"No, really," she pressed. "Did I send you the 'how

much I hate you' letter?"

He laughed. "That's not the one I got."

"Oh," she said. Looking down, she examined the polish on her nails, moving her hand back and forth, trying to catch the light of the lamp. "Then you got the wrong one."

"Oh," he said, understanding the game.

"You see," she started, looking up, but beyond him. She moved her gaze from point to point, never meeting his eyes. "I wrote two letters: a 'how much I hate you' letter and a 'how much I love you' letter. I guess I must have sent you the wrong one." Her eyes focused onto their target: his eyes.

He met her gaze, unwavering. "Of course."

Together, they laughed.

He shifted on the sofa. "I didn't expect that."

"What?"

"Your letter. At first, I thought it was something else. I didn't realize it was a letter. Then, when I did, it wasn't what I had expected."

She looked at the table, then out the window, then back at him. "What did you expect?" she asked.

"I expected you to back away from me, agree not to see me." He looked at her, softly. He reached out, grabbed her hand lightly, firmly.

"Is that what you expected," she ventured, "or what you wanted?"

He looked at her lips, her soft lips, the light from the lamp reflecting on them. He looked at her skin, so flawless, so smooth, so clear. So much like a fantasy. "I want you to be happy," he said softly, reverently.

"I am happy," she replied, surprised at his comment. She reached out her free hand, placed it on his. "I want you to be happy, too."

He sighed, leaned even further into the sofa. "I wish I could be happy."

She slid smoothly off the sofa, bending her legs under her as she did, coming to rest on them on the floor. She looked up. "You can be happy, Bretaigne. I can help you be happy."

He did not look at her. He looked at the moon across the room, glowing outside the window. He willed his eyes to not look at her. Irene saw the struggle on his strong face.

"I know," he finally offered. Then, his mouth formed the same words again, silently, no sound coming from them.

Irene saw tears welling in his eyes. She, too, felt on the verge of crying, but refused. "Then, why?" she asked, wanting to understand. He turned his face down to hers, the shadows flickering across the lines of his face. He looked into her eyes, so dark, mysterious.

He began to speak slowly. He told Irene everything about him. From his boyhood in Germany, his escape with his parents from a Germany that was changing under the leadership of Hitler. He told her of his involvement with the French underground, the death of his parents at German hands, his escape from Europe to the safety of America.

He told her the reason behind the letter. So desperately he wanted her to be the person he would spend the rest of his life with. He wanted it but doubted the truth could be so wonderful. The letter was not a test, a challenge for her to come to him, to fight for him; instead, it was an honest confession to her of the doubt he felt about her, about himself.

He stopped short of telling her about Carole and the fact his deal with her was too much for him to handle. He had hoped Irene would break off the relationship and provide him an easy way out of a deal he never should have made. The money was a lure dangled in front of him like a worm on a hook in front of a fish. He said yes before thinking through the consequences.

Through it all Irene listened, her head rested on his legs, without interruption.

The clock struck midnight. For almost two hours, Bretaigne had spoken, confessing to Irene everything except the truth. For nearly an hour, they sat in silence. As if at his command, Irene looked up at him, saw his dark eyes looking at her, love the driving emotion. As if in reply to a question from his mouth, she nodded, smiled. "Yes," she said.

"You don't care about -- "

She shook her head.

"You're sure?"

She lowered her head again, to rest upon his leg in answer.

"When?"

"I don't care," she said softly. "If we could just do it quietly, quickly."

"I know," he whispered, stroking her hair. "Carole?" She nodded her head against his leg. "We'll do it however you wish, my dear."

"Thank you, Bretaigne."

They rose quietly, packed nothing, drove to Connecticut where, at seven o'clock that morning, they became husband and wife.

Thursday, Early Morning, 19 July 1945

The sounds of a woman screaming filled the house.

Writhing in pain, Carole fell to the living room floor, sending a table and two vases crashing to the ground, shattering. John, polishing the wooden balustrade, turned at the commotion, saw streaks of blood as Carole's arms raked over the splinters of crystal littering the floor.

"Miss! What is it?" Carole's face contorted in pain. Her mouth worked but no sound came out. Carefully, lovingly, John raised her body from the floor, lowered her to the blue sofa. He dashed into the kitchen.

"Mrs. Kennison," he shouted at the cook's back, frantically waiting on the telephone for the operator to answer so he could summon the doctor. "Get some towels, soak them in water quickly, then tend to Miss Carole." The old woman turned, began executing John's commands but feverishly probed

John for information. Although the household staff knew of Carole's illness, told by Mrs. Kennison at Irene's orders, they did not know the full seriousness of her condition or the time left of her life.

"She fell onto the floor," John said, hanging up from telephoning the doctor. In an effort to save time, he had telephoned the Davis house, hoping to summon the closest doctor. After allowing the telephone to ring a half dozen times, the operator's voice returned, asking him whether he wanted to continue ringing. He told the operator the telephone number of the family doctor, reached him quickly. "She cut her arms up real bad when a vase broke. She was screaming something awful!" The face of the elderly man, another of Mr. Trent's most faithful and long standing employees, was coated in a layer of sweat, rivulets streaming down from his temples. He stood at an opened front door as Mrs. Kennison tended to Carole's wounds and waited for the doctor's arrival.

That afternoon, Irene Davis Fischer and her husband returned to a house in chaos. Mrs. Kennison, hearing the sound of the car from the kitchen, met them at the doorway, panicked and frantic.

"What is it, Mrs. Kennison?" Irene asked, dropping her handbag on the floor at the sight of this usually reserved woman in near hysteria. In tears, her throat choked with fear, the old woman told them the events of the morning.

Irene, frantic over Carole's health, ran toward the stairs. "She isn't here," Mrs. Kennison yelled after the retreating figure.

"Where, then?" Irene asked, one foot already on the stairs.

"The doctor insisted she go into the hospital right away. He said her condition was too unstable to allow her to remain at home until they knew what happened."

"What did happen, Mrs. Kennison?" Bretaigne asked. "Was it a fall? Was the baby injured?"

The woman turned to him. "I don't know. John was in the room when she began screaming or something. He said he heard the table crash after the screaming started, so he didn't think she fell. Oh, doctor," she pleaded with him. "Do something!"

"I will, Mrs. Kennison. Irene, let's get to the hospital immediately and find out what's going on."

They charged back out of the house, ran into the car still parked in the drive, and sped off to the hospital.

Slowly, Irene pushed open the door to the room, while Bretaigne stood at the nurses station, reading through the admitting doctor's report. Carole, pale and wan, lay in the bed. She stood there, watching the weak figure of her friend move only slightly with each breath. After a few minutes, Bretaigne rejoined her.

"They think she had early labor pains," he whispered into Irene's ear, standing next to her just inside the room. "They don't seem to think her pregnancy was such a good idea. Her doctor even suggested surgery."

"Surgery?"

"To remove the baby."

"NO!" she screamed in a whisper, her hand clutching Bretaigne's sleeve.

"Irene," he began, putting a hand on hers. "I told them how important the baby was to her and the pregnancy was what she wanted. They can't operate without her consent. I told them they would never get it."

"But what is her condition?"

"They're not really sure, yet. It's probably nothing. They've done some tests. The doctor should know tomorrow."

A middle-aged man opened the door, motioned for Bretaigne and Irene to come outside with him. "I don't want to alarm you unduly," he began as they moved into the hallway. "But she should remain in the hospital until the baby is born."

"She would not allow that," Irene said, standing nearer to her husband whose presence, she felt, lent credibility to her statement.

"I agree with Doctor Fischer's original prognosis," he said, "but the birth, the strain, the trauma, could jeopardize her. In the hospital, we can closely monitor her, be right there should she experience another episode like this one. Were she to fall again the pregnancy could terminate on its own. That additional strain on her body," he paused, looked at Irene, "could hasten the progress of the damage to her brain. There is no way to be safe unless she remains here under constant care."

"I'm sorry, doctor," Irene ventured, not needing to consider his comments. "She's been in superior spirits. A hospital stay would depress her needlessly. She would rather...." She paused, looked at Bretaigne. "If she had to chose, doctor, she would rather die at home. I've known her nearly her entire life and I'm sure she would rather be home, when the time comes."

"As you wish," the man said. "As for now there is no more you can do. Call me tomorrow and I'll tell you when you can expect her to be released from the hospital. We should know by tomorrow afternoon."

Thanking the doctor, Irene and Bretaigne walked out of the hospital and into the waiting car.

Saturday Afternoon, 21 July 1945

She picked through the hospital lunch eating very little. She was hungry: she knew she should eat; but being trapped in a hospital preyed too heavily on her mind. She should be out, planning, organizing, doing something, anything other than wasting the remainder of her life in a hospital bed. As she pondered an unappealing sandwich, the door to her room swung open.

"If you lose any more weight," the voice said, "you'll

have to chose another size for your wedding dress."

"Irene!" Carole shouted at the sound of her friend, moving her body around to sit up. The tray which had been resting on a bed stand upended. The sandwich toppled onto the bed sheet, slid off the bed, onto the floor.

"Oh, darn," Carole said, leaning her head over the bed to see the sandwich on the floor. "And I so wanted it, too."

"I'm sure you did," Irene said, having heard non-stop complaints about the quality of the food, the size of her room, the care she was receiving and having to be in the hospital in the first place. "But, I've got good news for you." She walked into the room, dropped her purse onto the wooden chair in the corner. She slid off her cloth jacket, setting it onto her purse, unpinned her hat, dropped it onto the jacket. "Whew!" she said, moving closer to the bed, leaning her hip sideways against it. "It's a scorcher out there." She waved her hand rapidly in front of her face, cooling herself.

"Hot?"

"Boy, is it! One of those depressions, or something. No wonder the banks closed! Who'd wanna work in this weather?"

Carole laughed at Irene's play on words. "It's so good to have you here, Irene. I'm getting stir crazy forced to sit in this bed with nothing to entertain me other than that old radio which doesn't get half the stations in the city." Carole waved in the general direction of a beaten console radio with a cracked plastic face. "What a life!"

"Well, that's all about to end," Irene said, cheeringly. "Bretaigne's out there talking to the doctor. It seems like everything's fine with you. The baby got squirreled up sideways or something, pinching on something in you, causing the pains you had."

"Thank you Doctor Davis!" Carole said, laughing anew at Irene's feeble attempt to explain the complex.

"Oh," Irene said, startled. "It isn't Doctor Davis."

"No," Carole noted. "I'm sure it'll be a long time before you're ever confused with a medical man."

Irene moved closer to her friend. "That's not what I mean, Carole." She turned her body sideways, resting her back against the bed. "Bretaigne and I got married Thursday morning."

"Irene!" Carole reproached. "But, you didn't!"

Irene turned her head, looked at Carole, the affirmation clear.

"Oh, but we were to have a double wedding, Irene. And now you've ruined everything." Carole pouted in mock indignation over Irene's actions. "But, she added, "I am happy for you both."

"Are you really, Carole?"

"Of course, Irene. How could I not be? Isn't Bretaigne just everything? The cat's meow as they say? What could I be but happy for you?"

"But, the double wedding."

"Don't let's kid ourselves," Carole said, pushing the bed sheets off her upper body. She scratched her arm. "It'll be a long time before I'm made a decent woman -- if ever." There was a pause between them, Irene not wanting the conversation to continue on the subject. Finally, Carole broke the moment. "Where? When? Tell me everything, Irene," she said, patting the bed, motioning for Irene to sit next to her.

Irene climbed onto the bed, reclined her body leaning on her right elbow, her head opposite to Carole's. "There's not much to tell, is there? We talked, had dinner when you were at the cinema and then drove into Connecticut to get married. It was terribly romantic. I mean, haven't you just dreamed of the man of your dreams coming to you, whisking you away to his castle?" She dropped her head back, closed her eyes, stretched her tired neck muscles. She lifted her head again. "It's wasn't a huge do, but it was wonderful."

Carole looked at Irene. "Is he?"

"Is who, what?"

"Is he the man of your dreams?"

"Yes," Irene whispered in response. "I think you picked

the best man in the world," adding, hastily, "for me. I cannot thank you enough, can I?"

"Be happy," Carole said. "That's thanks enough for me."

"I want you to be happy to."

"I am, Irene. I am. But," she added, kicking Irene through the sheets," I'd be happier getting out of this place."

"But that's the good news I came in to tell you originally!" Irene leapt from the bed, straightened her skirt. "We're here to take you home!"

Thursday Morning, 02 August 1945

He awoke. He glanced around the room, swung his left leg off the bed as he lifted his tired body from the sheets, pushing them aside. He sat there, on the corner of the bed, thinking. He turned, looked at the sleeping figure that represented his wife. "My wife," he whispered. What a comforting thought. He caught himself smiling at her, the heavy brunette hair framing her face as she slept.

Her eyes opened. "Good morning," she said. She turned her face to watch him watching her. "Did you just get up?"

He walked to the corner of the bed, sat next to her. "Yes," he said, running his hands through her hair. "I was just marveling at how beautiful you are in the morning." He smiled. From outside their room, they heard a light tapping sound. "Come in," Bretaigne said.

The door swung open. Irene and Bretaigne expected to see the figure of Mrs. Kennison standing at the door. Instead, the person they saw shocked them.

"Good morning, newly wedded!" It was Carole, her hands laden with a heavy breakfast tray. Irene bolted from the bed to help Carole with the heavy load.

"Great goodness, Irene! Sit down. I can handle a simple thing like breakfast in bed!"

"But, why Carole," Irene asked, perplexed, "when we

have Mrs. Kennison in the house? There's no need for you to do this yourself!"

"I said I could handle the breakfast-in-bed part. You don't think I actually cooked all this." They all laughed.

Carole bent her knees, placed the tray on the side table which stood by the door. "I haven't done anything special for you two since you ran away and got married -- other than scare you both near death when I got sick. So, I thought I would wake myself up early, go downstairs and supervise the preparation of a big breakfast in bed for you two. After all," she said, sheepishly, turning to face them. "I'm sure you'll be needing all the strength you can get over the next couple nights." Quickly, she corrected herself. "Days, I mean."

Carole began ferrying plates from the table to any vacant spot on the bed. When everything was spread before them on the blankets she stood, proudly. "So," she began, sweeping her arm in a manner which took in the entire feast, "Dig in!"

The three sat on the bed, ate like children at a slumber party. They gossiped; told stories; reminisced. For both Carole and Irene, it was as if the days when they were young had never ended -- the past recaptured. The thought of those happy days of their youth gone by struck Irene and tears began to course down her cheeks. Bretaigne sensed the intrusiveness of his presence at that moment, stole a croissant, stepped through the doorway, slowly closing the door behind him.

Carole looked at Irene. "Don't Irene," she said, her voice barely above a whisper. "Don't let's spoil this moment." She fought back the tears which threatened her own eyes. She sniffled, lifted her head and inhaled, deeply. "Why do you always do this to me, Irene? Every time, anymore, when we're together, you start."

Irene allowed her tears to flow freely, making no effort to check their course. "I don't know, Carole. I really don't." Irene looked at Carole. "Yes, actually, I do." She looked at the food on her plate, trying to steady her voice. Finally, she spoke. "I'm really going to miss you, Carole. I don't know what I'll do without you. All my life, no matter what else there was, there was always you. Wherever I went, whatever I did, you were there. Maybe not next to me, physically, but I could always feel you near me, in spirit, thinking of me as I was always thinking of you." She stopped. The tears stopped.

This moment became for them, as they both understood, the moment for their final goodbye. Neither woman knew as they sat there, knee to knee on the bed, when or if Carole's illness would ever allow them another moment like this, another moment to say those things which usually remained unsaid, which somehow never find the right moment to be expressed. Irene did not want those things to remain unspoken, all the feelings she had for the woman who sat in front of her, the woman who was her lifelong friend. She would never have to say "If only I had been able to tell her..." Filling in the last phrase over and over in her mind through the years she would be alone. "...that I loved her," or, "...that I appreciated all those little things she always did for me," or, "...that she was always able to make a bad moment better." This moment became not a moment for crying, but for saying those very things.

"Carole," she started, boldly, blindly. "I want you to know that I do now and have always loved you so very much. You have been so much to me. You are the sister I never had, the family I lost. You have been a mother, a best friend, a counselor. There would be no way, ever, if you were to live to be a hundred, that I could repay you all of that. I will miss you very much, but always I will hold memories of all that we did, everything that we shared, close to my heart and think of them, and you, often. I know that you are happy and I'm trying very hard to be happy with you, to be a best friend to you, to give you back the support you always, so freely, gave to me, never asking anything in return. I want this to be easy for you. I only wish I could have been a better friend to you, through the years, than I have been."

Carole reached out her hand, placed it very lightly on

Irene's arm. She looked deeply into Irene's eyes and said: "If I had been able to choose whomever I wished and given this person all the traits I admired so much and had this person for my very, very best friend, Irene, she could never have been to me half the friend you have always been. You have been so much to me. You were the little sister I never had, you were the family which so often left me alone. You were my mother after she died, you were my best friend. You kept my feet on the right path and for that, I will always love you and thank you. You've made these last days for me better, more fulfilling than a life of fifty more years could ever have been. Think of me after I'm gone, Irene. Remember the wonderful things we did, the good times and the bad times we shared. Those thoughts, my dear friend, will keep me alive, forever."

She grasped Irene's hand, squeezed firmly. "I have something to give you, Irene."

Irene looked up, met her hazel eyes. "What?"

"It's a gift, of sorts," Carole said. She grabbed Irene's wrist, gently, firmly. She pulled her hand closer to her, placed it lightly on her stomach. "This," she said, is your gift."

Irene searched Carole's eyes for some clue, something to help her understand. She said, "I don't understand."

"I visited Mr. Gordon some time ago."

"Your lawyer?"

"Yes. I needed to attend to so much unfinished business. You know, my will, things like that. I needed to tie up the loose ends. One of those loose ends is...." she pressed Irene's hand to her stomach to complete the sentence.

Irene looked blankly at Carole. "I don't understand, Carole. What is it you're telling me?"

"I have known for some time that were Philip to leave me he would never return. I have come to terms with this thought within my own mind." She twirled the ring on her left hand. "I decided to have this baby inside of me because it will be the one thing that will remind Philip of me, our love, always. I know, also, that I'll probably not see the arrival of autumn this year. I may not, in fact, see September. I feel something very strange within me."

"Are you in pain?" Irene asked, calmly.

Carole shook her head. She smiled. "It isn't anything like that, dear. No, I feel calm, somehow. It's really the most odd feeling, but I feel very calm. I think it's a feeling of peace, total and complete. I'm not sure, but, I think this is what happens when a person is about to die."

She shifted her legs on the bed, turned sideways, sat next to Irene. "Remember about my mother?" Irene nodded. "A very strange thought had occurred to me only a couple days ago about her. I was remembering when last I saw Mother, in the hospital, right before she died. I noticed something in her eyes, her face. I was young then, too young to have really noticed it or realized what it actually meant. But, a couple days ago, when I was knitting something for my son, her face came back into my mind. Remember how I told you I could so rarely think of her face?" Irene nodded. "I couldn't believe it! Right out of the blue, mother's face formed before me as if she were standing there. It was so easy. She was smiling, her eyes were glowing. It made me remember that last moment when she held my hand and said 'Be a brave little girl, Carole, there's nothing to be afraid of. It will be all right.' I finally understood, Irene. She was not telling me not to be afraid for her, she was telling me that, when the end comes, there was nothing to be afraid of. For so long I hated mother for leaving me, for telling me not to be afraid and then leaving me. Now, finally I understand. She was giving me the last piece of advice she would ever be able to, telling me not to be afraid of death. I only wish I understood it, then." She paused, remembering, then took a sip of coffee. "She died a few hours later."

Irene nodded. "Yes."

"Well," Carole continued. "I almost believe that she knew she was going to die on the operating table. I don't know how she could have known but I think she did. That's how I feel I look, now, the way mother did."

"You do, Carole. I can see it. But, I still don't understand about my gift."

Carole laughed. "Of course. At my lawyer's office, I drew up all the necessary papers."

"Papers? For what, Carole?"

"For you and Bretaigne to adopt my son, temporarily."

Irene smiled. The meaning of Carole's gift sunk in. "Adopt?" She paused. "Your son?"

"Yes," Carole said, excited, nearly bouncing on the bed. "Isn't it wonderful? My little boy will be yours until Philip comes home."

Irene rose from the bed. "I don't know, Carole, this seems -- "

Carole turned on the bed to follow Irene's walking figure. "What's there to know? You're married now and you'll take care of Philip's child until he returns."

Irene looked at Carole. "Until he returns?"

"Yes. The document grants you and Bretaigne total custody of my child until Philip returns and is able to take custody of his son. So you see, you will actually be babysitting until the war ends."

Irene suddenly felt a sickening, thick pain in her stomach. She took a step toward her friend, anger welling up within her. "What did you say?"

Carole smiled. "I said you'll be a babysitter until the war"

"Not that," Irene said, waving her hand to cut off Carole. "Tell me the part about Bretaigne and me."

"Well," Carole said, willing to comply, not thinking. "I said something about the legal document which allows you and Bretaigne custody -- " she stopped. Her eyes lifted to Irene's. She recoiled at what she saw.

"And you had this document drawn up when?" Irene pressed.

"A couple months -- " Carole stopped, fear and frustration gripping her heart like the cold hand of death. She dropped her head, covering her face with her hands, the realization finally clear. "Oh, my god."

"Yes, Carole," Irene said. "I've only been married since the nineteenth of July. That's barely,..." she ticked off the days. "Barely fifteen days! Hardly a couple months, wouldn't you agree?"

Irene stepped closer to Carole. "How could you have known so surely who I would marry, Carole? Why, Bretaigne and I only started dating a couple months ago. Before then, his name never crossed my lips. Why doesn't the document name Joe? I was all set about him a couple months ago. How could you have known, Carole? How could you have known?" Irene's voiced raised to a shriek. "I never gave Bretaigne a second thought until he asked me to go out with him, until you suggested -- " Her hand flew to her mouth. "Carole!" she shrieked.

Carole looked up to Irene. Finally, in answer to the painful pleading she saw in Irene's eyes, she said: "You're right, Irene. I arranged it all."

Thursday Afternoon, 02 August 1945

Carole sat on the edge of the bed not moving until Bretaigne came into the room minutes later.

"What did you say to her, Carole? She stormed through the living room up to the bedroom, changed her clothes, then left, slamming the front door behind her."

Carole slowly rose from the bed, flexing her legs. "I told her everything -- more, actually, than I had originally intended. I'm afraid I've ruined everything."

"What are you talking about?" he asked, running his hand through his black hair.

"I accidentally told her about the arrangement we made."

"Why?" he asked, moving further into the room, confronting Carole. "What would have made you tell her that?"

She walked away from him, toward the window

overlooking the terrace. "I didn't tell her. It slipped. I was telling her about the temporary adoption plans and, well, the rest slipped out."

"That's swell," he said, trembling, sitting on the bed's edge to steady himself.

"I'm afraid the deal may be off."

He looked up. "What do you mean?"

"Now that she knows you only married her for the money I offered you, she'll want out of the marriage before my child is born. I guess I'll have to make some other arrangements."

"You told her that?" he screamed, standing from the bed, crossing the room toward her. He grabbed her upper arms, violently turned her to face him. "Did you tell her I married her because of the money?"

Carole, frightened, looked up at him. Her mind raced, quickly searching for an answer. "I -- " she paused. "Well, actually, no I didn't use those exact words."

"What exact words did you use?" he shook her. "Tell me what you said to her!"

"What are you so upset about, Bretaigne? I'll still give you the money I promised and help you set up your private practice. This wasn't your fault. You did your best."

He shook her again wanting, rather, to strike her. He released her. She stepped backward, her path blocked by the window. She stood against the wall, her only security. "Bretaigne! What is wrong with you? It just means the annulment will come a little sooner than we had planned. I would think it would make you happy."

He walked away from her, trying to calm himself, trying to avoid the temptation to go over to her, shake her again. He ran his hand through his heavy black hair. Finally, he turned, faced her. "Don't you understand? I don't care about the damned money. You can have it all back for all I care about it."

She stood, searched his face, trying to find an answer. "What are you saying?"

He stepped toward her, looked at her, angrily spat out the words: "I am trying to tell you I did not marry Irene because of our deal! I married her because -- " he stopped, turned from her, walked across the room. He paced for a few moments like a caged animal, then sat on the corner of the bad, scattering breakfast dishes onto the floor.

"Good god, Carole. Can't you see? After I began to see Irene on a regular basis, I began to understand it was not you I thought I loved. It was Irene. Before, whenever I saw her, she was with you. You were my patient. I thought it was you that caused those stirrings in my heart. But, it wasn't." He rose from the bed, walked back to Carole. He remembered the day Irene kissed him in his office. How that simple, quick, impulsive action made all of the pieces to the puzzle fall into place. How like a door opening, or a sun rising did the truth become so clear to him. "That night, outside the Blue Panther. It wasn't you I was telling that I loved. It was Irene -- only, she wasn't standing in front of me. You were. She was standing down the sidewalk. Those words came out of my mouth. I was looking at you but my heart was speaking those words to Irene."

Carole looked up, surprise in her eyes.

"Don't you see what you've done?" He walked from her. "Now, she'll never believe I married her because I loved her. She will always think it was because of that stupid deal we made." He turned, faced her, his eyes meeting hers. "Yes, Carole. Without knowing it, you actually helped to bring us together. Now, you've helped to destroy it. All of it. Because you were too selfish to see beyond your needs, to see what Irene needed, or me. Because of your stupidity, Carole, you've just betrayed your best friend."

Tuesday, 07 August 1945

The flat, Midwestern voice made the announcement: "Sixteen hours ago, an American airplane dropped one bomb on Hiroshima, an important Japanese base. That bomb had more power that twenty-thousand tons of TNT." He continued: "It is an atomic bomb, harnessing the basic power of the universe." Then, he said. "What has been done is the greatest achievement of organized science in history." He concluded. "If they do not now accept our terms, they can expect a rain of ruin from the air, the like of which has never been seen on this earth. We have spent two-million dollars on the greatest scientific gamble in history -- " Harry S. Truman, president of the United States, paused, then added "-- and won."

Carole sat in the living room, listening to the speech on the Sonora radio. With the president's final words she looked across the room to Bretaigne who had been sitting calmly, reading, before the special broadcast preempted the music program they had been listening to on the NBC network.

He returned her look, but did not seem concerned with the words he had heard. His thoughts were miles away scouring the countryside of Maryland. Irene had not been seen or heard from since she left the house last week. At first, Bretaigne had searched Baltimore and the surrounding cities looking for his wife. He called the hospitals for an unidentified woman fitting her description. There had been one, dead on arrival; but it was not Irene. He called hotels trying to find her listed in the register. Called the police about any women recently arrested. Nothing. The police aided in the search, but found nothing. For days, Bretaigne neither ate nor slept. His search was relentless. Yesterday, Monday morning, he collapsed from exhaustion. The doctor forbade him from any more searching until he regained his strength. He issued a prescription which would insure his orders were carried out.

The tables were turned: Carole was now looking after and caring for the man who had first cared for her.

Thoughts of Philip filled her mind. "Do you think," she said, hesitatingly, "that this means the end?"

"I don't know, Carole. I don't know. For so long we've

heard the end of the war proclaimed but nothing ever comes of it. I wouldn't get my hopes up."

She sunk into the sofa. "Yes. Of course, you're right."

"I'm sure Philip is fine, Carole," Bretaigne said, emotionless.

She looked at the worn man who sat across the room. Slowly, Carole rose from the sofa, walked the distance between them. She sat on the floor at his feet. "You poor man," she said. "Here you are worried about Irene yet you can be kind enough to ease my fears about Philip. I truly underestimated you, Bretaigne."

He looked down at her, placed his hand at the nape of her neck, stroked it, lightly.

"You never underestimated me, Carole. Until I met Irene, I had no hope of ever loving again. I was so afraid that whomever I loved I would also lose, like my parents. In that way, Irene and I are very much alike."

Carole nodded.

Thursday, 09 August 1945

The Japanese city of Nagasaki lay in radioactive ruin. Since the Potsdam conference in Berlin in July, President Truman had awaited the Japanese response to the ultimatum issued by the Big Three: Truman, Churchill and Stalin. There was none. Truman met with Premier Stalin, head of America's ally, Russia, and Prime Minister Churchill of England to discuss the coming end of World War Two. After the first atomic bomb Japan did not concede defeat. After the dropping of the Nagasaki bomb Japan's wishes were unclear. Emperor Hirohito, long considered the puppet leader of Japan, was unsure. Should Japan surrender or continue to fight a war already lost?

Friday Morning, 10 August 1945

She sat alone, bunched in the corner of the sofa in her living room, thinking, as she had for each of the last eight days. Her mind was filled with so many thoughts, she did not dare to rise from her position. She had eaten little during the last week. Her time had been mostly spent crying, screaming in fits of anger, throwing objects around the room, beating her fists against a pillow on the sofa. She had not seen aforehand how clever her choice had been. Who would have thought to look for Irene in her own house? There had been knocks at the door, people looking through windows, but to the outside world, her house was still closed up.

After her marriage she had dismissed the house staff, closed the house intent on selling it, moving in with Carole through to the end. So there it sat, the huge Davis mansion, empty, boarded up, vacant. She had blindly walked around the lake to the only familiar refuge she knew other than Carole's house. The house she grew up in. Her house. There was some food in the pantry, the weather nice enough to keep a few upstairs windows open to prevent the house becoming stale. She made a few trips into town for other provisions, food and personal items, but she looked so different now, drawn, pale, listless. No one recognized her. She did not read the newspapers or listen to the radio. She did not know of the frantic statewide search for the missing rich woman. Was it kidnapping? Did she drown? One day she spotted policemen around the lake searching for a body, never connecting that it was her body for which they searched. Time had nearly stopped for Irene. In her mind, a couple days had passed, not a week.

She gave no thought to Carole or Bretaigne as they were now; but on how they were months before, when the deal was made. Through her mind filtered variations on the same scenario: who approached whom? How did the deal begin? What kind of money was exchanged? Questions which she could not answer including the worst one: why?

She could not understand the circumstances leading up to this moment. Now, she questioned her own actions. Why did she stop seeing Joe? Why did she kiss Bretaigne in his office? (In fact, she wondered if she initiated the kiss or had he. She could no longer be sure.) She questioned everything, from the fight in the Blue Panther (Did Carole arrange that, as well?), to Bretaigne's declaration of love on the sidewalk outside. The lack of connection between her world as it had been and the world in which she now found herself caused her mind to snap.

Her world was nothing but shades of grey as she bolted from Carole's house one week before. Slowly, colors were returning, but they were not the colors they had been before. She stretched her legs, her arms, arched her back, clenched her fists. She looked around the room.

Her world was unclear, but she had been able to come to terms with a few things: She loved Bretaigne without regard to the conditions under which they married. She remembered the night they decided to marry. He had been honest with her, she concluded, had told her the truth. Had he been lying, why the elaborate story of his escape from Germany? the death of his parents? his arrival in America? The problem with lies, she knew, was too few details. She also knew she loved Carole even after what she had done. But, she asked herself, just what had Carole done? "She tried to make me happy," Irene said aloud. "Carole was concerned that I would be alone, without anyone, so, she arranged for Bretaigne to take care of me. What's wrong in that?" Irene did not know in her heart if that was Carole's motive, but refused to question it. She put Carole's actions into perspective and did not want to risk upsetting the balance with matters of logic. Plus, she knew, as her safeguard, the marriage could always be annulled. False pretenses, she could claim, and would win.

It had only been a few weeks, she thought. Nothing major had been damaged by her marriage. She gave herself to Bretaigne freely, willingly and probably would have anyway even were he not her husband. No, that did not bother her. What bothered her was her lack of control, her inability to control what happened to her.

First, her mother leaving her, abandoning Irene, Matt, and her father. Then, the start of the war and her father's death, then Matt's. Joe's supposed death, Carole's accident, being fired from the plant, Bretaigne's kiss: all these things happened *to* her, not because of her actions. She was forced to react to events, not given the chance to act to cause or prevent them. Perhaps, she thought, this was how life was suppose to be: things going on around you, affecting you, without any contribution from you. Perhaps, she thought, she should be happy Carole arranged her marriage. Irene most certainly was not making any efforts to that end on her own behalf. Why not an arranged marriage? They worked for centuries. Bretaigne was a doctor, setting up in his own practice. He was handsome, kind, gentle. What more could she ask for? If life was to happen around her, why complain?

Time passed. Finally, Irene knew what course lay ahead of her. She must return to Carole, to the friend she had abandoned. Everything else could wait. She would allow herself to spend time with Bretaigne, to determine later what her course of action should be. Her mind was now organized, her thoughts had some pattern, some order even if they still made little sense. She would return, refocus on Carole, plan for the end. And maybe, if she was very lucky, she would be able to take her life into her own hands and tell Bretaigne she wanted a divorce.

The sound of the telephone alerted Carole who sat with Bretaigne in the living room reading the morning papers and waiting. Waiting as they had done each of the last eight days for word of Irene. Hope was raised, but only for a moment. Carole's eyes darted to the extension as she listened to the sound of Mrs. Kennison answering it in the kitchen.

"It's the police inspector, Miss Carole," the cook said, peering around the kitchen door. "Still nothing."

"Thank you, Mrs. Kennison," Carole replied, looking quickly to Bretaigne who said nothing. A few moments passed. Then, Carole heard a knock at the front door. A feeble knock, it sounded more like a small animal scratching at the wood for some attention. Not sure anyone was there, Carole walked to the foyer. Her hand pulled open the heavy door. It was Irene.

Friday Evening, 10 August 1945

Gently, she set the hairbrush onto the silver tray and lifted her eyes to the mirror.

The eyes that looked back were not hers. They were the eyes of a man who protested his love for her despite Carole's comments to the contrary.

"I know, Bretaigne," she said, resting her elbow on the vanity. "And I believe you."

"But, do you?" he asked. This conversation had been going on for nearly an hour. They were dressing for dinner, Bretaigne again bringing up the topic which Irene thought settled.

She turned her body, looked at him. "Bretaigne, I don't care about the money, the deal, or what Carole told me. I believe *you*." She needed only to look at the disheveled image which greeted her at the front door upon her return to know conclusively his love for her. She knew that any man who could fall so far in such a short period of time could do so from one of only two causes: a grave illness or a broken heart.

She rose, walked to the bed where he laid, reclined, wearing his shirt and tie. "Darling. You must understand what a shock it was. How the ground underneath me teetered when Carole told me the news; but I've had a lot of time to think about it, everything, every element that's made up our lives. Of course I would be lying to say I had no doubts; but the joy and happiness you have brought to my life and Carole's so outweighs that doubt as to make it insignificant. In fact," she laughed, stroking his cashmere dinner jacket, her eyes lifting to meet his, "we both should thank Carole. Her heart was in the right place -- right next to her wallet." Bretaigne allowed a chuckle to escape his controlled facade. "Dear," Irene continued, her hand caressing his face. "I don't care how it happened. I only care that it did. Carole's luck held as it has always -- and to complete her plan she picked two people already destined for each other. Everything is ginger peachy, my love. And so," she said, kissing his forehead, "are you!" She sprung from the bed, walked to the closet, pulled her dinner dress from the rack where the maid left it after pressing it and turned, coyly, to the man draped across her bed. "Care to watch me dress?"

The table was set with the best china, silver and crystal. It was a coming home dinner, a celebration dinner, an end-of-the-war dinner. Irene sat on one end of the long, dark wood table, Bretaigne on the opposing end. Carole sat in the middle of one side and faced the living room. She stretched out her hand to Irene, who met hers halfway. She stretched out her other hand to Bretaigne, who met hers. "So, we are together again," she said, smiling. She looked across the table to the empty seat. At her own instructions, Mrs. Kennison set a place for Philip.

"And," Irene added. "The war is over."

A few minutes before they sat down for dinner an announcer on the radio reported that Japan had surrendered. The war was finally over; Philip would be coming home.

"What is past, is past," Bretaigne added. "And, our futures have only just begun." Irene quickly looked to Bretaigne, then Carole. "I'm sorry, Carole," he said.

"Don't be. There's no reason for either of you to be sorry. Your futures have just begun and so has mine." She released her grip with Irene, patted her stomach. "If he kicks much harder," she said, laughing, "he might be born before dessert!"

The sound from the radio in the background was lost to the laughter from the three friends and the sounds of dinner being served. Strains of big band music filled the room as the laughter subsided. Suddenly, the music stopped, interrupted. Around the table, conversation stopped. Mrs. Kennison, about to walk through the kitchen door with the soup tureen, stopped, propping open the door with her foot. Silence filled the air.

They listened as another announcer came on the air. His words were quick, concise: earlier reports of the Japanese surrender were false. Mrs. Kennison pushed open the door, walked into the kitchen. Carole looked down at her food.

"It might not be over this moment, Carole," Irene offered. "But it's no longer a question of whether, but only of when. Philip will be back before you know it." Carole resumed her eating, a nod her only reply to Irene. She took a bite, chewed, looked at Irene, a blank stare in her eyes.

Irene watched Carole eat her food then rise slowly from the table.

"Carole?" Irene questioned.

Carole turned, looked at Irene. "I -- " she said, holding onto the table for support. A quizzical look crossed her face as she tried to maintain her footing.

Suddenly worried, Irene looked to Bretaigne, then rose. She walked to Carole's side, supported her. "Are you all right?"

Carole lifted her hands, placed them on either side of her head as if in pain. She looked to Bretaigne, then Irene. Her mouth opened as if she wanted to speak. No words came out, her body went limp and slumped to the floor, her eyes closed, a gasp escaping her lungs.

Sunday, 12 August 1945

Early in the day, an announcer interrupted the program on the radio. He announced the Japanese surrender and the end of World War Two.

As before, a later report confirmed that the rumor of surrender was unfounded.

Monday Evening, 13 August 1945

Irene had not left Carole's side since her collapse. She rode with Carole in the ambulance to Baltimore. Bretaigne followed in the car and spent as much time in the hospital room as not. No argument could convince Irene to return home, to rest, even to sleep in the adjoining room. Instead, Irene slept on the small metal chair next to Carole's bed.

Irene looked at the pale body which lay on the rumpled bed linens. She had long ago stopped crying for the injustice which lay stretched out in front of her. She saw the tubes running from the back of Carole's neck. She knew the dark liquid being pumped through them was the excess blood filling Carole's brain cavity. The doctors told Irene not to get her hopes up. These attempts were temporary. It was only a matter of time before they, too, would fail and Carole would die.

Doctors had been coming and going from Carole's room since she was admitted. They were conferring on the pregnancy, deciding how to handle it. They questioned whether a baby could be born at only eight months -- a whole month premature; whether Carole could be kept alive for another month or a couple weeks at least. Teams of doctors came and went; Irene could see signs of optimism fade quickly, their hushed tones and grave faces told her more than their words. Irene stressed to Bretaigne Carole's wish the baby be born healthy no matter what.

Carole faded in and out of reality, speaking rarely, other times looking around her then falling asleep. What words she spoke were disjointed, unclear. The doctors were unclear whether she would ever regain consciousness. Irene looked at the face on the pillow. It was difficult for her to watch life drain from her friend, a woman who had once been so alive, so vibrant. She reached her hand across the distance, moved a strand of hair from the otherwise unblemished face. She stroked the pale cheek lightly and heard the sound of humming. She stopped, the sounds of music filling the room. Irene concentrated on the sound and soon realized it was her own voice making it.

Hours passed. Irene looked up to the clock on the wall behind her. It was 11:30 in the evening. She turned to look out at the darkness through the window. She wondered what other people were doing at that moment, how soundly they might be sleeping. She turned back to Carole and gasped.

"Hello, my friend," Carole said.

"Hi, my friend," Irene responded.

"I'm in the hospital, aren't I?"

Irene nodded.

"Is it?..."

Irene nodded, again.

Carole exhaled, feebly, her strength almost gone. "And my baby?"

Irene squeezed Carole's hand. "The doctors haven't decided yet. They seem to want to wait until the very last moment to see if nature will take its own course."

Carole smiled. "They'd better hurry. There may not be much time left."

"Don't say that, Carole."

Carole squeezed Irene's hand, hard. "I need you to be strong for me now more than ever. You must let me do this my way, do you understand?" Her soft voice was firm. "You must promise me you will do as I have requested." Irene sat motionless. "Promise me, Irene." Carole squeezed Irene's hand very hard, pressing her engagement ring deep into Irene's skin.

"I promise you, Carole."

"More so, Irene, I want you to tell Philip, when he returns, that I was not afraid. It is very important that you tell him I was not afraid, that I did as my mother told me: faced death without fear. And then show him his son." She paused, closed her eyes. "Show him our son, Irene. Pick up the boy, put him in Philip's arms, tell him that because I could do this for him, I was happy. He will need your help, too, Irene. So, be strong for him the way you have always been strong for me. Will you?"

Irene nodded, her eyes growing tired, her hand still gripped by Carole. "I will, Carole. I will."

Carole winced as pain shot through her body. She bent her knees to ease the pain.

"Carole?" Irene said, rising from the chair. "Carole?"

"I think -- " she said, her face flushing, sweat beginning to form on her forehead.

Irene ran from the room, calling for Carole's doctor. Finding him, she rushed him into Carole's room. "What is it doctor? Is it the baby?"

The old man quickly surveyed the situation then rushed from the room. Irene stood over Carole's bed, her breath coming in quick gasps. She heard the doctor barking orders from down the hall, then turned as the door to the room flung open. The room was suddenly filled with doctors, nurses and others Irene could not identify. She backed into one corner of the room, clearing the way for hospital personnel. From the rapid-fire succession of orders Irene understood the baby was about to be born, that Carole had begun labor. She understood what the doctors had told her earlier: that the body, sensing its imminent death, might force an early labor. The doctors had been hoping, waiting, for nature to take its own course and Irene watched it unfold before her.

The room grew frantic. Hot. Irene felt sweat under her arms, running down her neck. She did not dare move. Each time she looked at the door, thinking of leaving, someone rushed in or out. She did not dare get in anyone's way, cause a problem, hurt Carole's baby. She decided to stay where she was. Her mind began to wander amidst the cacophony of noises in the room. She felt hot. "Why doesn't someone open a window?" she thought. "Am I the only person who is hot in here?"

Her mind went to the drinking fountain which stood against the wall only a few feet outside Carole's room. She looked around the room, saw the blue porcelain pitcher on the table next to her bed. She gasped as a nurse, turning quickly, bumped it with her elbow, sending it to shatter against the floor. Irene felt dizzy. Her legs grew weak. She stood, her body braced against the hot wall. She looked around at the people in the room, the obstacles between her and the door. The room around her began to tilt, tip, then spin. She put the palms of her hands flat against the wall. Her body slipped, the wall moved upward against the sticky silk blouse she had worn since Friday night. Her mind went blank moments after a resounding slap filled the room, followed by the sound of a baby's first, shrill cry.

Tuesday Morning, 14 August 1945,
12:02 a.m. Eastern War Time

Irene's strength returned suddenly, unexpectedly, as in a rush, a surge of adrenaline coursing through her body. She lifted her body, sliding along the wall into an upright position. The smile on her face spoke more eloquently than any words could as she walked quickly to Carole's bed, pushing aside doctors and nurses blocking her way. "My," she said, almost as if a prayer. She looked at the bloodied, wet form held by the doctor. It was Carole's healthy baby.

Irene stepped back a few feet as the doctor handed the baby in front of her to a waiting nurse who wrapped it in a blanket and took him to the makeshift cleaning table by the door. One by one the nurses and doctors filed out of the room, exhausted from their ordeal. As Carole's doctor made to leave the room, Irene stopped him, placing her hand on his arm.

"How is she?"

"Not well," the man said. He removed his glasses and looked directly at Irene. "I'm afraid its only a matter of a few hours at most." He turned away from her, opened the door. "I'm very sorry," he said, walking from the room.

Irene turned, walked back to the bed. Behind her, a nurse entered.

"The baby?" Irene asked. The nurse nodded, smiling. "Will you bring him in?"

Surprised, the nurse asked, "How did you know it was a boy?"

Irene smiled back. "I just knew, Nurse. I just knew."

The nurse looked to Carole. "Is she awake?"

"She is. Can you bring him, quickly?"

"We're just finishing weighing and cleaning him. I'll bring him in as soon as we're through."

Irene nodded. "If you could hurry," she said, stressing the urgency of the moment. Understanding, the nurse left the room. Irene stood over Carole's bed, looking down at her. She grabbed Carole's hand, squeezed. Carole's eyes opened.

"I was right, wasn't I?" she asked through a foggy haze.

Irene squeezed her hand again. "Yes, dear. Taylor is doing just fine. Congratulations."

Carole nodded, her eyes closed.

Irene spoke: "Carole?"

Carole's hazel eyes reopened. "Calm down, dear. I was just taking a little rest, that's all. Don't worry. I'm so tired now, I..." Her eyes closed again. Irene stood holding Carole's hand as the minutes on the clock ticked by. She watched Carole's chest move up and down, shallowly, slowly. Irene knew it was only a matter of minutes. Carole had lived long enough to do what she needed to do. Now she would be able to die, her life complete.

After another half hour, Irene heard a knock on the door. She looked up as Bretaigne walked in. He entered the room, dark except for a small light over Carole's bed, barely able to make out the figure of his wife. "Irene?" he asked, tentatively.

She motioned for him, smiled weakly. "She's resting."

"The baby?"

"As you would expect, Carole got her way again. He's fine. The nurse will bring him in a minute or two."

"Are you ready to be a mother, Irene?"

"Why?"

He walked to the chair next to the bed where Irene now sat. He squatted next to her, spoke quietly. "This," he said, handing her an envelope which had been torn open hastily. "I went home to get you a change of clothes and this arrived." He paused. "I'm sorry, Irene. Somehow, I don't think Carole could have planned for this but," he said, standing up, alternately bending his knees. "This is something we'll have to discuss later." He smiled to her, leaned down, kissed her forehead, squeezed her shoulder, then walked from the room. The door closed silently behind him.

She opened the envelope, read the words, placed the paper back inside the envelope and sighed quietly.

Tuesday Morning, 01:49

In New York, most radio stations were signing off. In California, some radio stations were completing the day's schedule of programming. Many people across the country were already asleep, preparing to awaken within a few hours; to venture back into their work-day worlds; to maintain the routine which helped them survive the many long years of struggle, of sacrifice, of devotion to the cause of a country at war. But for now, these people were in bed, their radios on, listening, half awake.

With some trepidation, some hesitation, apprehension, these same people stirred awake, struggled back to full consciousness when they heard the announcement: Japan had surrendered. This time it was true: World War Two was over.

Tuesday Morning, 01:54 a.m.

If one was flying an airplane, close to the ground, able to see the rough outline of the buildings which comprised the cities from the east to the west coast, one would have seen a sudden brightening as one by one, or in small groups, lights all across America were turned on by the hundreds and thousands. And, if one looked closely enough, one could see men and women streaming out of their houses into the recently empty streets.

By the thousands they began to scream, to cheer, to shout their joy over the final moment, this victory for which they had so long been fighting. VJ Day had finally arrived.

In the distance church bells rang signaling the beginning of a new, brighter day for America and the world. People ran to their cars, leaned on the car horns to announce that they, too, had heard; that they were happy; that the war had finally ended.

From within the small, darkened hospital room, Irene heard the revelry outside. A nurse popped her head in through the door and quietly whispered the news. "The war is over!" she exclaimed in a whisper.

Irene smiled, said "Thank you," in a small voice. She was thanking the nurse for the news and providence for the fact the war was finally over and that Carole had lived to see its end.

"What's wrong, Irene?" Carole asked.

"The war is over, dear," Irene said, forcing back tears. "The nurse just came in. Japan has finally surrendered."

Carole chuckled softly. "I thought it was only a dream. I'm so glad to hear that it's over. So glad." She paused. "And now, Philip will be on his way home. To me. To our wedding. To...." Carole's eyes drifted down to the envelope Irene had set on the bed and forgotten about. "What's that, Irene?"

Irene's eyes darted to the envelope. She had forgotten all about it; she should have placed it in her purse, out of sight. "What?"

"That envelope, there." Carole lifted her hand from under the blanket, reached feebly for it.

Irene reached it first. "It's a -- "

" -- telegram, isn't it, Irene?"

Irene nodded.

"From whom?"

Irene's mind raced. "It's..." she began, haltingly. "It's from Philip, Carole. Bretaigne just brought it. It was delivered to the house a few hours ago."

Carole reached for it. "Let me read it."

"No!" Irene answered too quickly. She tried to soothe the point. "Let me read it to you, dear. The light's not very good in here." Carole nodded as Irene fumbled with the envelope, her fingers trembling.

She pulled the telegram from the envelope. " 'My dearest Carole,' " she began, her voice tightening, clutched, strained. She felt her mouth go dry as she swallowed hard, pressed forward. "War's over stop My duties done stop Will return home as soon as possible to see you and marry you stop Looking forward to seeing Philip junior stop All my love to you Philip.' " Irene let the telegram fall to the ground, inhaled deeply, forced herself not to cry. She looked at Carole's face, wet with tears, and saw a smile stretch across it.

"I knew he'd be safe," she said, barely audible.

"You did, kid," Irene said, her voice choked to a whisper. "You did." She grasped Carole's hand as a knock sounded outside the door. Irene looked up as the nurse walked through, a bundle in her arms.

"Is she awake?" the nurse asked.

Irene nodded. The nurse moved forward with the baby in her arms wrapped warmly in a blue blanket. Taylor was sleeping quietly.

The nurse moved around to the window side of the bed next to Irene.

Carole's eyes opened. She smiled. "My son?" she asked. The nurse nodded, handed the bundle to her.

Carole placed her arms around the bundle as the nurse guided the baby to Carole's side not wanting to release him. Carole looked to the young woman. "I want to hold him, myself. Please." The young woman hesitated, released the bundle. Irene watched Carole's face as she held the little boy. Irene heard humming; but, this time, the humming came from Carole.

Carole lay there, humming to the boy who yawned, clutched his hand while waving his little arm, stretched, then fell fast asleep. Irene sat in the chair, breathing shallowly, afraid the noise from a single breath would disturb this private moment. The nurse stood -- in the same corner that, a few hours before, was occupied by Irene -- watching, struggling to hold back her own tears, watching carefully over the mother and child.

Minutes passed. Carole looked up, sought out the nurse. "I think it's time. I think you should take my son to the nursery now."

The nurse moved forward quickly, took the baby gently from Carole's side. She rounded the bed, then stopped. She turned, faced Carole, said quietly: "Miss Trent?"

Carole looked up. "Yes?"

The nurse stood there, her mouth opened, trying to form the words. Tears wet her face. Finally, she shook her head. "No. It's nothing, Miss Trent. I'll take your son to the nursery." She turned, walked through the door.

Alone, the pool of light overhead illuminating the two women, Carole looked at Irene, reached out, grasped her hand. She smiled. "Thank you, for this. For everything." Her eyes closed. After a moment, Irene felt the grip weaken as her hand fell loose against the bed.

Tuesday Morning, 02:36 a.m.

Irene and Bretaigne walked down the hall and out of the hospital. They emerged into the darkness of the evening. In the distance, they could hear the sounds of people celebrating, could see the lights of the city brighter than they should be at such a late hour. As they approached their car, Bretaigne broke the silence. "Did you tell her?"

Irene stood. She looked down at an object reflecting the moon's light. Bretaigne opened the passenger side door of the car. She walked toward the open door, the gravel crunching under her black patent leather shoes. Finally, she looked up at Bretaigne who stood, one hand on the opened door. "You know I couldn't have told her. It was hard enough as it was, Bretaigne. How could I have told her?"

He stepped around the door. "I had only just gotten in the door when he came. I was never so surprised to see a man in uniform in my life. I didn't know what to do. What to think."

Irene looked up. "A man in uniform?"

"Yeh," he replied. "Philip was an officer. I guess that means he rated someone other than a civilian."

They stood in silence. "What did you tell her, Irene? Anything?"

"She saw the envelope on the bed. I should have put it into my purse right away, to hide it. I told her it was a telegram from Philip and that he said he was happy the war was over, that he was heading home, ready to marry Carole. Words to that effect."

Bretaigne motioned Irene into the car, closed the door after her. He walked around the front of the car, opened the door, got in. He fumbled with his keys, then started the car.

"She was right," Irene said.

"About what?"

"After he left she told me she knew she would never see him again. So, in her own way, she was right."

"But, she always thought she wouldn't see him because she would die first, didn't she?"

Irene nodded. "I don't think the possibility ever entered her mind that his plane would crash. That *he* would die."

Slowly, the car pulled down the drive. "She never

planned on his not coming back," Irene said. "I guess this means Taylor is our child, doesn't it?"

Bretaigne nodded. "I looked through the legal papers after the telegram arrived. I think it does."

As the car pulled away from the hospital grounds, Irene allowed herself a backward glance. From behind the hospital she watched a white bird illuminated by the light of the full moon. It took flight upward, into the sky. "Goodbye, Carole," she whispered. Her eyes followed the brilliant bird as it joined another in flight. The two birds changed course and headed in the direction of West Lake.

The End

Made in the USA
Lexington, KY
02 June 2013